Adam Andrews Johnson

This book is a work of fiction. The characters, incidents, and dialogue are drawn from the author's imagination and are not to be construed as real.

The Mantis Continuum – Book Four

Edited by Brent Allan Northup

For information, connect with the author on social media.
Instagram @AdamAndrewsJohnson
Twitter @AuthorQueerotic
Facebook.com/AdamAndrewsJohnson

Acknowledgment

Massive shoutout to the three people who beta-read this book for me. Claire Rosalind, Joharra Harper, and Michelle Gilbert, you three are superheroes!
...don't worry, I won't try to eat your mantis glands :'-D
And to everyone in the Write Owls discord group, thank you all for the fun conversations and encouragement.

This book is dedicated to Christa

The end of the world is nigh!

THE MANTIS CONTINUUM

Prologue – Aftermath of the Massacre

Upon the hillside of Gunge, surrounded by the severed body parts and ruined corpses of the many slain monstrosities, Ronging approached the creature with the mechanical crown. The two naked former-humans were similar in many ways. Their skin tones were close, as were their hair and eye color. They also each possessed far too much *body* for a human. The extra arms and legs and fleshy bulges may have been unique to each monster, but both of them looked like an entire group of people that had been melded into the hideous amalgam of a single humanoid creature.

Ronging was not of a mind to make decisions, but his fellow monster had an air of authority and gave orders. None of that mattered to Ronging, and his pull toward the other creature was a need, which he obeyed.

When the other said, "Follow," Ronging did. However, if it had not given the order, Ronging still would have followed it, inexorably drawn to others like himself.

The pair of them left the bloody hills of Gunge and ventured into the wilderness, abandoning their home. The crowned creature spoke occasionally, and far more often than Ronging, but Ronging rarely paid attention or replied. He was waiting for his wicked craving to rise, even though that would not happen again for several years; he simply wanted to do his waiting with another of his kind. So Ronging followed, and the other led.

The sun and moon passed above, over and over again, until the crowned monster eventually stopped by the banks of a stream.

"I can already feel my desire beginning to rise," it said. "Not long now until I need to feed." It looked at Ronging.

Ronging did not respond.

"Ugh… that's why the rest of you weren't welcome anywhere except Gunge." The creature picked at the mechanical crown where the metal devise bit into its skin, and it continued talking to its unresponsive companion. "I was the only one of us allowed back into Teshon City and the Messiah Tower." It turned and looked off through the trees. "Come," it commanded.

They forded the stream, and a moment later, the edge of a village came into view. The two monsters slunk up to the back of a building.

Ronging hardly paid attention as his companion banged on the door.

A latch clicked and a tiny hatch opened. A completely normal-looking man peeked out.

"Why, master Lonklam," the man exclaimed in surprise, "you only just left us no more than six months ago. What brings you back so soon?" Another thought interrupted him. "Oh, no, your sister!" He looked fearful.

"What about her?"

"Hang on," the man said. He closed the little window and opened the door, and then he noticed Ronging. "Goodness me, you've... brought another of your kind to see us?"

The two monsters entered.

"Gunge has been destroyed."

The doorman was shocked. "But master Lonklam, how is that possible?

"I don't know. Now, what about Eccoodia? What happened to my sister?"

"I'm so sorry," the man said hesitantly. "Many of the Messiahs in Teshon City have been killed. Your sister, the Principal Messiah, was among them. I'm sorry, master Lonklam," the man repeated.

The monster named Lonklam asked, "Dead? The Messiahs are *dead*?" He added, "And the inhabitants of Gunge are dead." Lonklam picked at his crown and looked over at Ronging. "We belong nowhere."

Ronging seemed entirely uninterested in whatever was happening.

"Master Lonklam," the man said, "can I offer you a pleasure session? Most of the regulars are not in town because we did not expect you to come back so soon, but if you allow me to gather a few of your past lovers, I'm sure that we can arrange some distractions to help take your mind off your losses."

Lonklam stepped up to Ronging. "Stay," he ordered, and he left his fellow monster, following the doorman deeper into the building.

Ronging could feel Lonklam. He was near enough that there was no pull toward any others of his kind. The command to *stay* was the only thing in Ronging's mind, and he waited. Time passed for him with no thoughts, and the crowned monster eventually came back into the room. He led Ronging outside, and the two made their way into the trees.

Lonklam allowed his addiction to lead him, and his weird double mouth smiled as he spied his prey, and he was very pleased to know that his craving would not have the chance to overwhelm him.

The two twisted mutants came to the edge of a little back patio behind a café, and Lonklam rumbled, "I need!"✪

Chapter 1 – Thech & Jzuna, Part One

"Come on inside, you two!" called Thech and Jzuna's mother from the old sun-scorched front deck of their family home. "It's time for supper!" The cozy little cottage was positioned just outside of town and upstream from where the Hazel Cove Creek emptied into the sea. Thech and Jzuna were building a sandcastle close to the water's edge.

The woman smiled at her children, strange though they were, as they left their play and headed up the path that led them home. Thech and Jzuna each moved in their own unique manner, and their mother could not have loved the pair more.

The two youngsters did not bear the appearance of human children. Almost six months earlier, when their photonova gland activated, they changed.

It is often the case with Shift youths that they are rejected by their families and cast out. However, Thech and Jzuna's mother was delighted when it was revealed that her offspring were not only Shifts, but in fact exceptionally rare Biological Shifts.

When Thech and Jzuna were born, their mother gave them the name Mai, and a little over 12 years later, Mai's photonova gland activated. The child that was once a single individual became a *pair* of entities.

At the beginning of the change, Mai's skin started to excrete a thick slime that coated every inch of their body, and a mass began to form on Mai's chest. It slowly expanded over the next fortnight, until it was impossible for Mai to walk upright or lie down on their back without feeling crushed and having difficulty breathing.

On the morning of the 23rd day after the change began, Mai's mother awoke to find that the bulbous protuberance had sloughed off Mai's chest during the night. It lay in a clump beside the body from which it grew, but neither the humanoid form nor the fleshy mound beside it retained even the remotest semblance of Mai.

Over the course of the transition, Mai's mother was supportive and loving, even though she could not comprehend what was happening to her child. Mai was blessed to have such a compassionate mother. The woman's determination was strong, and she stayed by her child's side for those three long weeks of transformation.

At the end, Mai's mother stood above the two weird forms that lay motionless. She had become comfortable with the mucusy coating on Mai's skin, and she reached out and placed her palm on the child's chest where the mound had grown. Tears began to well in her eyes, as she realized their skin was much too cold. Mai seemed fine the whole way through the change, even when they were restricted to their bed, Mai had been upbeat and happy.

Neither of the slime-covered things moved, and for long moments, the woman stared at the two unique forms.

The body from which the mass separated was unrecognizable, did not look like Mai at all. Beneath the goo, its skin had taken on a subtle green tone, but it at least bore a vague resemblance to a human.

However, Mai's mother had never before seen anything like the great lump. It also appeared to be slightly green, and *it* was the first thing to move.

Like a single finger poking out, a small digit extended from the mound. It wiggled in the air, as if trying to feel if there was anything around it. Then the thing extended, and a snake-like tendril reached out that was longer than Mai's mother's arm. The rest of the slimy blob remained motionless, and as the questing limb came into contact with the humanoid form that was once Mai, the tendril froze.

There was a breathless moment, with Mai's mother's eyes fixed on the two entities, but nothing happened.

She waited.

At the top of the fleshy mound, something twitched below its ooze-coated surface. A single huge eye opened. It was larger than a watermelon and *not* part of a matching set. The lone eye blinked, gazing up at the ceiling, and then it looked over at the humanoid other.

Many more fleshy limbs, like the arms of an octopus, suddenly extended and reached out from the cycloptic mass. Each of the tendrils came into contact with the body and the creature fell still again, but then its one huge eye shifted to look at its mother.

She was gazing at the pair of beings, filled with terror and wonder.

"Mama," said a squeaky voice that seemed to come from the air all around the woman.

She could not determine the origin of the voice; the creature did not possess a mouth. Its one eye closed, and Mai's mother was even more surprised, as the creature lifted off the bed. It hovered in the air above the humanoid *other* who looked nothing like Mai, and it stared down at the motionless figure.

The bubbly voice came again from the mouthless form. "Thech," it said, "wake up."

The slimy child-shaped thing on the bed opened its eyes.

Mai's mother gasped in wonder. Tears streamed down her cheeks.

The tentacled eyeball rotated in the air and gazed at its mother. "Mama," the chirpy disembodied voice said, "I am your daughter. My name is Jzuna." She turned her huge eye toward the other figure, who sat up on the bed. "And that's your son, Thech. Mai is no more, mama, but now we are your children."

"And I love you!" their mother declared without hesitation. "You are beautiful," she added in a breathless voice, reaching out for the hovering monstrosity.

Jzuna extended one of her tentacles and wrapped the slimy limb around her mother's hand.

"I love you, mama, and Thech loves you, too," Jzuna said in her bright voice.

Thech rose and stood beside the bed. His expression was vacant, and his eyes were rolled up into his head. The boy's mouth hung open with his jaw sagging. His shoulders were slumped, and his arms were limp at his sides.

His mother stepped up and wrapped her arms around him in a tight hug, even though he was still coated in a thick layer of slime. Thech's limbs did not move, but he leaned into her.

"*Thech?*" the children's mother confirmed, looking at Jzuna.

"Yes, mama," she replied.

"And, *Jzuna?*"

"Yes, mama," her daughter repeated.

"Well, Thech and Jzuna, I love you both." Her gaze moved from one to the other and back again with awe. "I am now twice the mother," she declared with tears flowing. "Mai showed me how to be exactly the right parent. Thech and Jzuna, please teach me to do the same for both of you."

Jzuna was boisterous and energetic. She talked and laughed endlessly, and even though she was a hovering eyeball, she felt prettiest when her mother tied ribbons on her tentacles. The ooze that Jzuna's skin excreted caused the bows to slip off after a while, but they made her happy.

Thech's personality was reserved, but his mother could feel his subtle exuberance for life. All that Thech seemed to need was Jzuna. He followed her around with his awkward and lurching walk, rarely reacting to or interacting with anything other than his sister. The two were always together, and as long as they were close, Thech was content. On the rare occasions when they were apart, Thech would start moaning and grunting agitated wordless syllables until he was near enough to Jzuna again.

Besides the uniqueness of her now *two* children, and the way Jzuna floated, their mother was unsure what else their photonova glands granted them. In those first six months, neither Thech nor Jzuna displayed any gifts like what all other Shifts have. Their mother sometimes worried about her children's safety, aware that the two were targets for those who hunt Shifts, but the little family of three was happy in their lives together by the seaside stream.

The sun was setting, as Thech and Jzuna left the sandcastle they were building beside the Hazel Cove Creek. The two came up the path toward the cottage, and their mother smiled at them.

"I've made your favorite."

"Nubufish?" Jzuna exclaimed. Her tentacles started quivering in an excited way.

"Yes, indeed," her mother replied. "Take your brother and get him seated. I'll bring it right over." She plated them each a plump crispy fish, and she drizzled a little sauce on top.

She leaned down, planted a kiss on the top of Thech's slimy head, and wiped off her lips as she asked him, "Do you want my help?"

Thech's mouth hung wide, and his eyes were still rolled back, but he reached forward with an awkward jerking movement and grabbed ahold of the fish. He raised it toward his gaping maw and began to feed himself.

"Good boy," his mother said. She chuckled at his enthusiasm as he chomped down his dinner.

Jzuna hovered above her plate of food, focused on it with her one enormous eye, and the fish dematerialized. Her voice emanated from her unique mouthless body. "Mmmm! That was so delicious, mama."

Thech shoved the rest of his fish into the opening of his mouth, and he chewed for quite a while before swallowing his last bite.

Their mother could not have felt prouder of the two of them.

Before long, it was dark outside, and she helped her unique children into their beds. Because of the slime that coated both of them, Thech took to sleeping in a large basin with a sheet and a pillow. Jzuna, on the other hand, found an old fishing net that she wanted to use as a bed, and her mother draped it above Thech's basin for her. Every night he slept below his sister, and every morning, their mother washed Thech's bedding and Jzuna's net.

The three were happy.

Thech and Jzuna's mother loved them deeply. She prided herself on her acceptance of others, and she adored having children who were so unique; she celebrated them. Thech and Jzuna's mother was named Kynpri.

When Kynpri was a teenager herself, against her parents' rules, she secretly dated a Shift boy. Theirs was not a love to last, however, because the boy was murdered. It was never determined if a band of Demifae hunters or a Messiah did the horrible deed, but one morning at sunrise, the boy's headless corpse was found in the village square.

The loss only made young Kynpri more determined to be an ally for all Shifts. Long before she had a child of her own, she began volunteering with the small local division of Unity Between Humans and Shifts in Hazel Cove. The presence of the UBHS was much larger in Teshon City, but Kynpri joined this smaller chapter to do whatever she could in her community.

She could not have been more delighted when it turned out that her own child became a pair of Biological Shifts. Kynpri had perfectly loved Mai, and the woman's heart only grew when Mai changed. She loved Thech and Jzuna more than she could have imagined.

Since the devastation in the Teshon City underground, and the general acceptance of Shifts becoming part of society, even in the most remote regions, Shifts were now living out in public. Thech and Jzuna's mother tried to avoid crowds and only brought them into the Hazel Cove town center occasionally, and only early in the morning, but she always made sure they visited the newly opened Shift-owned café, Weirdo Beard-O's.

"Welcome to Weirdo Beard-O's!" called a jolly ginger man with a great bushy beard. Then he realized who was entering his establishment. "Well, hello there, Thech and Jzuna. Look at that, you two and your mother are my first customers this morning!" He was beaming at the trio, and his smile was a fissure of sparkling white amid the fiery red of his facial hair.

Thech lumbered away from his mother and over to the counter, leaning against it, and Jzuna floated up next to him. Her voice emanated from the air with enthusiasm. "Thech and I would each like a mistcream latte, please!"

"Right you are," the man replied with a chuckle. "Comin' right up."

"Thank you!" Jzuna squeaked. She and Thech headed outside through a glass door that led to the little shaded courtyard behind the café.

"Lovely day," the man said to the children's mother. "And for you?"

Kynpri smiled at him. "Nothing for me, thanks." She took out the rag that she always kept handy for the inadvertent little messes her children occasionally left behind.

"Oh, no, please!" the red-bearded fellow said quickly, as Kynpri went to wipe up the slime that Thech had left on the side of the counter. "Allow me," the man continued. "I'll clean up after him. You save that cloth for when you need it later." He came right around and wiped away Thech's slime with a smile shining through his red beard. "Not to worry, I've got a whole stack of these hand towels in the back."

A moment later, he was whistling a merry tune to himself and preparing the two beverages. He placed the steaming mugs onto the countertop.

"Here you are, milady," he said with a dramatic bow, "two mistcream lattes for the little ones."

"Thank you for making this wonderful place for Shifts," Kynpri replied to him.

"With so many fewer Messiahs now," the man commented, "the world has become a different place. The cultural impact of Shifts coming out and being part of society has been huge. Even though it's only been a short time since the fall of the Messiah Tower, it has made Teshon City much more welcoming." He looked proud. "I wanted to do the same thing here. I wanted Shifts," and he smiled toward the back patio and Kynpri's unique children, "*and* Bio-Shifts to know they belong, even way down in our little backwater village."

She picked up the mugs and said, "I can't even begin to tell you how much this place means to me and my children." Kynpri felt a lump rising in her throat.

"You and your two wee'uns are always welcome at Weirdo Beard-O's," he replied with a kind smile.

"Thank you. It's Bivon, right?" She tried to hold back her tears and cleared her throat hard, and the man nodded with a smile.

"Right you are," Bivon replied.

Kynpri joined her children outside on the patio. "Here you go, Jzuna," she said, placing one of the drinks onto a small table.

Jzuna was floating by the edge of the patio. The red-bearded owner of the cafe had planted flower bulbs around the perimeter, and Jzuna was admiring the blossoms that were just starting to bloom. She turned and drifted toward her drink, as the children's mother stepped up to her son.

"Thech, you ready?"

He leaned his head back and his mother poured the other drink into his gaping mouth.

Jzuna hovered beside the table and stared at the mug with her massive single eye, and the beverage began to drain until it vanished completely.

The cup remained.

"Mmmm!" Jzuna's voice hummed aloud. "Yummy!"

Thech also finished his drink, and he rocked back and forth with a subtle movement that his mother knew was an expression of his joy.

"Those were so good!" Jzuna declared. "Thech loved his, too. Thank you, mama."

The big jolly barista stepped out into the back area, carrying a plate of cookies, and he exclaimed with a chuckle, "I'm so pleased you're pleased." Bivon positioned himself in a small patch of light from the rising sun and added, "Fresh baked!" He held up the platter toward Kynpri. As she took a cookie for each of her children, the man winked at her. He then said to Thech and Jzuna, "Hey, kiddies, watch this."

Bivon squatted down and held up one hand in front of them. He looked at it in wonder, turning it one way and then the other, so the children could see either side of it. Right before their *three* eyes, the man's fingertips started to disappear! Then his hand vanished, and finally the man's forearm was gone. He looked at the empty space in pseudo-surprise, and in a blink, his hand reappeared.

Thech let out a single grunt of amusement, and Jzuna's peals of laughter came ringing out from the air all around them. Her tentacles waved in delight.

Then a strange voice came rumbling from the edge of the patio, and the sound of it halted the small group's enjoyment.

"I need!"★

Chapter 2 – Thech & Jzuna, Part Two

Lonklam's eyes fell on four life forms, and he honed in on the two photonova glands that were present. The bearded man with the tray of cookies looked shocked, and Lonklam thought he smelled most enticing. However, those wicked senses that allowed the monster to target his prey were not able to focus on the second photonova gland; he could only pinpoint one. Lonklam's powers of deduction were much weaker than they once were, and two *things* drew his attention. He did not comprehend what he saw.

A small human-shaped figure was standing beside a hovering blob, and somewhere *between* them was the thing that would satiate his monstrous desire. Their photonova gland felt different than any of the others Lonklam had consumed over his years of addiction, and he wanted it.

The man with the beard also possessed the answer to Lonklam's craving, but he was curious about the other photonova gland. There was something unusual and unique about it, and about the two weird entities.

There was also a woman on the patio, but Lonklam sensed nothing within her that could fill the void of his growing hunger. She screamed at the sight of the two monsters, and Lonklam lunged, but the patio behind the café was suddenly empty. The delicious-smelling bearded man, the two intriguing beings, and the woman had vanished.

Lonklam breathed the air. "They're still here," he growled to Ronging.

Thech and Jzuna, along with their mother and the owner of Weirdo Beard-O's were all invisible, and the red-bearded man was trying to silently coax the other three back into his cafe, but then the air exploded. Bivon was so startled, he inadvertently turned off his power, and the four of them reappeared on his patio.

Jzuna was attached to Thech's chest with her tentacles holding her firmly in place, and a radiance was coming from their three eyes.

The two monsters from Gunge were surrounded by what appeared to be a thin shell of fire.

"Don't hurt our mama!" Jzuna's voice roared from everywhere.

Lonklam's gaze shifted to the woman behind the two children. He grabbed one of Ronging's many arms, and Lonklam threw his fellow monster with all his might. Ronging passed through the flaming bubble, and he shrieked in agony as the radiation of Thech and Jzuna's power burned into him, but his body penetrated and was beyond the sheen of energy in an instant.

Ronging crashed into the two adults like a wrecking ball. The bearded man was knocked back into a table, and he fell to the ground. Ronging's impact with Kynpri was much worse. Her body was crushed beneath the monster's strange form, and she was broken.

Jzuna wailed, "*No!*"

Together with her brother, their powers grabbed hold of Ronging and Lonklam, and it was as if the two monsters were fired from a giant invisible catapult. Ronging and Lonklam were sent rocketing up into the sky above the treetops, and their weird bodies hurtled deep into the forested mountains.

Jzuna detached from Thech's chest, and they both turned to their mother.

The woman was in a bad state.

"Mama!" Jzuna cried.

Kynpri tried to reach out and touch her children, but her twisted body was in agony, and her limbs would not obey her commands. "I'm sorry," she gurgled to them. "Come... come closer, my babies. I'm... I'm... I..." her voice was failing her. They reached out to hold her, and tears streamed from her eyes as the cool viscous ooze of her children covered her hands.

"No, mama!" Jzuna wailed.

Thech was moaning and stomping one foot.

"I love..." their mother faltered, forcing her words to come out. "I lo... love you both." Her eyes shot to the owner of Weirdo Beard-O's and she said in a pleading voice, "Bivon, please, we have... have no one... no family."

He knelt by her side.

"Help my... my babies..." She coughed and blood splattered out of her mouth.

Bivon looked unsure and nervous, but he nodded and said, "I can take them. I know people who can help."

Kynpri turned to her two children, and in a raspy voice, she said, "Go... with him. Thech, Jzuna, I love... you both. I'm sorry, I can't..." but her voice failed. She turned her eyes to the bearded man.

"I can watch over them," Bivon said quietly.

Thech and Jzuna's mother looked with love at the faces of her unique children, and her life left her.

"*Mama!*" Jzuna cried.

The owner of Weirdo Beard-O's left the children, locked his shop, and he rushed across the street. He knocked urgently on his neighbor's door.

A moment later, two men who looked like they had just woken up opened it. They both seemed a bit surprised.

"Bivon?" one of them said to him. "What are you doing here? What's wrong?"

"You're bleeding!" the other added. "Please, come inside."

"It's not mine," Bivon said. "There's a body."

The two sleepy men snapped into action.

"Where?"

"At the café."

"Who is it?"

"A local woman whose kids are Bio-Shifts. Some sort of abominations came out of the forest and attacked the four of us on my patio."

"What happened to the children?"

"I'm taking them to Tophilogin."

"We'll handle their mother's body."

"She'll be honored."

"Those poor kids."

The two men followed Bivon to his café, and he unlocked it. They entered and the men froze at the sight of the strange children, and they were struck with how comfortable Bivon was with the unusual pair.

"I'm sorry, Thech and Jzuna," he said gently. "We need to leave. I'm sorry," he repeated.

"But mama," Jzuna whimpered, and her voice came from the air all around.

"I know," Bivon replied, "it's terrible." He looked at the corpse of the children's mother and held back his tears. "Come with me, please," he urged. "She's gone. I'm so sorry, but there are other people like you who can help."

He reached a tentative hand toward Jzuna, and he tried not to cringe as one of her slime-covered tentacles wrapped around his fingers.

"Come on, you two. Please, come with me." He coaxed them away from their mother's body and brought them outside, around his building, to where his old mobile beverage cart was parked. It had remained unused since he opened the café, and the top was covered in dry leaves.

Bivon took a breath, and he tried to speak with a positive tone of voice. "Thech, Jzuna, will you go on a trip with me?" He patted the cart. "I used to take this thing up the coast. I've got a lazy horse who can pull it for us. Will you come with me?"

He was surprised to have Thech respond to him.

The unique boy huffed a noisy breath, and he used his shoulder to nudge Jzuna where she floated, but her voice remained silent.

The children faced each other and there was a quiet moment.

Bivon watched them. "Kids, are you alright?"

They remained motionless and silent.

"Thech, Jzuna?"

Jzuna then spoke in a quiet voice. "Are you sure?"

Bivon turned back to ask what she meant, but Thech made a gentle hum noise.

"Okay," Jzuna said. She rotated in the air, and her one weird eye looked at Bivon. "Okay," she repeated.

He gave them a weak smile and tried to sound bright. "You may already know my name, from coming into Weirdo Beard-O's, but in case you don't, I'm Bivon. But you two can call me Beard-O, or if you'd like, I suppose you can even call me *Weirdo*," he added with a kind chuckle. "Why don't you bring me to your house so we can get some of your things for the trip; is that okay? I'll feed the horse so he's ready to go when we get back."

It was still early morning, and the sun was slowly climbing in the clear sky, as the children brought Bivon up the path that led to their home outside of town by the creek. Once inside, Thech immediately climbed into the basin he used for a bed, and he started quietly moaning.

Bivon knelt beside him. "I'm so sorry, Thech."

"That's his bed," Jzuna informed the man. Her voice sounded small.

"Should we take it for the trip?" Bivon asked gently.

"Yeah," Jzuna replied, "we can sleep in it together. Can we bring my ribbons?" and her disembodied voice choked on a sob. "I like my ribbons."

"You can bring anything you want," Bivon replied. He leaned over Thech's tub bed. "You're not gonna be okay, not for a long time, my young friends. And you should *feel* all those feelings. Let yourself feel the hurt and the angry and the sadness; feel everything that comes up in your heart."

"Thech has a really big heart," Jzuna's voice said from the air, and she sounded like she was crying. "Thech might be quiet, but he is so sweet. He's the best brother!" Jzuna declared.

"He's lucky to have you," Bivon replied. "Can I pick him up in his tub? Will he let me?"

"He won't mind," Jzuna said miserably.

Bivon carried Thech all the way back into town with Jzuna floating beside them. Clutched in her tentacles was a bag containing a few of the children's possessions. Bivon positioned Thech's basin inside of the large traveling cart, and he secured it so that it would not shift during the journey.

"I'm sorry," Bivon said down to the monstrous, slime-covered little boy, and he repeated himself to Jzuna. "I'm sorry, child."

Bivon got his horse and hooked the animal to his cart, and before long, the three Shifts were starting on their journey. They were at the very southern end of the Great Southtrack, headed north.

The road out of the village led into the forest, and Hazel Cove was almost immediately out of sight. Their first day passed uneventfully, and just after sundown, the lights of Port Judy began to flicker through the trees.

A few folks enthusiastically approached Bivon to order teas or coffee, pleased to see the traveling vendor back in their village after being away for quite a while, but he informed them that he was fresh out of everything. He convinced his potential customers that he was headed to Teshon City in order to replenish his stock, and that he looked forward to serving them on his return journey.

Bivon parked his cart at the northern edge of Port Judy, out of the way and off to the side of the next leg of the Great Southtrack. Then he poked his head into the cart.

"Thech, Jzuna, are you two hungry?"

"No," Jzuna mumbled, but Thech's head popped up over the lip of his basin. His eyes were still rolled up in his head and his mouth still hung wide, but he was facing Bivon. He grunted once.

"I'm sorry," Jzuna said to Bivon, but she did not say anything more.

"You have nothing to be sorry about, Jzuna. I know you're sad, and there's nothing that can take away your sadness. You don't have to eat if you don't want to."

"We *are* hungry," Jzuna replied. "It just feels like everything hurts."

Bivon looked concerned. "Are you injured?"

"No, we're both just... just sad."

Thech let out a single moan, and Jzuna's voice fell quiet again.

"Give me a few minutes to get some dinner going for us," Bivon said. He sighed. The heartbreak he felt for the children's loss had been weighing on his soul throughout the day, and he wished there was a way to ease their sorrow.

Bivon gave his horse some feed, and he organized a little circle of stones and collected kindling while the animal ate. After a few minutes, a fire was crackling merrily, and Bivon stuck a cast iron pan in the flames. He let it heat, then removed it and cracked four eggs onto the hot surface. They sizzled.

"Dinner's nothing special," he informed the children. "Just frying some eggs for us to put on slices of bread I baked yesterday. It's a little crusty and should be nice. Jzuna," he continued, "I've seen your mother help Thech with his drinks, does he need help with his food?"

"Only sometimes," Jzuna replied. Her voice sounded empty. "You can just put his on a plate."

"Jzuna, Thech," Bivon said to them, "I'm so sorry she's gone. Your mother was a remarkably compassionate woman."

Neither child responded.

He decided to let them sit in silence.

The eggs were nearly done, and he used a spatula to gently flip them. He took the pan from the heat and let the eggs finish cooking as he sliced four thick pieces of dense bread. He placed an egg on each and put plates in front of the children. Bivon kept two eggs for himself, and he watched Thech and Jzuna as he ate. Each of them consumed their meals in different ways.

Jzuna stared at her egg and slice of bread, and they dematerialized and disappeared.

Thech appeared to struggle getting ahold of his food, and when he did, it seemed to take the unusual boy a significant amount of effort to get it into his sagging mouth. Once he succeeded, however, he chewed it up and rocked back and forth in a content way. He was also surprisingly tidy as he ate. After a few bites, both children's dinners were gone.

Bivon took their plates and asked, "Did you two have any friends in Hazel Cove? Or family?" He could still hear their mother's words in his head, *We have no one, no family.*

Jzuna answered Bivon in a quiet voice. "Mama used to let us play with our friends when we were Mai, but when we became Jzuna and Thech, the other kids' mommies and daddies didn't want them playing with us anymore."

"I'm sorry that happened." Bivon sighed. "There aren't many of our kind in Hazel Cove or these other coastal towns, but up in Teshon City, there are lots of people like us. I lived there for a few years, and I made friends with many Shifts. Before I moved back to Hazel Cove, I'd even gotten to know a few Bio-Shifts, like you two." He cleaned the slime left by Thech's fingers off the plate. "Teshon City will be different."

It was dark, and the unusual little boy climbed back into his basin.

"I think we're just gonna go to bed," Jzuna said.

Bivon was used to hearing her bright voice like chiming bells at his café. She had always been full of life and enthusiasm, and it crushed Bivon to hear her sounding so empty. "Okay, Jzuna," he replied, "I'll dim the lantern and let you rest. I'll be out here beside the cart if either of you need anything. I hope you both sleep peacefully."

Jzuna joined Thech in the basin, and she wrapped her many tentacles around his arms and legs and neck.

Bivon could hear Jzuna quietly sobbing and Thech groaning, and beneath the starry sky, the big red-bearded man was also brought to tears✪

Chapter 3 – Kosephaji, Relliduna, & Pelipi; Part One

Relliduna fluttered his eyes open. "Kos… Koseph…" he started to say.

"I'm right here, Duna," Kosephaji said quietly. He wanted his hurt friend to hear a voice he would recognize.

Relliduna tried to reach up and rub his head, but he could not. His body would not obey the commands he was giving it. He could not move.

Kosephaji took Relliduna's hand. "You've been injured."

Relliduna groaned. His body felt wrong.

"Duna, try not to move," Kosephaji said, barely able to hold back his tears. He was overwhelmed with joy and sorrow, relief and anger. He brought one of his hands to his mouth and smothered a sob. The sight of Relliduna broke his heart, and he upped the dose of sedatives and sent his friend drifting back into unconsciousness. "You'll be okay, Duna," Kosephaji said in a choked voice, and he repeated himself at a whisper. "You'll be okay."

Relliduna was strapped to a gurney. His body was mangled. He had been attacked, and he nearly died.

"I'm so glad I got to you in time," Kosephaji whispered over Relliduna's sleeping form, and he headed into the next room.

On top of a table sat an enclosed glass box. Floating directly in the box's center was a light. The light flickered in time with a voice that issued from the box.

"Duna woke up?"

"Only for a moment," Kosephaji replied. "I put him back under. Duna needs more time to recuperate; he needs to rest."

The blinking brightened and said, "Kosephaji, I wish you'd let me go burn those people's souls, burn them to death!"

"Pelipi!" Kosephaji snapped. "Don't say such things."

"Why not?" the light asked. "And why shouldn't I go kill those people who did that to Duna?"

Kosephaji looked toward the other room. "More violence won't solve anything," he replied.

The light dimmed slightly, and the voice said with forced calm, "It won't be violence; I'll just kill them."

Kosephaji frowned at the light. "Pelipi, please, stop talking like that. Duna is safe now." He sighed. "He needs more medicine, so I'm going back to the alchemist down the street. I'll grab myself some dinner while I'm out."

Pelipi flashed and asked, "Bring me back some scorpions?"

Kosephaji let out a small laugh, and trying to tap into the sass that usually existed between the three friends, he said, "You're one demanding-ass bitch; you know that, don't you Pelipi?"

Pelipi scoffed up at Kosephaji from his box. "*You're* a bitch!"

"*You're a bitch!*" Kosephaji repeated in a poor impression of Pelipi's voice, and he let out another little laugh. "And yes, Pelipi, of course I will. I'm glad you're with us. I'm glad you're with me," he added as he headed outside and locked the front door.

Kosephaji pulled his jacket tight and turned down a narrow lane, but his attention was drawn by a booming voice.

"Alright, you minnows!"

Kosephaji was stunned by what he saw. On one of the Ru River docks stood a giant. The enormous man was easily over three times the height of everyone else, and his thighs were thicker than the waists of the folks who bustled around him. He was clothed in a patchwork garment that accommodated his huge frame.

Behind the giant, floating on the waters of the Ru was a ship unlike anything Kosephaji had ever seen. The vessel was monstrously huge. It was made of a combination of steel and wood, with porthole windows lining its sides. The gargantuan boat's deck sat several stories above the waterline, and its main mast towered over every building in Ruburge.

"Good to be back in the city!" the giant said in his booming growl, and he laughed so loudly that the people nearest to him jumped. "Enjoy your week, troop. We set sail at dawn in seven days."

The giant headed straight up the street in the direction of Kosephaji.

He's like Duna, Kosephaji thought to himself, and even though he was nervous and did not have any extra money, he spoke as the giant approached. "How much is it to book passage on your vessel?"

The giant seemed to ignore the question at first, but he noticed Kosephaji's eyes on him.

"Were you talking to me, boy?" the giant rumbled. His tone of voice did not sound aggressive, but the huge man was intimidating.

"I'm sorry, yes," Kosephaji replied. "There are three, I mean, two of us."

The giant scrutinized him and asked, "Is it two, or three of you?"

"Sorry," Kosephaji said again, nervous by the enormous man, "it's just... just two of us."

"My ship doesn't leave for a week."

Kosephaji nodded up at him. "I know, I heard you say that, and I think the timing works perfectly for us, that is, if we're able to book passage with you."

"What's your story, kid?" the giant asked.

Kosephaji decided to be honest. "I have a… a friend who is very special to me, and he's like you, one of the *others*."

"Your friend's a Shift?" the huge man said without a hint of reservation in his voice.

Kosephaji looked over his shoulders and quietly said, "Yes, I think so, but he's not big like you are."

The giant gave him a knowing smirk. "You're just a young thing, kid. Do you think you can handle a journey by sea? Are you good at anything?"

"I've always wanted to be a healer," Kosephaji replied halfheartedly, "but I wasn't good enough to be accepted into the organic mechanic apprenticeship. I am passionate about helping others, though."

"What exactly does *wasn't good enough* mean?" the giant asked. "How good are you?"

"My friend, who I just mentioned, was recently attacked and horribly beaten; he would've died." Kosephaji paused. "I want to take him and leave. I just want to take him away from here."

The giant looked serious, but there was gentleness in his voice. "People can be very cruel to our kind. I'm sorry your friend was attacked. Are you a Shift, also?"

"No, I'm just a regular person."

The huge man frowned. "Maybe you shouldn't think of people in terms of *regular*, or by comparison *irregular*."

Kosephaji was taken aback, and he was also frightened of offending the giant. "I didn't mean it like that!"

"I'm sure you didn't, but words matter," the giant replied. "You wouldn't want to say something like that in front of your friend. What's your name, kid?"

"Kosephaji."

"I'm Ogomo," the giant declared in his rumbling voice. "And look, I won't charge you or your friend for passage, but you'll have to earn your place on my ship. Act as an assistant healer to the Demifae on my crew, and you boys can both come with us."

Kosephaji was surprised by the man's generosity. "Thank you," he said.

"Do you agree to the terms?" Ogomo asked.

Kosephaji shrugged nervously and said, "Relliduna is really messed up. I don't think that he'll be able to earn his way on the ship."

Ogomo smiled and replied, "Kosephaji, the deal I'm offering is just for *you* to help my mystic. I don't require anything from your injured friend." His brow crinkled at the middle, and he added, "I'm sorry that happened to him. And what a lovely name, please tell it to me again."

Kosephaji gave Ogomo a sheepish smile and said, "Relliduna, but we all call him Duna."

"*We all*, are you sure there's only two of you?"

"Sorry, *I*," Kosephaji replied quickly, "I call him Duna."

The giant raised an eyebrow. "How old are you, kid?"

"I'm 17. Me and Relliduna and... I mean, just us, we *both* are."

"Alright, Kosephaji," Ogomo replied, "be here before dawn, seven days from now."

"Okay, we will. Thank you, again."

Ogomo nodded his massive head and continued wherever he was going.

Kosephaji stood alone for a moment, feeling stunned and anxious. *Is this the right decision*, he thought. He headed toward the alchemist, and Relliduna's twisted body lying in the gutter flashed into Kosephaji's mind. He solidified his resolve. *We need to leave this city.*

He pulled open the front door to a shop underneath a sign painted with the words *Squelious & Petonicat's Apothecary, Herbshoppe, & Tincturista* and a series of bells jangled as Kosephaji entered. He removed a crumpled paper from his pocket, looked down at the handwritten list of items, and started collecting the things he needed. They were expensive, and Kosephaji was grateful for Ogomo's offer of free passage.

An hour later, he was home again. He looked over at the sleeping form of Relliduna and sighed, as Pelipi called from the other room, "Did you bring me..."

"Yes," Kosephaji interrupted quietly, "I got you some scorpions. Let me give Duna this dose of eternal chili pepper extract first. Hang on a second." He added one dropperful of red liquid to the bandage on Relliduna's ribs, and he placed the other items he purchased onto a small table beside the gurney.

Kosephaji entered the second room, picked up the glass box with the light in it, and he placed it on a shelf by an open window. He unlatched and lifted its lid. "Here you go," Kosephaji said as he picked up a large handheld fan. He unscrewed the top of a jar containing several scorpions and poured them into the box, as he waved the fan toward the window. Kosephaji scrunched his nose. With a quick series of high-pitched sizzles, the venomous creatures were scorched to nothing, and a vile aroma worse than burnt hair accompanied the feeding.

"Thank you," Pelipi said with satisfaction.

"You're welcome," Kosephaji replied. He resealed the lid of the glass box and added, "I think I've figured out a way we can leave."

"Really? What do you mean? How are we getting out of here?" Pelipi asked in quick succession, glowing brighter.

"There was…" Kosephaji hesitated and said quietly, "a Shift man who captains a ship. He's leaving a week from today, and he agreed to take us."

"How do you know he's a Shift?" Pelipi asked.

"Oh, there was no mistaking that, and he confirmed the fact while we were talking. His ship had just arrived, and when they leave again, I think we need to be with them."

"How did you afford tickets?"

Kosephaji shrugged. "He's going to have me assist his healer in exchange for passage."

Pelipi snickered. "Did you tell him you didn't get accepted into the apprenticeship?"

"Yes," Kosephaji answered miserably, "I told him. His healer's a Demifae, anyway, so it doesn't matter; I'll just help however I can."

"So, one week left in Ruburge," Pelipi said wistfully. "The day can't come soon enough for me!"

"Duna needs to heal," Kosephaji replied. "I think the timing will work well."

Seven days later, Kosephaji was helping Relliduna hobble down the dark pre-dawn streets toward the docks. Relliduna was not in great shape. The two of them pulled a little wheeled cart behind them with a few bags on it.

Kosephaji could hear Ogomo before he could see the giant, and he said, "Almost there."

They turned the corner toward one of the countless wharfs that jutted out into the Ru River, and Relliduna froze. "What on earth?" he whispered.

"Bitch, I told you he was a giant," Kosephaji said under his breath.

Relliduna scoffed. "I didn't actually believe you." Kosephaji tutted at him, but Relliduna said, "Shut up," before his friend could say something else sassy. "Alright, I get it; he's a giant. *Look at that ship,*" and he added with a weak snicker, "bitch."

Kosephaji shot Relliduna a smirk, and replied, "It's quite a boat."

A very normal-looking man approached Ogomo, pointed at Kosephaji and Relliduna, and he whispered something up to the giant. The enormous man turned in their direction.

"You made it," he boomed. "Good for you, lads. Wasn't there a third one of you? Ahh, well, welcome aboard, and remind me your names."

"Kosephaji," he said as they approached, "and this is Relliduna."

Ogomo turned to a woman who was loading gear into a large crate. "Nahli, will you please show the boys to their cabin?"

Nahli replied, "Aye-aye!" She was a handsome woman, taller than either of the two new arrivals, and Kosephaji and Relliduna both looked up slightly to her. She was muscular, and her nose was crooked. "So, you're the one helping me," she stated to Kosephaji with a grin.

"Oh, you're the mystic?" he replied.

"That I am," Nahli informed him. "Up the gangplank, you two."

There was a railing on only one side of the walkway. Relliduna leaned against it as Nahli helped him limp onto the ship, and Kosephaji carried their few possessions onboard.

Nahli led them below deck to a small cabin. "Get yourselves settled in; we head out with the sunrise."

The world outside was beginning to glow with the light that seeped over the horizon before the sun had crested.

Kosephaji and Relliduna heard shouting voices from above them, and they looked up at the ceiling.

"Are you going to let me out, or what?" came the muffled voice of Pelipi.

Kosephaji hushed him. "Keep it down!" he whispered. "You're not supposed to be here."

"What you *mean*," Relliduna interjected, "is that you didn't tell the giant about Pelipi and he doesn't know there's three of us."

"Why didn't you tell him about me?" Pelipi asked, speaking more quietly. Kosephaji opened one of the bags and lifted the glass box out of it, as Pelipi added, "Are you ashamed of me?"

"No," Kosephaji replied emphatically, "of course not, I just thought it would be more expensive to book passage for three of us, and we can easily hide you. I've been helping hide you for years."

"I'm a person, too," Pelipi mumbled.

"I know you are!" Kosephaji replied.

The ship suddenly lurched forward, and Kosephaji wobbled on his feet. He managed to keep his balance, but the movement was too much for Relliduna. He teetered and Kosephaji reached for him, but he fell to the floor.

Relliduna let fly a string of curses in his native tongue, and he gritted his teeth against the painful shock that radiated through him.

"I'm sorry," Kosephaji cried, kneeling beside him. "Where does it hurt? Is it one of my treatments?" his eyes moved over the bandages that covered Relliduna's many injuries.

"My arm," he replied through his teeth. "I landed on it, and your OM treatment popped out again."

"I'm sorry," Kosephaji repeated. "It was the best I could do."

Relliduna took a hissing breath. "It's okay. I know you saved me. That fall just hurt."

Kosephaji helped Relliduna to the bed, and he examined his friend's arm. He readjusted the organic mechanic repairs he had installed while Relliduna was unconscious, but Kosephaji could tell that the healings he performed were barely sufficient. He had managed to save Relliduna's life, and gotten him to some semblance of being okay, but that was all he did, he simply kept his friend from dying. His skills were seriously lacking.

Pelipi's voice came from his box, and he sounded like he could barely believe his own words. "By the great river, we're on our way, bitches!"

Kosephaji rose from the bed. He peered out the porthole at the landscape, as it appeared to slide by the ship, but he could not tell how fast they were traveling. The journey to the riverside village of Mellini should have taken almost an hour, but less than twenty minutes after leaving Ruburge, Ogomo's ship raced past the little town toward the pink sand beaches of southern Xin and the sparkling sea beyond★

Chapter 4 – Kosephaji, Relliduna, & Pelipi; Part Two

"I found Relliduna's body on the street," Kosephaji said. He was talking to Ogomo.

The giant's ship was approaching the mouth of the Ru River, where its waters emptied into the sea, and the morning sun was climbing in the clear sky.

Ogomo was in a massive chair at the boat's stern, and even seated, he still towered over Kosephaji. The captain was curious about the few new people onboard, and he had asked about Relliduna.

"Someone beat him within an inch of his life," Kosephaji explained. "I found him bleeding in front of our house. He can't remember what happened to him."

Kosephaji sighed and continued, "I've been working at an organic mechanic parts and gear shop during the week, and I volunteered at an OM clinic on the weekends. I did some shoddy treatments that worked; they kept him from dying, but they're not very good. *I'm* not very good."

"It sounds to me," Ogomo's voice boomed, "like you saved your friend's life, and I think you ought to give yourself a little more credit. From what I've heard tell of organic mechanics, their old methods are challenging."

"No," Kosephoji countered in a downtrodden tone, "I'm just inept."

"You're not," Ogomo retorted. "That boy's alive because of you." His eyes caught sight of something ahead of his ship, and he smiled. As the vessel approached, he stood and said, "From this elevated position, these beaches are a lovely sight."

The pink sand stretched out as far as the eye could see from either side of the mouth of the Ru River. The rosy grains sparkled in the morning sunlight, and the view was indeed breathtaking.

Kosephaji had visited the southern beaches a few times in his childhood, but he now stared out at them with awe. He got to appreciate the view for only a matter of moments, because the ship was sailing straight out into the ocean at a serious clip, and the land behind was quickly shrinking into the distance.

"Get below, lad," Ogomo said to Kosephaji. "The crew's got some work to do, and we'll let you know when meals are served."

Kosephaji nodded and headed down to his cabin.

As soon as he closed the door, Pelipi said from inside his box, "What did he want? Why did he want to talk to you?"

Kosephaji hushed him. "Be quiet; Duna's sleeping."

"Not anymore," Relliduna groaned.

"That's *your* fault," Kosephaji said to Pelipi.

"He's slept enough. What did the giant want?" Pelipi asked.

"His name's Ogomo. Don't call him *the giant*. He just wanted to know what happened to Duna." Kosephaji turned to Relliduna and asked, "How are you feeling?" He began inspecting the mechanical repairs, cringing as he examined his mediocre work. "I need to patch a few things."

"I'm okay," Relliduna replied.

"Are you in pain?"

Relliduna gave Kosephaji a defeated look. "Maybe a little less," he said unconvincingly. "Everything kind of aches."

Kosephaji set about modifying his repairs to the best of his ability. "I wish I could take away your pain," he whispered.

There were several adjustments that caused Relliduna to hiss and wince away from his friend's ministrations.

"I'm sorry," Kosephaji mumbled more than once before he was finished.

"It's okay," Relliduna replied, taking Kosephaji's hand. "Thank you."

There was a knock from outside their cabin.

Kosephaji tossed his jacket over Pelipi's box and opened the door.

"Food's up," said a deckhand. Without another word, he turned and left.

"I'll bring you some lunch," Kosephaji told Relliduna, and he followed the man. He closed the door and climbed back up into the sunshine.

The healer waved him over to her. She was ladling a bowlful of stew. Kosephaji approached and she handed him the bowl.

"Thank you, erm…" he said, trying to remember her name. He could not. "I'm sorry, can you please remind me your name?"

"It's Nahli," she replied with a smirk. "Ogomo tells me you're not very good at medicine." She was quite a bit older than Kosephaji, but she spoke to him in a casual and playful tone of voice, almost as if she had been friends with him for years. "And you apparently can't remember names," she commented. "So, what *are* you good at?"

Kosephaji felt embarrassed. "I got rejected from the organic mechanic apprenticeship program in Tuilii la Ru." Nahli burst out laughing, and Kosephaji did not think he could feel more awkward.

Nahli eyed him. "I thought anyone could get into that apprenticeship! Aren't they desperate for fresh fodder? You seem like the perfect type for them to mold into their little minion." Nahli laughed again. "I don't mess with that OM stuff, but do you think you can handle helping me with my potions?" A puckish grin was on her face. "Here," she added, thrusting a second bowl of stew into his other hand, "for your friend."

A few minutes later, Kosephaji was back in the small cabin with his two companions. "You'll have to make do with cooked food for the rest of the trip after this," he said to Pelipi, holding the box by the round porthole window. He poured in the last of the scorpions and the fumes were sucked out and dispersed over the ocean.

Kosephaji and Relliduna ate their dinner while Pelipi talked, and his light blinked along with his voice. "It's hard to believe we're doing this. We left Ruburge, bitches. *We've left Xin!* This ship is huge, and it's so fast; where do you suppose we'll end up? Did the giant, I mean the *captain* tell you our destination?"

"I overheard him say that he was looking for someplace new," Kosephaji replied between bites, "someplace that isn't Xin,"

"How big do you suppose the whole world is?" Pelipi asked rhetorically. "Do you really think there are places where people view Shifts differently than the way Xinitians do?"

"Aren't you not supposed to use that word, *Shift?*" Kosephaji asked.

Pelipi's flickering light intensified. "Well, what else should I call myself, huh? Me and Duna *are* what we are. We're Shifts, and we should be allowed to be proud of who we are!"

"I agree with Pelipi," Relliduna added. "He's not wrong; we should be able to be ourselves. Most people say the word Shift under their breath, but that's not right, not to people like us."

"Yeah, gurl! I'm a Shift, and I'm proud," Pelipi declared.

"I hope there really is someplace that views us differently," Relliduna said to Pelipi.

Kosephaji set his spoon down in his empty bowl and said, "It already does feel like we're someplace new. We're on a ship captained by a Shift," and he tried not to let his voice drop as he said the word, "meaning someone like both of you is actually in charge here."

"By the looks of him," Relliduna added, "I would guess he's actually a Bio-Shift, like Pelipi!"

"Yes," Kosephaji chuckled, "and Ogomo's not in hiding... erm... not that it'd be easy for him to hide."

Pelipi continued talking. "What do you think we'll find, wherever it is we're going? Kosephaji, you said the ship is heading south; I have no idea what lies to the south. When I was a boy, my older brother took me to a map shop. Other lands around the world fascinated him, but bitches, I couldn't have thought it was more boring."

Relliduna snorted a laugh and winced at a fresh flash of pain. He took his last bite of stew and placed his bowl into Kosephaji's.

"I don't remember a single thing about the maps my brother liked," Pelipi added. "Kosephaji, I didn't think to ask, did you see any other Shifts in the crew? I'll bet the captain's got other Shifts working with him."

Relliduna quietly interrupted. "Hey," he said, and he fixed his eyes on Kosephaji. Pelipi stopped talking, and Relliduna spoke in a quavering voice. It sounded like he was trying to hold back tears. "Thanks for not... I don't know, not giving up on us, or abandoning us when we became Shifts."

Kosephaji was surprised. "What do you mean *became?* You've both always been Shifts." He looked from Relliduna to Pelipi and back again. "Even though when we were kids and it was dormant inside of you, and even though it feels weird for me to use the word

Shift without it meaning something bad," he paused and gathered his thoughts. "When it came out first that you, Relliduna, and then you, Pelipi, were both Shifts… I don't know, I still just saw you as Relliduna and Pelipi, that you'd *always* been Relliduna and Pelipi." Kosephaji let out a wry laugh and added, "There was a brief time afterward that I thought I might be next, thought I might be one too, but nothing ever happened for me."

"And we love you just the way you are, gurl!" Pelipi declared, blinking brightly.

Kosephaji smiled and rolled his eyes at his friends. "Let me take these bowls back to the cook."

The following four days passed similarly. The crew ate twice daily, once in the late mornings and once in the late afternoons, and Kosephaji took each meal to Relliduna and Pelipi in their cabin. He was only called to help Nahli with a few minor injuries crewmembers sustained, and he spent the rest of his time in the small room with his two companions.

Late on the fourth evening, there was a knock on the cabin door, and the deckhand who alerted them of mealtimes said, "Cap'n wants to see Relliduna." The man turned without any further explanation and descended a flight of stairs that led deeper into the bowels of the ship.

"Me?" Relliduna asked the empty doorway. "Erm… okay… he hasn't wanted to talk with me before."

"That's weird," Kosephaji said. "Do you want me to go instead?"

"If he wants to talk to me," Relliduna replied, "I don't think it'd be a good idea to send you in my place."

"What do you suppose he wants?" Pelipi asked.

Kosephaji shushed him. "Keep your voice down!" he said under his breath. "The door's open." He turned to Relliduna. "Duna, do you want my help getting above?"

"No, that's okay, I've been getting a little better each day. I think I'll be alright."

He left Kosephaji and Pelipi in the small room and hobbled up the narrow flight of steps to the deck of the ship. It was impossible for him to miss the giant.

Ogomo was seated at the back of the boat. He raised a hand and waved Relliduna over.

Relliduna joined him, feeling very small next to the giant.

"Haven't seen land since we left Xin," Ogomo said in a casual way that still boomed. "Just ocean in every direction, as far as the eye can see. It's breathtaking, mesmerizing, hypnotic."

Ogomo did not speak for a moment, and Relliduna asked him, "Where are we headed?" Even his voice felt small.

Instead of answering, Ogomo asked, "How many people have been staying in your cabin?"

The giant's question caught Relliduna completely off-guard. He knew Kosephaji had told Ogomo there were only the two of them, and for a split second, Relliduna considered doubling down on Kosephaji's lie, but he blurted out, "Three!" He followed it with, "There's three of us! I'm sorry, we weren't trying to lie to you. The third one of us is... not... really... a person?"

Ogomo let out a friendly chuckle. "I knew there were three of you before you even got on my ship. I knew there was a stowaway." He gave Relliduna a kind smile that did not seem to go with his accusatory words, and he continued. "One of my crew calls himself a Shift-Seer. He's a Shift who can detect other Shifts. He could feel your Bio-Shift friend, even though we couldn't see him, but I wasn't going to stop an injured Shift and a hidden Bio-Shift from escaping Xin. Incidentally, how are you hiding him?"

"He doesn't take up much space."

The giant studied Relliduna's face for a moment before continuing. "Some Shifts in Xin manage to make a way for themselves, to thrive. Others keep themselves hidden for their entire lives, and good for them! But any Xinitian Shift who wants to leave and has the means to do so, I support them. I support you, Relliduna," Ogomo added, "and your other secret friend is welcome with us on my ship. Thank you for telling me," he added with another grin.

"My... my friends all call me Duna," Relliduna said.

Ogomo raised an eyebrow and smirked. "Are you saying we're friends? Do I get to call you Duna?"

Relliduna gave the enormous man a sheepish smile and nodded.

Ogomo let out a booming laugh and said, "Well, Duna, you and your hidden friend, and your human companion who's helping you, you three are all welcome!"✪

Chapter 5 – Ilya, Part One

Ilya often made trips into the forested mountains around Teshon City. "I'll see you three in a few days," she said to Dozi, Harakin, and Sumi.

"Have fun!" Harakin replied.

"Yeah," Sumi agreed, "I hope you have a great time."

"Be safe," Dozi added with a warm smile.

Ilya's feet lifted off the ground, and she soared high into the sky above the city. She always left after nightfall, when the streets were empty and it was unlikely for someone to see her flying.

Every flight felt good to her, as she flexed her powers, speeding through the sky in defiance of gravity. The solitude in the mountains was something she treasured. There were several locations around the area that had become favorite spots, and it took Ilya an hour at most to fly to any of them, but that night, she wanted to explore. She rose higher above the mountains than she usually did, and the forest whipped by far below her as she sailed through the night sky. Exploring may have been the reason she told herself, but Ilya just wanted to fly.

High in the atmosphere, the cold wind whipped, but her body was unaffected by the low temperatures. She loved her gifts, was *in love* with her gifts, and she embraced her powers, corkscrewing and spiraling and looping in the air with exuberance. There was a time in Ilya's life that she wished she had been born a human, but those feelings now belonged to a completely different person, the one she used to be. She was ready to unleash her powers.

One hour of flight stretched into two, and still Ilya soared for the sheer joy of it. She was above even the highest mountain peaks, yet there seemed to be no restriction to how high she could fly. Even in the thinning atmosphere, her powers protected her. Ilya could breathe effortlessly, and she climbed until the blue of the sky thinned to the inky blackness of space. She could see the curvature of the earth.

Ilya's soul felt enraptured in the flight. She was the person who she was always meant to be.

From her extreme altitude, she paused to look back, but she could no longer see the glow of Teshon City. Her eyes were drawn to lights that flickered in a number of distant regions, indicating other human habitations. Then she looked inland, toward the moon that was starting to rise. It was not full, but it was bright, and it illuminated an off-color patch of forest beneath it on the far horizon. Ilya commanded her powers to take her toward it.

The spot slowly drew nearer as she flew, and the moon continued to slide up the sky. It was over an hour later before Ilya could make out what she was seeing. The sight of dead trees was not unusual, but this anomalous grey patch of forest in a perfect circle was strange. She approached and realized that the trees appeared more than simply dead; it was almost as if the very pigment of the wood itself had been sapped. The grey of the spot below her was pale and the trees looked more like enormous dried bones.

Ilya could see a person, and she came in for her landing, but it was as if her powers sputtered and failed. She stumbled, lost her footing, and fell to the grey dirt.

A man came rushing toward her through the trees. He looked to be several years older than she, and he was very distressed.

"Who are you?!" he asked loudly, but there was no anger in his tone.

"Blah..." Ilya groaned. "What's wrong with me?" She pushed herself upright, but then she staggered and leaned against the trunk of a dead tree. She brought her palm to her forehead.

"You shouldn't be here!" the man declared urgently. "It isn't safe for you!" He was wringing his hands together anxiously. "Please," he implored, "I know you're a Shift. I'm one too, but my power makes people sick, and it's much worse for other Shifts. You need to leave!"

Ilya reached out and took one of his hands.

He looked shocked and tried to pull away from her.

"I'm Ilya," she said. "What... what's your name?" Her head was starting to spin.

"*Please*," he repeated, "you can't stay here! It's my power; it sucks the life out of everything. That's why I have to live alone deep in the forest."

"That's so tragic," Ilya replied in a quavering voice. "You can't turn it off?"

"No," he answered, "I was told that it started before I was born and made my entire village sick. It killed my mother, and the town was abandoned. I was raised in isolation, but when I was able to take care of myself, I left and headed out here to live away from anyone I could hurt."

"I'm so sorry about your mother," Ilya said. Her legs were getting weak. "But there must be something that someone could do. I have a friend who built a device that made another Shift's mantis gland invisible. Maybe she could…" her voice got caught in her throat as a wave of nausea rippled through her. "Ugh, I don't feel good."

The man looked excited. "Do you think your friend has a way to turn off my mantis gland?"

"I don't know, maybe; I'll ask her when I get back to Teshon City, but it's far."

"Listen," the man said, "all I need to do is leave you alone, and you'll recover immediately. But will you come back? Will you bring your friend? I don't want to be this *thing* anymore. Please."

"What's your name?" Ilya asked again. She dropped to her knees.

"Unadi," he replied, "my name's Unadi."

"I'll come back, Unadi, but it's gonna be a while," she mumbled. She felt very weak.

"Thank you, and I'm so sorry I made you sick." Unadi turned his back on Ilya and ran.

A moment later, he was no longer visible through the moonlit trees, and a short time after that, it felt to Ilya like a blanket of illness suddenly lifted off her. She blinked her eyes a few times and stood up as if she had not felt ill at all. Testing her powers, they obeyed her perfectly, and her feet rose off the ground.

"Okay, Unadi," she said to the dead trees, "let's see what Olona can do for you," and with the gibbous moon nearing its zenith in the dark sky, Ilya took off back toward Teshon City★

Chapter 6 – Unadi & Olona, Part One

Unadi was in his shack. The little building stood at the dead center of the lifeless grey circle. He was anxious for Ilya to return with the friend who he hoped would be able to turn him into something other than a perpetual devourer of life. He could not remember a single other time in his existence when he hoped a person would come *into* his region of death. Now it was his sole thought.

The hours of night continued to slip by, and Unadi tried reading to distract himself. He selected an old reprint of a technical manual that one of his tutors insisted he take with him into his self-imposed isolation, and his eyes moved over the information he found so boring. Unadi ended up flipping through quite a few of his books in an unfocused way. One of the volumes was on the origins and development of early organic mechanics. Another told of the rise and fall of the Oselian Empire. There was even a banned book in his possession, which contained details from several illegal scientific research projects. Many experts at the time of its original printing considered the contents highly controversial.

None of the books helped.

Unadi was completely fixated on the idea of no longer being a Shift, and all he could do in the moment was wish for Ilya to hurry back. He had no idea where Teshon City was. She told him it would be some time before she could return, but Unadi kept checking his window for any sign of her. *Looking* was unnecessary; he would feel Ilya's presence again the instant his power started to afflict her and the friend she mentioned.

The hours slowly dragged until the dawn was beginning to glow. Then the day came and went. Another and another and another slipped away, yet there was no sign of Ilya, and Unadi lost hope that she would return.

Early on the sixth morning, Unadi was startled. To his surprise, he could feel Ilya; she was back! He instantly honed in on her and raced through the dead trees in the direction of the life forces he could feel himself absorbing. Two women were walking toward him, and any frustrations he felt during his time of waiting were instantly replaced by joy that he could barely contain.

"Unadi!" Ilya called out to him as he approached. "This is Olona. She thinks she can help, but not on her own." Ilya was instantly woozy, but Olona was not affected as quickly by Unadi's powers.

He initially had doubts about the young woman, but then Olona spoke.

"I need to go with you to discuss how this will work. Ilya has to fly back and get someone else we need. Once you and I are far enough away and she can fly again, it's going to take her quite a while before she returns, so I'll need to have some space away from you for that interim."

Unadi was surprised and impressed. "You already understand what's going on?" He looked at Ilya.

"I told her all about our encounter," she answered, leaning against a tree as a wave of dizziness washed over her.

Olona continued. "I accepted everything Ilya told me as correct and factual, and I've been preparing for this trip to you with that mindset. I think we're going to be able to help." She gave Unadi a confident smile, and she dug in her bag and pulled out a device wrapped in cloth.

"That's the thing I told you about," Ilya said to Unadi.

Olona went on, "You're going to wear this halo, which I've reconfigured to focus on your mantis gland. When our other friend gets here, she will use her unique siphoning ability channeled through the halo, and the combination will deactivate your energies of absorption." She placed her hand on his arm. "I can't even imagine how much heartache your powers have caused you, but Unadi, are you sure you want to do this?"

"Unquestionably," he replied without hesitation.

"Alright, let's give Ilya her space so she can head back to Teshon City."

"Yes, okay, right," Unadi replied.

Ilya turned and started staggering into the living trees, as Olona followed Unadi into his lifeless realm. After several minutes he informed her that Ilya was again beyond the reach of his powers, and just as he said it, they saw her lift off and soar into the morning sky. Soon he and Olona arrived at his little dwelling; she was just beginning to feel unwell.

She removed the device from her bag, unwrapped it, and handed a single piece to Unadi. "Bring this to your forehead," she instructed, and her voice was a little weaker than she expected. "I need to configure the two components."

Unadi stood still with a small piece of machinery that looked like a partial star shape held against his brow, while Olona made a few adjustments to a separate square contraption in her hand. She brought it up to the device he was holding and it beeped.

Olona smiled. "Done," she informed him, taking back the portion from him. She wrapped it, stowed it in her bag, and applied the final setting to the square she was holding. It folded in on itself and became a little solid cube. The object had no external components, and its outside was plain. Olona looked up and said, "This is going to work." Then she noticed Unadi's books. She did a double-take and gawked at them. "*How is that possible?*" she asked.

"How is..." His eyes followed hers. "How is what possible?"

Olona brought her fingertips to the spines. "Where on earth did you get these books?" She looked over at him. "People where I'm from in Xin talked about these, and how they no longer exist. I've read books inspired by and based on these books, but I'm totally flabbergasted that you've got original copies here!"

"I'm from the mining village of Bahlim," Unadi explained. "It's an old Oselian salt mine, and in the valley below is one of their libraries. It's carved right into the side of the mountain, and the salt keeps the moisture low enough to preserve books indefinitely."

Unadi continued. "In my dead region, nothing can decay, so the books are still preserved in my presence. Do you want to read them? Since it's going to be a while before Ilya returns, and I can't stay near you for much longer, why don't you take a few books outside of my region? I'll wait here until I can feel both of you again, and then I'll come to you."

"There will be three of us next time," Olona reminded him.

"How long do you think it will be before Ilya gets back?"

"Six hours, at the very least," Olona replied. "It was a three-hour flight, one way. We left *really* early in the morning. Once she gets back to Teshon, she'll likely eat and rest for a bit. I wouldn't expect her to return before this evening. I packed myself some food for while I wait."

"You really did think this through, didn't you?"

Olona gave Unadi another smile. "If you're alright with it, I'd love to stick several of these books in my bag."

"Please, take all you like!"

"Thank you, Unadi." Olona packed quite a few of them, and she left.

After a short while, Unadi could no longer feel her; Olona was in the dense forest just outside of his area of effect.

Right at the edge of the ring of death, she found herself a comfortable spot, lit a joint, and she started to read. Olona poured over the volumes as the hours slipped toward noon, and she was astonished by some of the information she came across.

In a massive tome titled *The Awesome and Terrible Collapse of the Many Nations of Oselia*, Olona found a chapter about organic mechanic experimentation combined with genetic enhancements. The physiological manipulators had created living cybertronic weapons and armor, which sounded to Olona very similar to some of the procedures she had performed on herself. The technical information contained may have bored most others, but Olona was fascinated by what she was learning.

Stuck in a book called *A Retrospective Look at the American Empire After the Devastation*, she found an old photograph with an article titled *The Cursed Village*. The picture was of a hillside village, and on the back, the words "The mining community of Bahlim Town before the ghost sickness" were written in scratchy letters. The newspaper clipping was not dated and there was no publication information.

*

> When a strange plague struck the hillside village of Bahlim Town, people started claiming that the old mining community was cursed. It began in the year 224 AE, and the townsfolk called it the ghost sickness. The illness affected only a few children at first, but then some of the elders contracted it, and the disease slowly continued to spread. Over the course of several weeks, the ghost sickness proved to have no preference for its hosts. Livestock, and even crops were afflicted; it seemed that nothing was immune.
>
> Some of the inhabitants of Bahlim Town fled their village, and each of them made a complete and immediate recovery by simply venturing to the valley below. For most, that confirmed something in the town was the cause of the ghost sickness. To be healed, all a person needed to do was leave the village, but many of

the people wished to remain in their homes on the hill, and the first deaths happened several painful months after the initial spread.

Wise folk and scribes came from all around the neighboring region, and they tested many theories, but they struggled to determine the cause behind the ghost sickness. The community water was not tainted. No strange vapors were emanating from the old mine. The illness seemed to be entirely connected to the village itself, and the rumor of Bahlim Town's curse spread throughout the land.

Eventually, the reason for the suffering was found, and it came from a very unexpected place. A pregnant woman was the only person in the village who did not get sick, and it began to occur to some of the healers that she was the carrier. It was not her fault, nor was she to blame for the so-called curse, but the disease seemed to relate to her directly. The ghost sickness did not cause its victims immediate bodily distress, but before she gave birth, everyone who insisted upon remaining in the village had become ill.

She was not persecuted for the suffering, and in fact, many wise women and men spent time trying to purge it from the pregnant woman. Groups of three or four healers would venture up the mountain, spending a day and a night with her, and they left as the sickness began to affect them. Many tests were performed over the course of the woman's third trimester, including on her blood, urine, and saliva. The midwives examined her entire body and declared that they could find nothing wrong with the woman or her pregnancy.

At the end of her nine months carrying the baby, her labor pains began to strike, and at that point the midwives refused to let any of the other wise folk visit her. The traveling healers remained in the valley below.

During her hours of labor, the ghost sickness became more severe, and those assisting with the birth were not able to stay for more than a few hours before needing to return to the lowlands, away from the source of the curse.

A brutal 18 and a half hours later, a baby boy was born. He was not frail or malformed, and he was alert from his first breath. The infant seemed entirely unaffected by the ghost sickness.

However, his mother immediately succumbed. The symptoms of the disease hit her like a crushing boulder, and before the eyes of the midwives, her life began to eke away.

She could feel her existence extinguishing, and she reached for her child. With her final breath, she spoke his name. "Unadi," she whispered, and she died.

Unadi's mother was not the first woman to die in childbirth, but the midwives were shocked at her instantaneous deterioration.

The babe was cleaned and wrapped in a blanket, but things in the village were getting worse. No one was able to hold Unadi for more than a few minutes, before they too fell ill.

Another team of midwives was called in, and by that point, everyone in the village was in a terrible state. The new group was warned against touching the child, lest they also suffer the worst of the disease. At first, some of them refused to believe the ghost sickness was somehow related to an infant, but a few hours after he was born, most of the midwives refused to touch him.

Over the course of Unadi's first week of life it was determined, and there could be no doubt that the infant was the source of the sickness. The villagers were forced to evacuate, and the child was left as Bahlim Town's only permanent inhabitant. Several people recommended euthanizing the baby and returning the village to its former state, but that idea did not come to fruition, nor was banishing the infant alone an option. It would be years before Unadi could fend for himself.

No one was able to be in his presence for much time, so a group of compassionate and determined volunteers began working in teams to care for the baby. Two nurses at a time would climb up the path to Bahlim Town, following a set schedule and giving the others their space for recovery.

Even among the group of Unadi's caregivers, most refused to lay a finger on him. Within a matter of minutes, those who *did* insist upon sharing their parental affections with the child were stricken by the strongest symptoms of the ghost sickness. They stated that it was necessary for Unadi to have the physical contact of another human, and a few of them were willing to suffer for his sake.

Without exception, every single living being that stayed in the presence of little Unadi for too long ended up dying. Before his first birthday, the patch of death that stretched out and surrounded Bahlim Town had become a stark indicator of how far the ghost sickness reached.

Within the patch of death, no leaves grew on the dry trees. Not a single needle still clung to any of the evergreens. The grass and clover and moss that once blanketed the forest floor were dead and grey. Low bushes that used to thrive in the shade of the canopy above were now little more than scraggly knots of twisted branches. Even the soil itself no longer teemed with life. Bacteria, viruses, protozoa, and any microscopic life that existed too close to Unadi also died.

*

The article just seemed to end, and Olona wondered if there was more to it that had been lost, or if that was simply the extent of the story. She also got the impression that someone who knew Unadi in his youth had written it. Folding the paper around the photograph, she stuck them back into the book.

As the sun reached its peak, Olona decided to break out some of the food she had packed.

During the several days before Ilya returned to Unadi, Olona constructed a harness. It allowed Ilya to fly with an extra person much more easily. Olona built a few compartments into the harness that allowed them to carry some supplies and food, since she knew her time in the forest was going to be extensive.

Olona unwrapped one of Dozi's meat pies and enjoyed a bite. It was delicious. She pulled a thin paperback from her bag and examined its cheap-looking cover, scrawled with letters that read *Reprint Edition Six: The Parisian Experiments, Years 14-19 AE – Terminated.*

She began to read.

The small booklet was written in the first-person perspective, and much of the information contained in it shocked and disturbed Olona. She read every word of the entire thing while she ate, but partway through, one section in particular caught her attention. She paused and reread the paragraphs aloud.

"Within the crystalline structure of every photonova gland that we've extracted resides a minuscule trigger mechanism along with a single droplet of watery fluid. When the internal switch is flipped, which happens after the onset of puberty, a tiny limb instantaneously extends and retracts. The trigger's firing causes a cavitation bubble to form in the liquid. This action is only achieved by a single other organism in nature, the stomatopod colloquially referred to as the mantis shrimp. In the lab, we've been calling photonova glands *mantis glands* and the nickname has been picked up by some of the staff."

Olona stopped reading and asked in surprise, "The word *mantis* doesn't have anything to do with an insect? I thought it was something about praying mantises this whole time."

She continued reading aloud. "In the ocean, the mantis shrimps' cavitation bubbles collapse in on themselves. Within photonova glands, there occurs an extraordinary phenomenon. A pinprick wormhole actually opens to the universe, and the glands' access to cosmic energy provides these evolved individuals with their powers."

Olona scrunched up her face. "*Mantis* really doesn't have anything to do with bugs?" she asked the little book.

Its contents went on to reveal that the practice of pinealectomy surgeries had been performed on living humans to remove diseased pineal glands from inside their heads, and that several Shifts – a term which the paperback never actually used – had briefly survived having their photonova glands removed by the same procedure. None of them had lived longer than 36 hours.

When Olona finished reading the small book, she looked at the front cover again. "Years 14 through 19 of the Advanced Era. So, this study happened *right* at the beginning, right when people realized their kids were not just going through puberty, but they were Shifts. I wonder when the term *Shift* was first used."

Realization set in for her. "Wait a second..." Olona took a sharp breath. "These experiments ended only 19 years after Shifts first appeared in the world, which means the oldest that any of these test subjects could have been was 19." She gasped. "They were all just kids!" She stuffed the book back into her bag, muttered, "Gross," and she took out Unadi's *Organic Mechanic Practices, Vol. 2*. It was a large book.

"Time to distract myself with something *not* horrible." Olona sparked another joint, breathed a cloud of smoke into the air, and she opened to the publishing notes. "Year 59?! Being printed in 59AE makes this book almost 150 years old! Wow," she marveled.

The book kept her focused for several hours, as she poured over information about all sorts of things that fascinated her. It had been written by the very people who invented the practices, and Olona was enthralled by it until the sunlight started to fade.

Lahari's voice eventually called out to her from above. "Olona!"

She closed the book, stood, and stretched. Olona yawned wide.

Ilya came in for a landing, and her and Lahari's feet touched down.

"You must be exhausted," Olona said to Ilya. "You've been flying nonstop for hours!"

Ilya did not look tired at all. “Flying energizes me, and the longer I fly, the more I want to! My brain is telling me it’s getting close to bedtime, but I don’t feel exhausted, not like I might after a strenuous hike.”

Olona looked curious. “Unadi let me borrow some old books that have a lot of information I wasn’t expecting, and tons of stuff I didn’t know.” She picked up one and started flipping through it. “I think it was this book that said something about mantis glands providing Shifts with unlimited energy for their powers, and that using those powers didn’t require your own strength. Hang on, where is that part I read earlier?” She kept flipping.

“So where is he?” Lahari asked.

Olona looked up from the book. “Unadi said all we need to do is walk into his region,” she explained, pointing at the dead trees, “and he’ll immediately be able to feel us and come running.”

“Let’s do it,” Ilya said, and the three women entered his lifeless circle.

By the time Unadi ran up to them, Ilya and Lahari were already feeling the first symptoms, and he froze in his tracks at the sight of Lahari. “*What?*” he managed.

“Oh, yes,” Olona said, “we probably should have mentioned our Bio-Shift friend to you. This is Lahari.”

“I know,” Lahari said to Unadi. She struck a very subtle version of one of the dramatic poses Auntie Peg liked to strike. “I’m weird,” she added, “but I think Olona is right; I think we can turn off your mantis gland.” A wave of nausea quavered through her and she leaned against a tree.

“You’re a… Bio-Shift? I’ve only read about your kind.” Unadi’s initial surprise at Lahari’s appearance had quickly shifted to wonder. Then he noticed Ilya was carrying a large sack on her back. “What’s that?”

“It’s a tent. We’re going to need to stay here in your forest tonight, *outside* your ring.”

“You won’t need to stay on the outside if we turn off my mantis gland,” Unadi replied. “How did you three even orchestrate all of this?”

Olona answered for the two Shift women, who were feeling worse by the minute. “We had to write out a pretty specific timetable, and we needed to plan for food and water. It also took me a few days to build a harness for Ilya to carry us. She had expressed how much it would mean for you to no longer have this power."

"It's a curse," Unadi retorted.

"Here in the forest," Olona continued, "you were too far apart to have discussed a plan with you ahead of time, so the three of us figured out how to make it work to come and help you."

Olona dug in her bag again and removed the halo in its cloth. She unwrapped it, held two pieces, and handed the third to Unadi. "Hold this against your forehead again, and I'll attach these to it."

The three parts connected and slid into each other, folding flat and forming a delicate halo.

"This used to protect another Shift friend of ours from being detectable to monsters," Olona added, and she turned. "Lahari, please, hold this. It's a channeler."

Lahari extended her scaly blue hand, and Olona placed the metal cube onto her palm.

"Just reach forward," Olona explained, "so that the channeler is between you and Unadi. When you use your powers, they will flow through the channeler and into the halo." She turned to Unadi. "And the combination of her powers and my organic mechanic gear will disengage your mantis gland." She gave him another smile and felt confident that she was explaining things clearly.

"*How* is everything going to work exactly?" Unadi asked her. He looked entirely perplexed.

"Yeah," Lahari added weakly, "what are we actually doing?"

Olona took a deep breath and puffed out her cheeks. "You don't need to do anything, just use your power, and it will go through the channeler and the halo, and Unadi's mantis gland will deactivate."

"That's it?" Ilya asked. She leaned against a tree.

"The two machines will do the rest between them," Olona replied.

Lahari and Unadi looked at each other.

"I'm ready," he told her.

Lahari nodded, extended her blue scaly arm forward with the cube in her hand, and she activated her powers✪

Chapter 7 – Lonklam & Ronging

Ronging lumbered toward the sound of his companion's voice. They were high in the forested mountains and had been separated. Thech and Jzuna's powers sent the two monsters on a flight that had left them both far from any human habitation, but neither of them was injured from the fall. Ronging's flesh had been scorched, but he would heal quickly.

"Ronging! Where are you?!" came Lonklam's voice from a distance.

Ronging trudged through the snow but the cold did not affect his strange enhanced body; he did not care that he was deep in the high forest. With his craving recently satiated, he merely desired to be near one of his own kind.

"*Ronging!*" Lonklam roared again.

A moment later, the monsters caught sight of each other. "Finally," Lonklam said as Ronging drew near to him. "My body begins to burn. I needed to feed on one of those Shifts, and I was denied. We must return to the village."

Ronging did not reply.

"Come," Lonklam commanded, and his desire drove him.

It was a day and a night before the two monsters made it back to Hazel Cove, and Lonklam led Ronging to his contact again. It was before dawn when the monster pounded on the door.

A moment later, the little window opened.

"Master Lonklam," the doorman said in surprise, "what are you…" but Lonklam slammed into the door, breaking it open and knocking the man back. He fell to the floor and looked up at the monster in alarm. "Master Lonklam?!"

"*Where is it?*"

The doorman quavered, "Where is what?"

"I can feel it on you," Lonklam growled. He grabbed the man with his multiple arms and pulled him very close to his mouths. Lonklam breathed his scent, but the doorman was not who he was after; humans were not his prey.

"Where is it?!" the monster roared, throwing the man back to the floor. Lonklam stormed past him, and his unearthly senses drew him toward a flight of stairs. He climbed them awkwardly, with the doorman close on his heels.

"Master Lonklam," he cried out in distress, "there's nothing up there for you! I live upstairs with my family. My shop is down below and the pleasure dungeon in the basement can be made available, even though it's very early in the morning, but please don't go upstairs!"

Lonklam ignored every word and reached the top of the flight. He grabbed a door handle, and the man's urgency increased.

"*That's my son's room*; he's just a boy! There can't be anything you want in there. Please, master Lonklam, let me take you downstairs and we can get you whatever you need."

Suddenly, the monster cried out in rage, and he smashed through the door like a tornado. Shrapnel splinters of wood darted through the air, and the man's son awoke in fright. Lonklam grabbed the boy and used his frail little body like a battering ram, smashing the child into and *through* the second-story wall of the building. The boy was dead before he could scream. The monster fell, holding the child's corpse, and Lonklam landed on the hard earth with the boy beneath him.

From the hole in the wall above, the boy's father let out a wail of anguish, as he watched Ronging and Lonklam disappear into the woods with the twisted corpse of his son★

Chapter 8 – Tragedy

The sun was setting over the grey spot of dead trees deep in the forest.

Unadi and Lahari suddenly screamed, startling Ilya and Olona.

Lahari was using her powers, pouring them into Unadi through Olona's channeler and halo. There was no illumination, no sound besides their shocking screams; no change at all was apparent to Ilya or Olona. She checked all the devices she was monitoring, but there was no indication that anything had gone wrong.

Before Ilya could ask Olona what was happening, Lahari and Unadi's voices died and they both fell to the grey earth✪

Chapter 9 – Lahari, Part One

Lahari was standing in a glowing blackness. It was bright, and there was light coming from nowhere. She was standing on a black planet. It was not an earth-sized planet, but a tiny planet, and Lahari could see its curvature.

Above her head, the sky was a bright black that shimmered like onyx, speckled with moving stars that swirled and overlapped in impossible patterns.

"Hello? Hello? Hello?" Lahari echoed. "Anybody? ...body? ...body?"

The dizzying movement of the sky was hypnotic, and she stared at it for timeless ages that melted away, and there was only the black universe, in which Lahari was the only life. All else was stone and stars.

She began to walk, and the patterns above looked more chaotic. It did not take her long to make her way to the opposite side of the miniscule planet, and there she found a door lying flat on the ground. Lahari reached down and gripped its handle. She turned and pulled.

As the door opened, so did the void behind it, and Lahari was sucked into the yawning darkness. She tumbled endlessly, falling deeper and deeper into nothing. She opened her mouth to cry out, but she made no sound.

There was only silence.

Far below, Lahari began to see a flickering, and as she drew closer, she could tell that she was seeing water. However, she no longer felt like she was falling, but instead, it felt like her body was being drawn upward, almost as if she was flying. Her flight slowed until she was hovering *below* a pool of black water on the ceiling of this cave of nothingness.

Then she saw a light. It was not a bright light, and it was coming from deep in the pool above Lahari. Like a tiny fish, the light moved through the water toward her until it was at the surface, opposite from her levitating form.

Lahari reached out one arm, and her hand entered the pool. She gently wrapped her fingers around the light, and she lifted it from the water. Droplets dripped up into the ceiling pool from her knuckles.

In her palm, Lahari held a flower. Its petals were pale blue with luminous yellow at the edges. She lifted it to her nose and breathed its fragrance. It smelled of oleander. She knew it had a wanting, and she knew she could talk to it.

"What do you need, little flower?" she asked, her voice returning to its echoing resonance.

"I want to go home," the flower responded.

"Where is your home?" Lahari asked.

The flower did not reply.

Lahari looked around the darkness, but she could see no means by which to exit the center of the black planet.

"Where are we?" she asked.

Again, the flower did not answer.

Lahari looked up into the depths of the pool of water on the ceiling above her, and she allowed her body to be drawn into it. First her hand with the flower, then her arm and head, and the rest of her entered the water. She rose deep into the pool.

Lahari ascended until she reached the bottom, or maybe it was the top.

Is this your home? Lahari thought to the flower.

The flower replied in Lahari's mind. *It is.*

Why did you leave?

To come find you, the flower stated, *so I could bring you to my home.*

Why have you brought me to your home?

The flower did not answer.

What can I do? Lahari asked the flower with her thoughts.

Do what you can! the flower declared.

Lahari pondered what the flower meant. She released it, and it floated in the ceiling pool.

Then Lahari activated her powers, and she focused them on the flower.

The flower, the water, the darkness, the black planet, and the swirling patterned sky overhead vanished.

There was nothing, not even Lahari★

Chapter 10 – Pleasure Island

Kosephaji, Relliduna, and Pelipi spent a lot of time above deck as the ship made its way south. It had been 11 days since

Relliduna was attacked, and he was continuing to recover. He hobbled about the ship, chatting with all the hunky deckhands. One of the crew found a cane in the ship's hold that assisted Relliduna immensely. Its brass handle was shaped like a fish that was *very* phallic, and Relliduna thought it was amusing.

A few crewmembers figured out a way to secure Pelipi's box to the main mast so he could remain with everyone above. He talked – and *flirted* – with many men and women of the crew, blinking in delight as he chatted to his heart's content.

"We're almost there," Ogomo boomed to Kosephaji one morning as the sun was starting to rise. He chuckled. "We'll likely arrive at the archipelago by late afternoon today. This chain of islands is... well, it's one of a kind," he concluded with a smile.

With the sun still high in the afternoon sky, the boatswain in the crowsnest cried out, "*Land ho!*" and a short while later, the ship arrived at the largest island of the Uodila Archipelago. The anchor splashed and sank to the bottom of the harbor waters.

The island chain was many days journey from the mainland, and several of the ship's supplies were running low, so Ogomo went to the market on the wharf to place the orders for what he needed. He smiled as he watched his crewmembers head in different directions for their shore leave.

"Enjoy your time here, you salty minnows!" he boomed to them with a laugh.

A lovely breeze was blowing in from the ocean, as Kosephaji assisted Relliduna down the beach. He was holding Pelipi's glass box by its handle. After a short distance, they found themselves in front of a seaside shack with a sign for fried fish and *finifa*. There was a little note describing finifa as a locally made fruit-medley liqueur. Relliduna set Pelipi's box down on a table beneath a broad umbrella.

"Pelipi, it feels so weird to have you out in public with us," Kosephaji said, as he and Relliduna each took a seat in the shade.

"I believe what Ogomo told us," Pelipi declared. His light blinked with enthusiasm. "He said this island is run by Shifts, and I feel completely safe and comfortable being out!"

Relliduna looked around. "Ogomo wasn't lying." He pointed. "Look, there are three Bio-Shifts over on the pier. They're just sitting out in the sun and fishing. One of them looks like... a frog."

"Do you two think we should *stay*, as in stay here?" Kosephaji asked.

"This little village is so isolated," Relliduna replied. He looked out at the waves. "It's beautiful, and I'm glad the trip brought us to this little slice of paradise, but it's so far from everything."

"And Ogomo said the people who live here have a hard life," Pelipi added, "and not only due to the remoteness."

"My, *my*, 'ello there, cuties!" said a cheery round woman who came out of the fried fish shack. Her skin was weathered from her years of island life, and a little grey streaked her long braided hair. "You lads interested in nibblin' what I gots to offer?" She gave them a kittenish smile; she was easily twice their age.

"Are you flirting with us?" Pelipi blinked at her.

The woman looked down at him with only momentary surprise. Then she stroked a fingertip along the edge of his box, as if a talking flashing light in a glass case was the most common thing.

"Don't you know it's rude to question a dame's motives?" she asked, and she let out a boisterous laugh. "What'll it be for you three on this fine afternoon?"

"I don't suppose you've got any scorpions, do you?" Pelipi asked.

The woman looked curious. "Well, now, I've never had that request made of me before, and believe you me, I've been requested *all* sorts of things." She shot the trio a wink.

"What a tease!" Pelipi said merrily. "I'm so glad we stopped here at your place."

"As am I," she replied with a broad smile. "Now, what can we figure out for you, since I'm fresh out of scorpions?" The woman chuckled. "Do you want something raw?"

"He eats mostly live insects and scorpions and spiders and stuff," Kosephaji explained.

The woman perked up. "How about a nice little crawler? I don't serve them, but they's usually in the shallows. *Dolo!*" she called aloud, surprising her three guests.

A tall, muscular young man strode around the outside of her shack. He was shirtless, wearing only an apron and a pair of very short shorts. His feet were bare, his hair was dreaded into tidy locks, and he rippled with muscles.

Kosephaji and Relliduna gawked at him.

"Hello, Dolo," the woman cooed to the beefy hunk. "Do you think you could catch our guest here a crawler? I think it'd be the perfect meal for him." She looked down at the light in the box and asked, "You are a *him*, right? Didn't mean to assume."

"Yes," Pelipi replied, "the three of us are boys."

Dolo smiled at Kosephaji, Relliduna, and Pelipi, and he headed out into the surf.

The woman's eyes moved over Dolo. "Mmm, mmm, *mmm*," she hummed to herself. "Couldn't you just sop him up like a biscuit?"

Relliduna snorted and Pelipi let out a single laugh.

Kosephaji whispered a breathy, "*Yes!*" and his friends both giggled at him.

Pelipi asked between his blinking titters, "What do we call you?"

The woman crossed her arms under her substantial chest, and her cleavage bulged. "Just call me Mama."

"He is very good-looking," Kosephaji murmured to no one in particular. He was gazing out at Dolo, who was bent over with his hands in the shallows.

Relliduna reached out and squeezed Kosephaji's arm.

Mama started to say, "He's a bit of..."

"*Caught one!*" Dolo blurted out, standing upright and raising a small creature above his head.

"What's a crawler?" Relliduna asked.

"They's an invasive species of sea urchin that ain't got no natural predators in these waters," Mama explained. "They gorge themselves on everything at the bottom of the food chain. Ain't much eating on them, so we don't often fish'em."

"I can't wait to try it!" Pelipi declared.

Mama smiled. "And what about you two fellas?"

"What's delicious, Mama?" Pelipi asked for Relliduna and Kosephaji. "That is, besides *you*," he added playfully.

"Aren't you just a wicked scamp?" Mama replied, giving the top of his box a little slap. She turned to Relliduna and Kosephaji. "Might I offer you both a basket of fried fish? I can do you spicy, and mellow." She gave them a coy smirk.

"That sounds good," Relliduna answered. "I'd take a spicy basket."

"Oh, I'll give you a spicy basket, alright," Mama cooed to him.

Relliduna blushed.

"I'll take a mellow fish basket, please," Kosephaji added.

"Some like it hot," Mama said with a wink. "I'll have them right out for you, lads. And how do you want me to prepare the crawler?" she asked Pelipi.

"He eats his food raw… or rather, *living*, whenever he can," Kosephaji explained.

"Dolo!" Mama called out again, as the muscly cook began to head back around the shack. "Leave that."

He placed the spiny thing onto the tabletop, and Mama stroked one finger along the man's collarbones.

"Thank you, Dolo," she said in a sultry tone. "And please start one spicy basket and one mellow basket."

Dolo gave the table of three guests a dashing smile, and he headed into the shack.

"Wow, he's really good-looking," Kosephaji repeated.

"It's nice keeping someone around who's easy on the eyes," Mama commented. "Now, how's about I bring you something strong to drink?"

She followed Dolo, and when the woman was gone, Kosephaji asked, "Pelipi, how on earth are you *still* a flirt, even though you're bodiless?"

"It's a gift," Pelipi replied with a sarcastic and elevated air. "It just comes natural." He laughed. "And I couldn't help but notice you two boys eye-fucking that side of beef."

Relliduna guffawed and Kosephaji snapped, "*Pelipi!*"

"That was a bit raunchy," Relliduna added.

"He is hot, though," said Kosephaji.

"You like 'em big and dumb, don't you?" Pelipi asked.

Kosephaji let out a dramatic gasp, and Mama popped back out of her shack with a trio of beverages before he could respond to Pelipi with something sassy.

"Here you go, boys, three finifa. Wrap your lips around these. Can you drink?" she asked Pelipi in his box.

"No, Mama," he replied, "but the boys can share mine. Or maybe you'd like to take a load off and join us for a spell! We'd love your company."

Mama gave his box a knowing grin, and she said to Kosephaji and Relliduna, "I'll let you two lads share the third finifa. Be out in a jiffy with your food." She headed back inside.

"You're awful!" Relliduna said to Pelipi.

Pelipi laughed and his light was radiant.

Just as Mama was returning, Kosephaji commented, "I think I could stay on this island."

"Oh, you don't want that," she responded to him. "These islands are brutal to us year-rounders. We's just on the cusp of storm season, too. This paradise ain't for the faint o' heart."

She placed baskets of fried fish in front of Relliduna and Kosephaji. Relliduna's was topped with a chili pepper, and a slice of pineapple came on the side of Kosephaji's.

"Tell me," Mama said to Pelipi in a come-hither voice, "how do I feed you?"

"*Mama,*" he gasped, "I think I'd be blushing right now if I had a body!"

"I can do it," Kosephaji interjected. He stood and picked up Pelipi's box.

"Bye, Mama!" Pelipi called out in a singsong voice as Kosephaji carried him a little way down the beach.

The sun began to set.

Kosephaji lifted Pelipi's lid and said with a laugh, "You really are awful!"

"I know; I know. Awfulness is one of my finer traits."

Kosephaji scoffed playfully, and he dropped the entire crawler into the box. A shrill high-pitched noise ripped through the air, and accompanying it was a noxious cloud that almost made Kosephaji dry-heave. He took a few steps back, as the stink wafted out to sea on an ocean breeze.

"By the great river!" Pelipi cried out in delight. "Mama! That was delicious! Mama, can you hear me? I've never eaten anything like that before!" His light was very bright.

"Pelipi, I don't think she can hear you," Kosephaji said, trying to catch his breath. He coughed a few times. "I'll bring you back over there in a second. That was horrible."

"I can't help it!" Pelipi whined. "I'm sorry that the way I eat is so gross to you."

Kosephaji laughed. "Don't be a pouty bitch! Gurl, you're one of us. You know I love taking care of you." He sealed Pelipi's box and picked up his friend. "And just look where we are."

Kosephaji held the glass box in his hands and extended his arms toward the sea. He slowly rotated, allowing Pelipi to take in a panoramic view of the ocean, then the coast, and around toward the island. Kosephaji kept turning with Pelipi's box until the coast on the opposite side came into view, and then the ocean again filled the horizon.

"It's breathtaking," Kosephaji said. He began to head back over to the table and added, "Pelipi, I'm so glad you're here with us."

Mama had planted herself in the chair beside Relliduna, and she was drinking the third beverage.

Relliduna raised his glass of finifa to Kosephaji and said, "This is really good."

Two hours later, the sky was an inky indigo and the stars were flickering. Torches burned around Mama's shack, and shadows danced to the sound of music being played somewhere not too far away.

Kosephaji and Relliduna were drunk. The two of them were whispering to each other in lusty voices about Dolo, and Pelipi was laughing at his inebriated friends.

"Why don't you guys go talk to him?" Pelipi encouraged.

"It'll take a lot more of *this*," Kosephaji said, eyeing his drink, "before I have the guts to talk to him."

"I just want to touch all those muscles," Relliduna added. "So yummy."

"Yes, I am!" declared Mama, who exited her shack with another round of drinks. By then she had learned the trio's names.

"Please, join us, Mama!" Pelipi urged.

"How would you like another crawler, Pelipi?" she countered with a cheeky grin; she had fed him several since sunset, and she did not seem to mind the stench.

"It really doesn't bother you?" Kosephaji asked her.

"Not in the least! Pelipi is an absolute delight!" Mama picked up his box. "Come along with me," she said to him, and she headed down the beach. She placed him on the sand and said, "You sit tight while I find you another crawler." Mama hiked up her skirt, flashing Pelipi her bustle and a wink, and she stepped out into the shallows.

The water started to glow in front of her and Pelipi asked, "How are you making that light?"

"It helps me find you a crawler," she replied, not answering his question. She shuffled a few steps, leaned her face close to the water, and then she laughed aloud in surprise and stood bolt upright. "That's cold!" she cried out. There was a matching pair of wet patches on the fabric of her shirt where it covered her breasts.

Pelipi let out a boisterous laugh.

"You got me wet," Mama teased, "and I found you another treat." She held up a very large crawler.

Kosephaji and Relliduna could hear Pelipi and Mama cackling together from a ways off, and then the loud sizzle of her feeding him.

"What a flirt!" Relliduna said with a snicker.

"I like that he's enjoying himself," Kosephaji added. "I almost feel like he'd be better off staying here. What's the name of this island again? No matter how many times you tell me, I just can't seem to remember."

"That's 'cause you're drunk!" Relliduna snorted a laugh; he was also feeling much drunker than he was trying to let on. "And anyway, Pelipi belongs with us, not here."

"Oi, lads!" boomed Ogomo's voice from down the beach. "We need to leave! Finish up and head back to the ship!"

"What's this then?" Mama asked, as she returned with Pelipi.

"I guesshh we need to go," Relliduna slurred, unable to maintain his composure.

Kosephaji giggled and said, "Duna, yer drunk."

Mama placed Pelipi's box on the table, and she stepped up to Relliduna, so that she was standing right over where he was seated. Beneath her damp shirt, Mama's large erect nipples were like gumdrops, and they were very close to Relliduna's face. She wiggled back and forth in front of him and asked in a breathy voice, "See anything you like, Duna?"

"Erm… we need to… uh…" Relliduna looked toward Ogomo's ship. "I… umm…"

Just as Kosephaji was finishing his last sip of finifa, Mama suddenly leaned down and planted a passionate kiss right on Relliduna's lips. He made a little noise of surprise and Kosephaji choked on his drink, coughing and sputtering. Pelipi burst out laughing and his light blinked energetically.

Mama's tongue quested into Relliduna's mouth, and he found himself giving in. To his surprise, he even found himself enjoying the woman. A moment later, Mama took back her lips, and she was wearing the sweetest of smiles.

"Aren't you just the cutest thing?" she said, gazing into Relliduna's eyes. She turned to Kosephaji and Pelipi. "The three of you are welcome here with Mama anytime."

Kosephaji and Relliduna rose nervously from the table. Mama was a little intimidating, and yet they were not sure that they were ready to leave her.

"*Bye-bye, Mama!*" Pelipi called out, as Kosephaji helped Relliduna stumble in the direction of the ship.

"Well, *that* was unexpected," Kosephaji commented.

Relliduna scoffed. "Even more so for me!"

"I, for one, loved it!" Pelipi declared from his box. He was tucked under Relliduna's arm. "Was that your first time kissing a woman?"

Relliduna blushed even more than he already was; he was grateful that it was dark out. "Yeah, I've never kissed a girl before."

Pelipi laughed. "Mama is *not* a girl," he said. He then asked, "Kosephaji, did it make you jealous that she kissed Duna?"

Kosephaji guffawed. "You mean, instead of her kissing *me?* Of course not!" Relliduna had kissed a few of the boys who he and Kosephaji fancied back in Ruburge, and Kosephaji thought it was very cute that Mama kissed his friend. "Maybe it surprised me a little." Kosephaji giggled and added in a quiet voice, "I've never kissed a girl either."

"You big idiots," Pelipi said through his laughter, "Mama is *all* woman!"

Kosephaji then commented, "I will say, I do feel a bit drunk."

Relliduna snorted a laugh. "So do I," he admitted.

"Sorry to cut your fun time short, lads," boomed Ogomo from the dock, "but there's a storm coming, and we'd best be on our way before it makes landfall."

Kosephaji looked at the stars. "But there isn't a cloud in the sky and there's barely a breeze."

Nahli spoke up. "One of the locals is a Shift weather-manipulator and he warned us that it's headed this way. It'll hit Uodila before dawn."

Relliduna handed Pelipi's box to Kosephaji, and Nahli helped Relliduna make his way up the wobbly gangplank.

"Ogomo, we've been having the best time!" Pelipi told the giant, and his light flashed intensely. "Thank you for bringing us here."

"My pleasure," Ogomo boomed with a laugh. "Sorry we can't stay. Get onboard with Duna, you two." He smiled at them. "We shove off as soon as the last of us arrives."

Nahli helped Relliduna down to the cabin and Kosephaji followed with Pelipi.

The alcohol had diminished Kosephaji's inhibitions, and before Nahli headed back upstairs, he asked her, "How come Ogomo lets you be part of the crew?"

"You mean, because Demifae usually hunt your friends' kind?" she asked in reply, nodding toward Relliduna and Pelipi.

"Yeah," Kosephaji said, "how'd you become friends with him?"

Nahli smiled. "Ogomo is my baby brother."✪

Chapter 11 – The Journey North, by Sea

Ogomo's massive ship left the Uodila Archipelago with the tropical storm in hot pursuit, but his vessel was fast, and the voyage to the southern continent was uneventful. The nation was called Phanisia, and Ogomo docked at a port on the small coastal island of Philletri. Even though he only planned to resupply in Phanisia, he gave his crew a three-day shore leave. None of the crew bothered to venture from the island onto the mainland.

Phanisia was not like the Uodila Islands, with its open Shift community; the region was much more akin to Xin. Its people only spoke of Shifts as the *others*, and they only ever spoke of them rarely. The nation of Phanisia was small. Part of the lands were mountainous, and the rest were plains that stretched to the sea. The capital city of Tostrijia was far inland, on the foothills that led up to the vast mountain range.

For Kosephaji, Relliduna, and Pelipi, the time on Philletri Island passed quickly. They stayed at an inn that overlooked the ocean, and Kosephaji and Relliduna spent most of the time in their rented room with Pelipi. At the end of the brief stay, the crew restocked the necessary supplies, and soon the ship was ready to venture back out onto the open ocean.

"All right, you scoundrels," Ogomo boomed, "shove off!"

The sails billowed and the ship quickly picked up speed.

"Don't you just love the salty smell of the sea air?" Ogomo asked Nahli.

They were standing at the bow.

"It doesn't smell much different than it did on Philletri," she replied to her enormous little brother.

"No, no," he said with a smile, "there's something different about the air farther away from land." He took a long sniff and let out a contented sigh.

The two of them fell quiet and listened to the sounds of sailing.

Eventually Nahli asked, "Is it time?"

Ogomo boomed a single word. "Yes."

Nahli smiled and said, "North."

"Yes," Ogomo repeated.

"*Home*," Nahli declared with relish.

The giant rumbled a chuckle and said again, "Yes."

When Ogomo was a youth and still a normal-sized boy, he was very close with his much older sister. They lived together in Teshon City. Nahli was 22 before Ogomo turned 12, and she had gone through a Demifae enhancement. She worked at a shop called *Abernathy's Apothecary* for only a fortnight, but the Demifae owner and his assistant were cruel, and because of them Nahli questioned her decision.

Unbeknownst to anyone at that time, Ogomo's photonova gland had activated, and he began to grow. Nahli was one of the first people to see him, and she was shocked by the condition of her brother. Overnight he had grown several inches. He was already taller than she, but young Ogomo's body did not grow evenly, and his proportions looked unnerving, even terrifying.

The oversized boy begged his older sister to help him, but Nahli's Demifae training caused her to hesitate. She knew that she could achieve so much with his photonova gland, but Nahli's compassion and the love she felt for Ogomo made her banish the thought, and she chose her brother over her history as a Demifae.

They left Teshon City together. Neither she nor Ogomo knew about the community of Biological Shifts living beneath the streets, and the two of them fled the city on foot and headed south. They made their way past the string of coastal fishing villages until they reached the wilderness at the southernmost end of the Great Southtrack. By that point, Ogomo had already been getting bigger for a week, but there were a full three weeks of his body's growth before it stopped. At the end of it, he was well and truly a giant.

Into those forested mountains along the coast, the two ventured. Against all the odds, over three arduous months after Nahli and Ogomo left Teshon City, they arrived at a rise in the land that gave them their first view of the vast rolling plains of Xin.

They also came across a monster.

Out of the trees lumbered a naked humanoid creature. It had far too many arms and legs and other parts. The monster roared, and it charged.

Ogomo, the nearly 20-foot tall 12 year old, did not understand what he was seeing. From his elevated height, the creature appeared roughly the same size as his sister, but everything about the thing looked wrong.

The hideous human-like beast pounced, and Ogomo swatted it with his enormous hand. The giant boy's strength was even greater than his size, and the creature was sent hurtling back down the hill and into the trees.

Ogomo scooped up his tiny older sister and ran. They made it into the grasslands and hurried south along the coast until the sun set, and they saw no sign of the monster again.

For a further two long months, the pair trekked along the coastline south until the land eventually curved east, and Nahli and young Ogomo got their first glimpses of the pink sand beaches of southern Xin. They finally came to the fishing village of Mellini, but the locals did not like the look of the giant boy, so Nahli and Ogomo traveled still farther. The two headed north, following a mighty river and a rumor they heard of a major metropolis upstream.

Nahli and Ogomo made it to Ruville a full six months after they left Teshon City, and outside of town, they made a home for themselves that could accommodate Ogomo. The two lived in the Ruburge region for years, and in that time, Ogomo became fascinated with the ships that sailed the Ru River, and he connected with other Shifts who had a similar interest in seafaring vessels.

On Ogomo's 27th birthday, his ship was launched. It had taken him and his companions over four years to build it, and it was unlike anything that sailed the Ru River or the seas beyond in those days. He and Nahli traversed the southern ocean for two adventurous years. They explored uncharted regions and visited remote harbors. A few of the original crewmembers were replaced by other sailors, and over that time, Ogomo gathered himself a loyal bunch of shipmates. Eventually, he added the trio of teenage boys.

With Relliduna doing a bit better and Pelipi attached to the mast, chatting endlessly with the crewmembers, Kosephaji spent more time with Nahli. He helped prepare ingredients for her potions and medicines. It was easy work, and she was very pleasant company.

On one morning, a few days after leaving Philletri, Kosephaji was with Nahli in her workspace, and she asked, "Are you in love with him?"

Kosephaji's voice cracked. "Am I *what?* Am I in love with who?" he asked, fully aware of exactly who she was talking about.

Nahli gave him a knowing smirk. "You can tell me. I won't let your secret slip."

Kosephaji checked over his shoulder, as if he was about to divulge a big secret, but he whispered, "I don't know what you're talking about."

Nahli playfully cocked her head to one side. "How *long* have you been in love with him?"

"Always," Kosephaji breathed aloud before he could stop himself. He looked at the floor, as if it was the most interesting thing in the room.

Nahli let out a sweet little laugh. "It feels good to say it aloud, doesn't it?"

"I don't really want to talk about..."

"I'm sure you don't," Nahli interrupted with a chuckle. "It's hard to admit to yourself your feelings, especially *aloud* and especially in front of someone who's almost a stranger."

Kosephaji was very embarrassed.

"Do you like him the way he is?" Nahli asked. "He talks to a lot of people. Are you sure you're not gonna get jealous?"

Kosephaji looked up with a smile. "I love that about him. He can make friends anywhere, and I love occasionally being along for the ride."

"Does he *know*?"

"No," Kosephaji mumbled, "I don't think I've ever made it clear. We've always been friends, and we're affectionate with each other, but I mean," and he whispered, "we've never kissed."

Nahli smiled wide and recommended, "Maybe you should tell him how you feel."

The old Oselian port of Teshon City was over 2000 nautical miles away from Philletri, and 10 days passed at sea before the boatswain in the crowsnest let out an enthusiastic, "*Land ho!*"

"Teshon City!" boomed Ogomo.

Kosephaji thought this was as good a time as any, and he surprised Relliduna by taking his hand and interlacing their fingers.

Relliduna looked into Kosephaji's eyes.

"Duna, I just wanted to take a second with you to try and get the words out about the way that things have been making me..." Kosephaji paused and scrunched up his face. "I mean, there's stuff that I think it would be good if it was, I guess, made less, I don't know... ambiguous?" He took a frustrated breath. *Come on,* he thought to himself, *do it!* Kosephaji stared at Relliduna. "Duna, I..." he began, "I love..."

Ogomo's ship crashed into something and everyone went flying.

Kosephaji and Relliduna were sent sprawling to the deck. Other crewmembers fell around them. Some were thrown overboard, and a few others became tangled in the rigging above. One man fell and landed on the deck, on his head, and he died instantly.

With the lights of Teshon City in sight, the ship had run aground, and it was sinking★

Chapter 12 – The Journey North, by Land

The sun was beginning to set, when Bivon saw the lights of Seven Rivers flickering through the trees. Thech and Jzuna were still hidden in the back of his cart as he led his horse through the town square.

Just like in Port Judy, several of the village residents approached Bivon to order warm beverages as the evening cooled, but he informed them that he was on a supply mission and would be happy to make them their drinks when he returned.

Unlike in Port Judy, Bivon parked next to an inn. He gave his horse some food and peeked into the back of his cart.

"Thech, Jzuna, the man who owns this tavern is a real fan of my coffee. I should be able to trade him for a nice meal."

"I didn't think you had any of your drink stuff," Jzuna replied. "You kept telling people that you couldn't make them anything."

Bivon smiled. "I'm on this journey for you two; I'm not here to make drinks for anyone. I also don't want people noticing you. Wait here," he added. "I'll be back in a few minutes with some food."

He grabbed a sack of coffee beans. They made a hushed dry rattling noise, and Bivon left the children in his cart.

The door to the tavern was propped open, and as he entered, he called out, "Ogre?! Where are you, you old mackerel?"

A skinny elderly woman with gray hair stepped up to him. "Ain't you heard?"

"Heard what?"

The woman sucked her teeth and looked Bivon up and down. "Ogre ain't here no more. Ogre got hisself chopped up."

Bivon let out a confused laugh. "What? What are you talking about?"

"He got hisself killed. Ogre always were an arsehole," the woman stated with a frown.

"He was not the most pleasant person to be around," Bivon agreed. "When was this? Can you tell me what happened?"

"Been a while now," she said.

Bivon scratched his chin through his beard. "I haven't been to Seven Rivers since I moved back to Hazel Cove over two years ago."

"Weren't quite that far back, but yeah, about then. Nobody don't know nothin' 'bout what happened. Said they just found him all chopped to pieces. Didn't see it meself," she added, "so I don't rightly know."

"What exactly do you mean?"

"He were all in pieces, weren't he?" the woman replied by means of an explanation. "That's what they said." She pointed at the sack of coffee beans. "Whatcha got there?"

"Oh, well, I was hoping to trade this for a nice meal." Bivon opened the mouth of the little bag and wafted its contents toward the woman. "Ogre used to like my coffee."

"S'alright," she replied, "I'll trade ya. Whatcha wanna eat?"

A few minutes later, Bivon was beside his cart again, and he called out quietly, "I'm back with some food." He heard Thech grunt and asked, "You kids ready for a little supper?"

"Yes, please," Jzuna's voice replied. "Thech is really hungry."

Bivon pulled back the flap of his cart and set an enormous bowl of stew onto a small table. "Here you go," he said, ladling a bowl for each of the children and keeping the rest for himself. He sliced three more pieces of bread and placed one beside each bowl.

"Thech needs help," Jzuna informed Bivon, "but I should be able to do it."

"Okay, let me know if you need my assistance."

Jzuna hovered above Thech's bowl and reached down with several of her tentacles to carefully lift it. She brought it to her brother's wide mouth and poured in a little of the chunky stew. He chewed, swallowed, and Jzuna poured in a little more.

Bivon smiled at the pair, and his heart broke for them again.

After a few minutes, Thech's bowl was empty, and he started chomping on the piece of bread.

Jzuna then turned her attention to her own dinner. Just like the latte back at the café, the surface of the stew slowly drained down until all of it and the bread were gone.

When Bivon finished eating, he cleaned out the bowls and headed back inside to return the oversized dish. When he reappeared, he was smiling.

"I think you're going to enjoy these," he said, and he held up his hands toward the children. In both of his palms were clusters of bright red fruit. "Give these sun-cherries a try."

Thech's arm shot forward, but his jerky motor functions made it difficult for him to control his movements. The boy's eyes remained perpetually rolled up in his head, and Bivon wondered how Thech even knew where anything was, but he did seem to have an awareness of his surroundings. Bivon shifted his hand beneath

Thech's questing fingers, and the boy snatched the fruit, shoving them into his mouth. He hummed in delight as he chewed.

In Bivon's other hand, he could feel the fruit beginning to weigh less, as Jzuna caused the sun-cherries to dematerialize.

"Those are delicious!" her voice squeaked. "Thank you."

A little while later, when the three were again settling for sleep, Bivon could hear the children making quiet sad noises from inside his cart like the night before, but they were soon asleep.

The following day, the trio made the journey to the village of Brokenpointe. They arrived just after sundown, but they did not enter the much larger fishing community. Bivon led his horse and cart along a path that circumvented the perimeter of the town, hoping to draw less attention, and he parked at the northern edge of Brokenpointe by the final leg of the Great Southtrack.

Bivon left Thech and Jzuna in his cart, and he headed into a small market to procure a little food for their dinner. It was only a matter of minutes before he returned with some sausages and a chunk of hard cheese to go with the remaining bread, but Bivon froze.

An unnerving aroma of roasted meat filled the area, and there was something acrid to the smell. Bivon stepped up to his cart, and right next to it, he saw the source of the scent. His stomach lurched.

A burned and blackened skeleton lay smoldering at his feet; much of it glowed orange like hot charcoal. The jawbone was not attached to the skull and one of the skeleton's arms lay separate from the rest of the mutilated body. Large chunks of scorched flesh clung to the lower half of both legs, and the hand of the severed arm was still in pristine condition. Clutched in the unburned fingers was the hilt of a sword, and a portion of its blade was smeared with a thin clear coating that glimmered in the rising moon's light.

Bivon heard noises from inside the cart.

"Thech? Jzuna?" he said under his breath. "Are you okay?"

Jzuna's voice was whimpering, but Bivon could not make out what she was saying.

"It's me," he said, and he slowly drew open the back of his cart.

Thech was protectively standing in front of Jzuna, and a threatening rumble was issuing from his gaping maw.

"Oh no," Bivon whispered, "Jzuna!"

Right inside the cart, lying limp in front of him was one of the unique Biological Shift girl's tentacles.

"What do I do?" Bivon asked. "Can we fix it? Can we heal you? Thech, please let Jzuna get by you so I can see. I'm not going to hurt you or her."

Jzuna nudged her brother and he moved out of the way. For being only a giant eyeball with tentacles, Jzuna managed to express an enormous amount of emotion without a word. She looked frightened and in pain; Jzuna looked like she wanted her mother.

"Can I see?" Bivon asked. "What happened?"

Suddenly Jzuna's voice cried aloud with choked sobs. "There was a man, and he had a sword, and he cut off one of my arms! He opened your cart, and he called us a bad word, *and he chopped off my arm!* He grabbed some of your stuff and was stealing it, and I'm sorry, I think we burned it up when we told the fire to eat him."

"You did... that?" Bivon asked, trying not to look down at the charred remains.

"I'm sorry we burned your stuff," Jzuna repeated in a whimper.

"Oh, no, no, no! Don't you worry about that; let's take care of you. Can I please see? How bad is it?"

Jzuna's voice sounded pitiful. "Look what he did!"

Her one huge eye stayed focused on Bivon, as her hovering mass rotated partway to the side. She extended the gory stump of her hacked tentacle, and another of her slimy limbs was wrapped around it, cradling the injury.

"Oh, Jzuna, honey, I'm so sorry. I can't believe it all happened so fast. I was only gone for a few minutes," he added

"It's okay," Jzuna whimpered. "I'll be okay."

"Do you want something for the pain? Did your mother ever give you medicine? I don't know how it will work for you, since you and Thech are so unique."

"I'm okay," Jzuna repeated, and she lowered into the basin that the two children used for a bed.

"What should I do with the..." Bivon began to ask, but Thech made his question moot.

The weird boy snatched the severed tentacle and thrust it into his wide mouth. He chewed, swallowed it, and then he joined his sister in their tub.

Bivon sighed. "I'm sorry," he whispered again. He stepped around to the front of his cart. "I'm going to move us away from *that*." He did not look back at the corpse. A few minutes later he turned down a quiet side street where the three spent the night.

Neither of the children ate dinner.

The next day, they began the final leg of their journey, but Jzuna's spirit had darkened. The tragic death of her and Thech's mother was compounded by the attack she suffered the night before. She was in pain, and when Thech climbed out of their basin, Jzuna remained at the bottom of it.

"I'm just gonna stay here," she mumbled.

Bivon did not know what to do, but when Thech clambered up and positioned himself at the front of the cart where Bivon usually sat, the big man climbed up beside the boy.

The final day's travel brought them to their destination before the sun began to set. Thech clearly knew when they arrived at the edge of Teshon City, because he began rocking in his seat with an excited energy as the cart rolled between the massive old base's gates.

"Jzuna, honey," Bivon called back to her, "you're really missing quite a sight. If you're feeling up to it, maybe just take a little look at the city."

Jzuna's massive eyeball peeked over the lip of the tub, and the view was indeed lovely. She levitated out of the basin and hovered behind Bivon and her brother.

Entire sides of buildings were decorated. Some were painted with vibrant murals and others were patterned in geometric rainbow colors.

"Oooh," Jzuna's voice cooed at the sight. "It's so pretty!" She then asked Bivon, "Could I please have something to eat?" She had eaten nothing in a day and a half.

"Absolutely!" Bivon replied. "Are you feeling a little better? How's your arm?"

Jzuna held out her damaged tentacle, still clutched by another limb. "It hurts, but maybe not as bad."

"Oh, I am so glad to hear that. Thech and I have been worried about you, and we're glad you're okay. Now, let's see what we can find you to eat." Bivon rummaged around in a sack of supplies and provided a few options for Jzuna.

She psychokinetically consumed an apple, seeds and stem and all, and then she dematerialized a tin of fish Bivon opened for her. She left the tin behind.

Bivon stopped his cart beside a street vendor and ordered a pair of little stuffed rice dumplings for Jzuna, one savory and one sweet.

When they vanished, she declared, "Wow, those were yummy!"

"Oh, good. I'm so happy you felt like eating something."

A few minutes later, Bivon turned his cart down a quiet side street, and he parked it in front of a house.

"Thech, Jzuna, why don't you two wait in the back," he recommended. "I have friends who moved here recently, and I think they'll be very excited to meet you, but first let me check and make sure we're in the right place, and that they're home. This is *my* first time to their new house as well."

He walked away from the cart, and the two unique children heard him knock on the door. It opened, and there was what sounded like pleasant conversation that lasted only a moment.

Bivon then cried out, "Wait, *wait!* I don't want you to surprise them!"

Thech and Jzuna were startled as the flap to the back of the cart opened, but standing outside it was just a little girl. She looked excited and curious, and more than anything, she looked happy.

"Oh, wow!" the girl said to Thech and Jzuna in a loud squeaky voice. "You two are like magic!"

Bivon quickly appeared behind her and said, "Thech, Jzuna, it turns out my friends are *indeed* home." He looked down at the girl. "I'm sorry, please tell us your name. This is Thech and Jzuna," he added.

"My name's Fennah!" the child declared. Every word out of her mouth sounded more excited than the one before.

"Why don't we step back, Fennah," Bivon suggested, "and give Thech and Jzuna a little space to get out of my cart. They've been in there a long time. It was a long journey," and he smiled at the girl.

Bivon looked at Thech and Jzuna, and he said, "And this is Tophilogin."

A little round man stepped up behind him and said, "Hello, children! Welcome to my home." He jabbed his thumb in Bivon's direction with a smile. "This silly goose insists on calling me by my real name, but you can just call me *mystic*."

The two unique children came out into the setting sunshine, and the mystic's breath caught. Evening was close, and the fading light sparkled on the coating that covered Thech and Jzuna.

"Aren't you both just incredible?" the mystic gasped. "My daughter, Lahari, is also a Bio-Shift, and I am so excited for you two to meet her! She's not here right now," he added, looking at Bivon, "but I'm sure she'll be home soon." He turned back to Thech and Jzuna. "My husband, Theolan, is inside making dinner. Please, you three, join us for a meal."

As the group entered the house behind the mystic, Bivon asked little Fennah, "How did you become friends with Tophilogin?"

The mystic answered for her. "Princess Fennah is the last surviving member of a royal house that existed until recently, down in Xin."

"You're a princess?" Jzuna asked.

The mystic and Fennah looked all around the room because Jzuna's voice seemed to have no point of origin.

"I used to be," Fennah replied, turning back to Thech and Jzuna, "but now I'm just Fennah." She sounded like she did not mind the change to her life at all. Her eyes moved back and forth between the two Biological Shifts. "Which one of you is talking?"

"I am," Jzuna replied, wiggling her tentacles. She then asked Fennah, "What happened to your family?"

"Jzuna," Bivon gently interrupted, "maybe that's a little too private."

"It's all right," Fennah replied in her bright voice, and she answered quickly. "My family was killed, and it was really bad, but they were always killing people, and they always said that people wanted to try and kill them too. I think it's better now that they can't kill anybody else."

The little girl continued chirping out disturbing things in her merry way. "My daddy killed my uncle and my auntie because they killed my mommy's cousins. And my daddy also made the sergeant kill a bunch of people in the throne room, and my daddy made everybody watch, even me. Oh, and my mommy really wanted her *own* daddy to get killed, and she used to say that a lot. Then one day they told me my grandpa was killed. Everybody was always killing everybody."

Fennah added in a quiet voice, "I thought I got killed also." She immediately became boisterous and flowery again. "But I *didn't* get killed, and I know that a lot of people got killed, but now they're not killing anybody, and that's so much better!"

She stopped speaking, and Bivon and Jzuna did not know what to say.

"And we are so glad," Theolan declared as he came in from the kitchen, "that you are away from all that killing and can grow up like a normal little girl." He was wearing a frilly apron and large flower-print oven mitts, but he was not carrying anything hot.

"Yes," the mystic agreed, "recent days have been brighter for many of us."

"Our mama got killed," Jzuna said quietly, and her voice came from all around them.

"That's true," Bivon confirmed. "Thech and Jzuna have no one." He let his words trail off, and all of them turned to look at the two unique children.

"Oh, kids," Theolan exclaimed, "I'm so sorry!"

The mystic stepped up to Thech and Jzuna, and he countered Bivon's words. "You two are *not* alone."✪

Chapter 13 – Bivon

The aroma of roasted food permeated the air in the kitchen. A large shank was resting on the counter with a tea towel on top of it. The meat was steaming, and it smelled delicious.

"Bivon, there's an extra chair in our bedroom," the mystic said. "Do you mind getting it? Fennah, maybe you could lead the way."

The little girl grabbed the big red-bearded man's hand, and Bivon smiled as she brought him down the hall. A moment later, the pair of them returned, and Fennah asked, "Can I sit between Thech and Jzuna?"

Bivon turned to the siblings. “Would that be okay with you two?”

Jzuna replied in a brighter tone than Bivon had heard her use since the death of their mother. “Yeah, alright!” Her brother huffed and Jzuna added, “Thech and me both want Fennan to sit between us,” and the little girl let out a delighted squeal that made Bivon laugh.

Theolan plated chunks of the roast meat for everyone, but Jzuna spoke up again. “I’m not really all that hungry.”

“Right,” Bivon replied, “Jzuna, you just ate quite a large snack.”

“Would you like a little something?” Theolan offered.

His husband added, “It’s quite yummy!” The mystic then leaned in and whispered to Jzuna, “I’ve already stolen a few bites.” He beamed at her and she let out a giggle that warmed Bivon’s heart. “And look at this!” the mystic continued. “I’ve made a lovely salad.”

Onto the center of the kitchen table he placed a large wooden bowl full of vibrant and rainbow-colored ingredients. Lettuce leaves of pale green, burgundy, emerald, and magenta were mixed with pieces of bright stone fruit and dark berries. There were sunflower, pumpkin, and black and white sesame seeds. On the side was a creamy dressing that would provide umami and spice.

Jzuna looked in the bowl. “Okay, I’ll have a little,” she chirped. Fennah and Thech sat together, but Jzuna paused by the table and looked over at her brother. “Oh, Fennah,” her disembodied voice said, “I need to help Thech eat, but after he’s done, I can be on the other side of you.”

“You need to help Thech eat?”

“Yeah, sometimes.”

“Okay,” Fennah said, “I don’t mind waiting until he’s done eating.”

The mystic chuckled and asked, “Jzuna, honey, what do you need to help feed Thech?”

She looked at the plate that Theolan placed in front of her brother, and then she turned back to the mystic. “Do you have a big spoon?”

“We certainly do,” he replied, and he began rummaging through a cluttered drawer. He found what he was looking for and passed it to Jzuna.

One of the unique Biological Shift girl's tendrils coiled around the utensil's handle. "Thank you," she said, and she floated over to her brother.

The three men joined the children at the table, and they all started to eat, but they found Thech and Jzuna distracting. Jzuna was very focused on her task; she managed to feed her brother without spilling anything. He chomped down each bite she served him, as the others tried not to stare and continued eating.

"Isn't this just scrumptious?!" Bivon declared through a mouthful of food.

A few minutes later, Thech's dinner was gone, and Jzuna drifted around the table and over to Fennah's other side. The little girl let out another giggle when she was between the pair, and Thech hummed.

"Thech likes you, Fennah," Jzuna squeaked, and Fennah burst out with peals of gleeful laughter that were contagious to everyone else. Then Jzuna focused on her small plate of food. The rest of them stopped eating again, as her meat and the little pile of salad began to dematerialize and disappear.

The mystic gasped and said, "Remarkable!"

"Hey, your food is shrinking," Fennah stated in confusion, but then all that was left on Jzuna's plate was a little chunk of bone.

"I liked that a lot!" her voice said all around them, and Fennah could not help but laugh even more.

After the lovely meal, Bivon carried Thech and Jzuna's basin into the mystic's house.

Theolan shifted a few chairs in the sitting room and made a space for the children's tub. "This placement is only temporary until we set up a room for both of you," he told them.

Bivon knelt in front of Thech and Jzuna. "Will you two be okay staying here without me for a little while this evening? I'm hoping to run out for a bit, but I'll be back later tonight."

Fennah answered for them. "Oh, yes, Thech and Jzuna, let's go play!"

"Bivon, at least take one of these for the road," the mystic urged, holding up a tray of freshly baked cupcakes.

Bivon grabbed one and headed outside. He walked through the quiet streets as the moon began to rise, nibbling on the cupcake, and he made his way out of Gate Town toward the crumbled ruins of the Messiah Tower. He stopped as he approached.

"You murdered so many of us," he said bitterly to the rubble. "You've killed my friends. You've killed my family and lovers, and you deserved what you got."

Bivon stood staring for a moment longer in silence, remembering those whom he had lost, and without another word, he turned and headed back into Gate Town. At the border of Shifton, he entered a quiet tavern and took a seat at the bar.

"Give me something strong," he requested before the barman could even ask.

"Y'alright?" a drunk woman managed to say. She was seated two chairs down from him.

"Haven't been back to Teshon City since the Tower fell. I needed to go see it for myself." He then added in a quiet voice, "Messiahs killed a lot of my friends over the years."

"My mosht heartfelt condolences," the woman slurred, sidling down the two seats and positioning herself next to him. "I'mma have one o'them, too," she said to the man behind the bar. She turned to Bivon. "What brings ya back to town, then?"

He sighed. "A couple of Bio-Shift kids from Hazel Cove lost their mother, and I brought them up here to stay with some people."

"Oh no, them poor chil'ens," she said.

"Yes, it's very tragic," Bivon responded.

An hour, and several strong drinks later, he was feeling rather forthcoming, and the woman was even drunker. Bivon had shared quite a lot about Thech and Jzuna and their mother, none of which the woman had retained, and he opened up about the mystic and Theolan.

"We used to be together," Bivon said in a wistful tone, "Theolan and I, and when we met Tophilogin, the three of us connected, and we quickly fell in love. I adored being in a throuple; it can be so satisfying." He sighed. "I've always enjoyed having many partners, and we let each other be free. The two of them continued to grow closer, though, and eventually I stepped back and let them enjoy their lives together." Bivon took a sip of his beverage, and he made a goofy grin, dribbling a little and whipping his chin.

He continued to ramble, and he sounded proud. "I've had countless lovers since, but I still adore Theolan and Tophilogin. I love them both deeply, and I'm not jealous or upset that I'm no longer part of the relationship; the two of them are *best* together. They are so good, and they immediately took in the children I brought up from Hazel Cove, just like I knew they would." He smiled again and reiterated, "They are such good men."

Bivon turned to the woman. She was asleep with her head on the bar.

"Cheers," Bivon whispered, and he clinked his glass against hers.

It was very late when he stumbled back to the mystic's house, and he spent the rest of the night in his cart.

Bivon was unaware of what happened.

Ilya had returned★

Chapter 14 – Lahari, Part Two

The front door of the mystic's house burst open, and Ilya rushed in with tears streaming down her cheeks. She was holding Lahari's limp body in her arms✪

Chapter 15 – Saved?

Ogomo's ship was capsizing. It leaned in the water dangerously, and the bow was quickly sinking below the waves. The life rafts were lowered, and several small boats were spotted racing from the mainland toward the sinking ship.

The weight of the water filling the hull caused a major portion of it to suddenly dislodge, and the section still above the waves lurched. Many people were thrown into the churning surf, and the rest of the ship began to be swiftly sucked beneath the roiling surface. Anyone left onboard dove from the destroyed vessel.

Kosephaji found himself surrounded by debris, and he was not even sure how he got into the water.

"Relliduna!" he cried out. "Where are you, Duna?!" Seawater filled his mouth and the surging waves made it nearly impossible for him to see anything as he bobbed at the surface. "*Duna!*"

Kosephaji could hear other voices shouting nearby, and he kept catching glimpses of a boat heading straight toward him. He reached one arm above the waves as high as he could, and a moment later, powerful hands were pulling him onto the deck of a small boat.

A brutal club connected with the side of Kosephaji's head, and he was swallowed in darkness.

*

"*Relliduna!*" Kosephaji shouted, sitting upright with a start. He was on a hard cot in a cold, tiny, gray room.

"I'm right here," came Relliduna's weak voice.

"Duna!" Kosephaji said a little quieter, looking over at his companion. "Are you okay? Where are we? *Where's Pelipi?*" He brought his hands to his throbbing head.

"I'm fine," Relliduna replied in a hollow voice. "I don't know what happened to Pelipi. I don't know what happened to him. I made it onto one of the lifeboats, but all of us in it were immediately arrested when we got to shore." He sighed and added, "These cells are some sort of old Oselian construction that prevents Shifts from using our powers."

Kosephaji looked surprised. "You can't do the *thing?*"

Relliduna raised his hand between them, but nothing happened. "Some sort of power-dampening stuff must be built into the walls or something."

Kosephaji rubbed his head where he had been hit. "Do you know what happened to Ogomo or Nahli?"

Relliduna shrugged. "Either they drowned in the shipwreck, or somehow they escaped, but I couldn't see them from where I was in the lifeboat, not even huge Ogomo."

Kosephaji looked hopeful. "Maybe Pelipi is with them and they're all safe."

Relliduna did not reply.

"How long was I unconscious?"

"You've been asleep for hours. I wasn't sure if I should wake you up or not. I didn't know what I was supposed to do, but I'm glad they locked us up together."

Kosephaji understood; he did not like the thought of waking up in the cell alone.

"I requested we be put together," Relliduna added, "and for some reason, they did."

"Any idea who *they* are?" Kosephaji asked.

"I guess we made it to Teshon City," Relliduna answered, "but I don't have a clue who runs this place."

Kosephaji squinted at a flash of pain in his head, and he took a deep breath. After a moment, he asked, "Do you have any idea what time it is?"

Relliduna looked up at the cell's tiny window and then back at Kosephaji. "The ship wrecked in the afternoon, and the sun set hours ago. It's still the night of the crash, but I don't know, maybe it's close to dawn?"

"Duna, do you know why..."

"No," he interrupted, "I don't know why they arrested us. No one's told me anything and no one has come in here since we've been locked up."

Kosephaji turned to look up at the window and asked, "What's that light?"

Relliduna's eyes moved back to the room's tiny exposure to the outside world. "That's not the sunrise?"

Kosephaji got to his unsteady feet and stepped up to the wall, but the window was too high for him to see anything except the sky. "No," he said, "that's not the sunrise. Duna, come here and let me lift you up." He interlaced his fingers together and bent his knees.

Relliduna stepped up to the wall and onto Kosephaji's hands. He was lifted and managed to get ahold of the window's ledge. He pulled himself up, peeked outside, and was very surprised by what he saw.

"Hello," boomed Ogomo.

"Ogomo?!" Kosephaji hollered from below Relliduna.

Nahli called back, "Let's get you two out of there! You boys better step away from the wall. Do you have anything that you can use to shield yourselves?"

"This wall is not long for the world," Ogomo added with a rumbling chuckle.

"Flip the cot up on its side," Relliduna recommended as Kosephaji lowered him back down to the floor of the cell. "Let's get behind it. I don't know what they're going to do out there, but Ogomo is holding the biggest hammer I've ever seen!"

Outside of the prison, Nahli stepped up to the wall and smeared a thick paste on the rough surface.

Ogomo spoke into the opening of the little window. "Nahli has put some brittle butter on the outside of the wall and it's about to shatter. Stay back!" The giant hoisted his massive warhammer over one shoulder, and he roared as he swung it with brutal force at the wall.

It connected.

Nothing happened.

"Well, that was anti-climactic," Nahli said, looking at the outside of the prison wall, and then at her brother's hammer.

"Why didn't it work?" Ogomo asked her.

She stepped up and examined the wall more closely. "Huh... this isn't normal concrete. Look at the space where your hammer connected. The brittle butter made that very specific spot brittle, but the effect was supposed to spread out."

Ogomo stepped up to the window and said to Relliduna and Kosephaji, "Sorry, boys, we're going to need to figure something else out. That didn't work at all."

Alarm bells pierced the air.

"I think they're onto us, baby brother," Nahli said. "Let's go!"

The window above Relliduna and Kosephaji lit up with the glow of a flickering light; then it faded.

"Hoist me up again!" Relliduna shouted over the shrill ringing. He peaked outside and gave Kosephaji a very loud play by play. "Ogomo and Nahli just climbed into some sort of weird boat at the water's edge. The thing's hatch is closing..." Relliduna paused. "By the great river, it submerged!"

Kosephaji helped him down and declared, "I can't believe they tried to break us out."

"I can," Relliduna retorted over the blaring alarm. "Way back at the beginning of our journey when Ogomo wanted to talk to me alone, he made it clear how much he supports other Shifts and Bio-Shifts. I was surprised that he was outside the cell, but I shouldn't have been. I wish that he had succeeded and we were leaving with them right now."

The screaming alarm died and the harsh silence returned, only to be filled with a sudden rattling at the cell door of keys being forced into locks and locks being released. The door swung open and a group of armed guards entered the tiny room, shouting at Kosephaji and Relliduna. The two of them could not make out what the men were saying, and they were dragged into a larger grey room and forced before a panel of severe-looking officials seated behind a wooden table.

"We had nothing to do with that escape attempt!" Kosephaji blurted out.

A woman stepped in front of him and Relliduna, and she snapped at the officials, "Why haven't these young men been released?! You already know their story. They've done nothing wrong and you are holding them without reason or just cause. You should have let them go last night with the others! As an advocate of the people, I demand their immediate release."

One of the men behind the table responded in a tone that sounded exhausted. "Milady Troonbien, we know your stance. We are also advocates and are just trying to keep the citizens of the city safe."

"By locking up young men for nearly drowning in our harbor?!"

Her fellow leader sighed. "No, we just wanted to make sure they are not a threat."

"*These two boys?*" she asked incredulously. "You were worried these boys might be a danger to our great city?"

The leader looked past her. "What brings you young men to Teshon City?"

Kosephaji and Relliduna turned to each other.

"We're from Xin," Kosephaji replied, "and we just wanted to find someplace that was more accepting."

"Look, boys," the man said, "we're not trying to treat you like criminals, and we're sorry you spent the night in a cell."

His apology surprised Kosephaji and Relliduna.

"Madame Troonbien, there," and he nodded to the woman in front of them, "insisted that we speak with you lads at first light. We questioned everyone else who we pulled from the harbor until the wee hours, and again, sorry we didn't get to you two last night. It just got too late. Everyone else has already been released."

Madame Troonbien turned to face Kosephaji and Relliduna. "You were the final two detainees. The rest of your crew are free." She looked at Kosephaji. "We know you got hit by one of the harbor officers, and we apologize for that too."

"We just want to make sure the city is kept safe," the leader at the table added.

"That's what we're looking for," Relliduna replied, "someplace safe and better to live than where we grew up."

The woman turned back to the panel of officials. "Are they free to go?"

Several of the leaders nodded and made dismissive gestures, and a woman seated at one end of the table answered, "Yes, they can go."

A man entered the room and quickly escorted Kosephaji and Relliduna down a long hallway and up a flight of stairs. They were ushered through a very plain door and suddenly found themselves standing in the rising sunshine. The door to the prison slammed behind them.

Relliduna let out a relieved sigh. "I'm glad that's over."

"They didn't even ask us our names," Kosephaji said.

"Let's try and find Ogomo."

"What about Pelipi?"

Relliduna's face fell. "I don't know how we're supposed to find his glass box, lost at sea."

Kosephaji looked down a few of the streets outside the prison. "I don't like this neighborhood. Let's see if we can find some part of town that's nicer than this."

"Should we head toward the water first and see if we can find Ogomo and Nahli?"

"You said they went underwater. How are we supposed to find them? It's morning and I'm hungry," Kosephaji added. "Let's get something to eat first and then decide what our next course of action should be."

Relliduna conceded and the two headed through the narrow streets. Before long, they came to an enormous pile of rubble at the city's center, and they needed to find a way around it. Many of the surrounding blocks were nothing more than warehouses and abandoned storage facilities, but eventually they came to a long straight street, and quite a ways down it they could see a bright sign leading into a neighborhood.

Kosephaji and Relliduna stopped at the first open pub they came across, and quite a few other folks were already inside, enjoying their breakfasts. The two took a seat at an empty booth and a mustachioed man strutted up to their table.

"Morning, gents! What'll it be for you?" He pulled out a tiny notepad and an even tinier nub of a pencil.

"Coffee," Kosephaji said.

"*Please,*" Relliduna added, rolling his eyes at Kosephaji, and he asked, "what's good here?"

"Have a slab of the chef's brekkie casserole. It's got veg and sausage and chili and fluffy eggs; it'll fill you gents right up."

"We'll take two, please," Relliduna replied, flashing their waiter a smile.

The man made a quick note and said, "Coming right up." He turned and entered the kitchen.

"He's not bad to look at."

"That mustache, though?"

"I think it's sexy."

The two boys giggled together.

Less than a minute later, steaming mugs of black coffee were in front of them.

"Cream and sugar'll be right out," the waiter quickly said, and he zipped off to other customers.

Kosephaji and Relliduna watched him hurry away.

"He's got a cute..."

"*Oi, lads!*" barked a gruff voice that Kosephaji and Relliduna did not know, but they recognized the man who approached them from Ogomo's ship.

"You're Z'Mantri, right?" Kosephaji asked.

"*Z'Matri,*" the man corrected. He had spent almost none of the voyage outside of his own cabin, and neither of the boys had ever spoken to him. "I felt you," he said, nodding to Relliduna, "as soon as they let you both out."

"Oh," Kosephaji said, perking up at the information, "you're the Shift who can sense other Shifts, right?"

Z'Matri nodded.

"Do you know where Ogomo and Nahli are? They tried to break us out."

"They're in Shifton," Z'Matri answered. "The narrow streets and alleys of Teshon City ain't made for someone his size, but there's a region inland near the city gates where he fits in better. When them prison guards didn't let you two go last night with the rest, Ogomo made the plan to bust you out."

"Wait, wait!" Relliduna interrupted urgently. "You're the one who knew Pelipi was with us before we joined the crew. What about him?! *Can you sense Pelipi?*"

Z'Matri furrowed his brow. "I'm sorry, lads. Ogomo asked me to try and find him, but I haven't been able to feel him." He concentrated, but then he looked from Kosephaji to Relliduna. "Nothing, sorry, can't feel your friend," he stated.

"No," Kosephaji breathed.

Relliduna frowned. "Can you feel other Shifts no matter how far away they are? Maybe Pelipi is beyond your range. Maybe he's..."

"I can feel Shifts on the other side of the planet," Z'Matri stated. "I can feel a child's photonova gland activating right *now*, and I can feel that the child is on the opposite hemisphere."

Kosephaji and Relliduna's food arrived, and Z'Matri handed the mustachioed barman some local money.

"Eat," Z'Matri commanded the boys, and the three did not speak until their breakfast and coffee were gone.

"This way," Z'Matri said, and he rose without another word.

Relliduna and Kosephaji followed him out into the Gate Town streets.

Kosephaji grabbed Relliduna's hand. "Pelipi can't be dead," he whispered. "He just can't be." He could not stop the tears that welled in his eyes, and he brought his free hand to his mouth as a sob wracked his body. Kosephaji had managed to care for Pelipi and keep him protected for the five years since his photonova gland activated and he changed.

Now he was gone, unceremoniously and without warning; Pelipi was just gone★

Chapter 16 – The Kids & the Queens, Part One

When Ilya brought Lahari's unconscious body home, Theolan rushed off to see if any of their friends were available to watch over the three children during the night while the mystic treated his daughter. Bivon had left the group a little while earlier, and Theolan and the mystic did not know where he was, but his cart was still parked in front of their house.

Theolan found Dotty Marbles, and she was happy to oblige. She now led Thech, Jzuna, and the ex-princess Fennah through the darkening Shifton streets.

"Alrighty there, kids! We're almost to Peggy's clinic." Dotty Marbles may have initially been surprised by the two unusual Biological Shift children, but she also fancied *herself* as unusual; she had been happy to take them. She turned the trio of youngsters down a side street, and a moment later they stopped in front of a drab building. "Let's try not to make too much noise," she said, pulling open the door. "There are patients resting."

Ninyani stuck his head out into the hallway at the sound of Dotty Marbles' voice, and he was surprised to see the children with her. "Hi, Dot!" he said with a wave. He added, "Hi, Fennah," and his eyes moved to the two very unique Biological Shifts. "*Hi!*" Ninyani repeated to them in an excited voice.

"Jzuna, Thech, this is Ninyani," Dotty Marbles said quietly. "Honey, where's Peggy?"

"She's making tea," Ninyani replied.

"Thank you, dear. Kids, why don't you come with me into the kitchen." Dotty Marbles led them down the hall and into a small cafeteria. "Peggy!" she called out.

"Dot?" came Auntie Peg's voice from an alcove. She stepped out and was startled by Thech and Jzuna. "My goodness! Why, hello there. I'm Auntie Peg," she informed them, "but you can call me Peggy. What interesting individuals *you* are!"

Thech let out a little huffing breath, and Jzuna sheepishly said, "Hello."

Auntie Peg looked around at the sound of her voice, seemingly coming from nowhere and everywhere.

"Isn't that neat?" Fennah chirped. "It's like Jzuna's talking right into your ears!"

"Can we make a cup of tea for each of you?" Dotty Marbles asked the children, and she nodded Auntie Peg back into the alcove.

"What's going on, Dot? What is it? You seem… excited."

"Yes, and I know I shouldn't be," Dotty Marbles said apologetically. "Those two kids' mother was just killed, and something has happened to Lahari; she's in a bad state." Dotty Marbles took Auntie Peg's hands, looked her in the eyes, and said, "I think it's time!"

The people on the night shift started arriving at the clinic, and Auntie Peg greeted them one by one, filling each of them in on the condition of the current patients. A few minutes later, Auntie Peg, Dotty Marbles, and Ninyani were ready to head home with the three other children.

"Aren't we having tea?" Fennah asked.

"Oh, right, sorry, dear," Dotty Marbles replied. "Let's make some when we get to our house."

The six of them headed outside, and a couple of blocks from the clinic, the queens stopped at a food cart. They ordered each of them a basket of fried shrimp.

"Thech doesn't need help with these," Jzuna informed Fennah, as the vendor placed the food onto a little table beside the cart.

Dotty Marbles looked curious and asked, "Jzuna, do you need help?"

"No, thank you," Jzuna answered, and Thech's arm shot out like a viper. "He's good," she reiterated to herself as her brother struggled to get his hand where he wanted it to go, but as soon as he had one of the crispy plump shrimp in his fingers, he shoved it right into his wide mouth. Jzuna focused on the food in her basket, and it began to disappear.

"Peggy and Dot, watch this!" Fennah squealed, pointing at Jzuna's shrinking food. The others could not help but to stare.

Jzuna stopped focusing on her food, and her enormous eye looked up at the other four. Auntie Peg, Dotty Marbles, and Ninayni quickly shifted their gaze to their own meals, but Fennah just smiled at Jzuna.

It was very dark by the time the group arrived at the queens' home.

"In we go," Auntie Peg said in a singsong voice.

The house was a small space they had made their own with Ninyani, and once several candles were burning, their home was very cozy indeed.

"Why don't we figure out beds for you three?" Dotty Marbles suggested. "Ninyani, can you please get a blanket out of the closet?"

"I'll grab one of the pillows off of our bed," Auntie Peg added.

"Thanks, doll!" Dotty Marbles patted the couch. "Fennah, we'll set you up on the sofa here by the window so you can watch the stars as you fall asleep." Ninyani spread a blanket out for the girl, and Dotty Marbles turned to Thech and Jzuna. "Now, what are we going to do with you two?"

"We normally sleep in a little tub," Jzuna told her.

Auntie Peg recommended, "How about the bathtub? Do you kids want to come see if this will work?" They followed her into the privy chamber, and Thech and Jzuna approached the large basin.

"It's a lot bigger than our bed," Jzuna replied. Thech swayed side to side, and his sister rotated in the air toward the queens. "Thech likes it, but is it really okay if we sleep in it? And what if you need to use the potty during the night?"

Auntie Peg smiled, and behind her, Dotty Marbles smothered a laugh; she knew what Auntie Peg was about to say. "Thech, Jzuna, you don't need to worry about Ninyani or Dot or me, but would it make you uncomfortable if Fennah needed to use the potty during the night? Because she's the only one who might need to come in here to use the potty."

Thech let out a little grunt and Jzuna said, "No, it wouldn't bother us if Fennah needed the potty."

"Ninyani and Dot and I can all use a *different* potty if we need to, even outside on a bush," Auntie Peg explained, and Dotty Marbles snickered. Auntie Peg added, "I'm sorry you have to sleep in the bathroom."

"We don't mind," Jzuna replied.

Dotty Marbles asked, "Do you two want a pillow or blanket?"

"Our mama used to give Thech a pillow and a blanket, but we haven't been sleeping with them since we left home."

"Would you like one now? We can give you either if you'd like.

"I think we're okay without," Jzuna said, "and we *are* pretty sleepy."

"Alright, let one of us know if either of you change your mind. We'll let you sleep, and we'll keep the door cracked. Good night, children."

Auntie Peg opened a bottle of wine and poured glasses for herself and Dotty Marbles. Ninyani gave each of them a peck on the cheek and headed into his own room. The queens could hear quiet sounds coming from their bathroom until the two unique children were asleep, and soon Auntie Peg and Dotty Marbles also retired to their boudoir.

The next morning, everyone rose early.

Before Ninyani changed out of his nighty, he collected the blanket and pillow Fennah had used.

"Good morning, Ninyani," the girl said with a yawn and a stretch. She added, "Good morning, Thech and Jzuna and Peggy and Dot."

"Good morning to you, princess," Dotty Marbles replied.

Auntie Peg stepped up to the four children and said, "We forgot to make tea last night, and therefore, I think we should get ourselves a little something fun today."

"And we shan't be staying in," Dotty Marbles added. "It is time for adventures!"

Thech lumbered over and stood next to the queen.

"Good morning, Thech," she said down to him, "are you excited to come with us?"

"Yes," Jzuna's voice squeaked from the air all around them, "Thech is looking forward to being with you and Peggy."

Auntie Peg asked, "Jzuna, how's your hurt arm?"

She held out her tentacle. "It's a little better."

"That is wonderful news!" Dotty Marbles declared. "I think you should have an iced mistcream."

Jzuna's one huge eye opened even wider, and she squealed, "We love Bivon's mistcream lattes!"

"Marvelous!" Auntie Peg replied with a cackle that made Fennah and Jzuna giggle. "He does make good coffee, and we should get some to start the day. However, we are going to give you something a little different; iced mistcreams for the four of you!"

"I can have one, too?!" Fennah asked in her chirping voice.

Dotty Marbles leaned down in a playfully conspiratorial way and said, "Let's go see what we can find. Follow me, children. It's time for fun!"

"Where are we going?" Fennah asked as they all headed out the front door.

"Are we going to Perrikleg's Icies?" Ninyani guessed.

Dotty Marbles replied in a dramatic and mysterious voice. "Is that where we should go? There are quite a few options in the neighborhood. We need to pick the perfect place for our first time enjoying iced mistcreams with Thech and Jzuna. Fennah, do you have a recommendation?"

"I've only gotten one from Chilly Squilly's once," she squeaked.

"Theirs are pretty good," Auntie Peg said. "But what do you think, Dot, about taking them to Frozone the Frozen Zone?"

"I've been wanting to go there!" Ninyani replied. "That's the place, Fennah, the one I've been telling you about, the one with the pool out front!"

Dotty Marbles grinned. "We know you've been interested in visiting."

"Let's see where the road takes us," Auntie Peg recommended.

They turned a corner and Dotty Marbles recognized where her beloved was leading them. "Ahh, so you're thinking Tolfer's Bistro for breakfast before iced mistcream, Peggy?"

"I am, indeed."

Ninyani let out a little squeal. "I've only been there once!"

Dotty Marbles laughed. "That's true. You kids are in for a real treat! There's a whole children's area out in the back with a jungle gym and slides and tunnels, and there are usually other children to play with. Peggy and I have only been there the one time with Ninyani, but I think you three are going to love it! Jzuna and Thech, there was even a Bio-Shift boy working behind the counter."

"It's owned by a few of the UBHS leaders," Auntie Peg informed them. "And in fact, we are almost there Fennah, what do you think you'll order?"

The girl answered without thinking twice. "I'm getting whatever Jzuna and Thech get!"

"There's the sign," Dotty Marbles said, pointing at the brightly-colored letters that spelled out *Tolfer's Bistro* on an old piece of driftwood hanging above the entrance.

They headed inside and the four children approached the counter with the queens behind them.

"We'd like three mistcream lattes, please," Jzuna requested for herself, her brother, and Fennah.

A jittery man behind the counter replied, "Comin' right up," and he zipped over to the coffee grinder. "And for you?" he asked, looking at Ninyani.

"I think I would like the same, please."

"I'd actually be happy with one of those as well," Dotty Marbles requested. She waved toward Auntie Peg. "This one will probably need a *double* shot of your double-black."

Auntie Peg made an innocent face at the man, and he set her separate drink to steep as he continued working on the five mistcream lattes. When a timer went off, he strained the double double-black.

"Here you are, milady," he said quickly, handing Auntie Peg her dark thick drink.

A moment later, the five matching beverages were also ready, and the group headed out onto the patio to play. It was already a little crowded with children and several sleepy-looking adults.

Fennah and Ninyani were each holding their own drinks, and Auntie Peg and Dotty Marbles carried Thech and Jzuna's beverages outside for them. The two queens selected a large table in the shade and sat down to let the children enjoy the play area. Ninyani left his drink on the tabletop, and he headed right for the line of children waiting below the slides. Fennah took a seat with her feet swinging beneath the chair and Auntie Peg sat beside her.

However, Thech and Jzuna were standing off to the side of the patio doors.

Auntie Peg turned to them. "Is it a little overwhelming? There's a lot of things to play with."

There were two slides, and one was a corkscrew. There was a jungle gym of tubes large enough for the children to climb through, and next to it was a set of monkey bars.

Up against the exterior wall of the café was a large wooden board with a lion's head painted on it. A hole had been cut from the wood at the lion's mouth, and a tube led from the back of the panel to a basket full of small brightly-colored balls. A little girl was attempting to throw them into the lion's mouth.

Jzuna then spoke, and her voice sounded sad. "Our mama died in a spot like this."

"Hunnies!" Dotty Marbles cried out, rushing over to them. "We didn't mean to bring you somewhere that would make you think about those things."

"It's okay," Jzuna responded before the queen could say anything else. "We just got sad for a minute, but Thech likes you and Peggy, and we're sorry we're a burden."

"Oh, my stars and moon and planets!" Auntie Peg squawked, jumping up from her seat and joining Dotty Marbles with them. "You two are not a burden. You both are absolute delights!"

"We are so sorry that your mother is gone, children," Dotty Marbles added. "Nothing can replace her. It's going to be hard for a while, but you two are so strong, *so strong*."

The four of them joined Fennah at the table where she was still seated. Half of her beverage was already gone.

Auntie Peg called out, "Ninyani, your latte's getting cold!"

"I'll drink it in a minute!"

Dotty Marbles sat down and asked, "Thech and Jzuna, do either of you need help?"

"Yes, please. Our mama always helped Thech drink his drinks. I can help him with food sometimes," Jzuna added, "but I'd probably spill his mistcream latte, and he really likes it."

"I've got this little one," Dotty Marbles declared, putting her very large arm around Thech's tiny and slimy shoulders. "You don't mind if I give you a hug, do you?"

Thech let out a quiet hum noise and leaned his head back.

"He's ready for you to give him his drink now," Jzuna said.

"Oh, thank you for letting me know, Jzuna," Dotty Marbles replied with a smile. She picked up the steaming beverage and poured a tiny bit into the boy's gaping maw.

"He can drink more than that at once, and the heat won't hurt him," Jzuna added.

"Sounds good," Dotty Marbles said, and she poured in a little more.

"And what about you?" Auntie Peg asked.

"If it's just sitting on the table, I can drink it," Jzuna answered. "But I think I only want to drink half of it, and then go play for a little bit, and then have the rest after."

"I think that's a splendid idea!" Dotty Marbles declared, pouring more of Thech's drink into his mouth.

Jzuna focused her enormous single eye on the beverage, and the surface began to lower as she drained it a little more than halfway down. "Mmm," she hummed in delight. "That's so yummy! And Thech really likes his, too. Thank you, Peggy and Dot."

The queens chuckled at Jzuna's enthusiasm, and they watched her float over to the basket full of bright balls. The other child who had been playing was now waiting in line for the slide with Ninyani, and Jzuna was by herself. She focused on the painted lion face.

Auntie Peg and Dotty Marbles watched her, and they were confused and astonished to see several of the balls float up into the air seemingly on their own. They drifted toward the mouth of the lion, entered the hole cut in the wood, and they rolled down the tube back into the basket again. Jzuna's voice burst out with giggles of joy, and Auntie Peg took her beloved's free hand and squeezed her fingers. Then she saw Ninyani. "Dot, look," and she subtly nodded toward the slide.

The girl who had been throwing the balls at the lion's mouth was now behind Ninyani. She noticed Jzuna and was gawking at her, but Ninyani turned and whispered something to the girl, and she looked at him with a surprised smile. The queens did not know what Ninyani said, but the little girl let out a loud *aaawww!* Then she and Ninyani hugged, and they both climbed the ladder up to the top of the slide.

Dotty Marbles smiled at Auntie Peg, and she turned back to Jzuna's brother. Her arm was still around him. "Thech, would you like to save half of your drink, like your sister did?"

He stayed leaning against her arm and kept his head tilted back.

"No? You want to drink it all now?"

He remained in the same position, and she poured the rest of his mistcream latte into his wide mouth. When it was gone, Thech brought his head upright again with his eyes still rolled back and his mouth still hanging strangely. He let out two quiet grunts.

"Are you happy, Thech?" Dotty Marbles asked him. "Would you like to go over and play with your sister?"

He did not move. Thech just continued to stand where he was with her forearm over his back, and although his eyes were blank, he was facing directly at her.

"Don't you worry, honey," Dotty Marbles said to him with a smirk, "you go right ahead and stare; I *live* for people staring at me! You're not gonna make *me* uncomfortable." She let out a cackle and Thech huffed a little breath of amusement.

"Dot," Auntie Peg whispered, "I think he likes you."

Jzuna's laughter rang out again, as another group of balls floated up to the lion's mouth and rolled back down the tube to her.

Ninyani walked over to the table and took a large drink from his latte.

"Is it even hot anymore?" Auntie Peg asked.

"I don't like it to be too hot," he replied.

Six matching bowls were delivered to their table a moment later, and Dotty Marbles said, "We ordered each of us the same thing, nothing special, just steamed fish on rice. There are a few different sauces you can add."

Dotty Marbles fed Thech his food, and when he was done eating, he pulled away and she lifted her arm from his shoulders. He lumbered over to the basket of brightly-colored balls, where his sister was still playing, and Dotty Marbles gave herself a quick wipe with a towel she had hidden in her purse.

Auntie Peg looked impressed and whispered, "You planned ahead?"

Dotty Marbles gave her a cocky little smirk. "Thought we might need it, and I don't mind what they leave behind, not one bit."

She stuffed the rag into a separate smaller bag that was also hidden inside her purse.

"Seriously, who are you?" Auntie Peg teased quietly. "I love the way you're so into these kids."

The group stayed and played at the bistro until almost noon, at which point Dotty Marbles declared, "I think it's time for lunch."

Out on the street again, Auntie Peg said to the four children, "I wonder what's at the end of this lovely boulevard," and she pointed. "Lead the way, Ninyani."

"But I don't know where we're going," he replied.

She winked and said, "We're going *that* way."

Ninyani smiled and began to lead the small group down the street. A moment later, he could see a sparkling ahead of him, and he exclaimed, "The water, you're taking us to the water, but why? I thought we were getting lunch."

"We most certainly are," Dotty Marbles replied. "Head for that boat straight in front of you."

"We're getting lunch on a boat?" Fennah asked.

Dotty Marbles burst out, "*We're getting lunch on a boat!*" and the other five laughed.

There was a very small sign that Ninyani did not notice until he was about to step off solid ground. "Café Zular? As in, the Zular who I know?"

"One and the same!" Auntie Peg replied. "At night, she's a fabulous performing queen, but during the day, Zular runs this lovely little restaurant."

The boat was a wide flat barge, permanently anchored in its position on a short canal the Oselians had built over 200 years earlier that led into the Grey Shallows. Zular's restaurant was a tiny hut at one end of the boat, and tables were positioned across the rest of it. Several people were already eating.

Ninyani saw Zular through the window of the little food shack. She was taking someone's order, and he scampered over to be next in line.

Auntie Peg waved for the others to follow him, and she and Dotty Marbles stepped up behind the four children.

"Hi!" Ninyani said exuberantly.

"What can I getcha?" Zular asked.

"I know you!" Ninyani declared.

Zular smiled. "Have you been here before?"

Ninyani's expression fell; she apparently did not know him. "No, I saw you at the Gate Town fundraiser."

"Oh, you've been to my performances," Zular stated.

"Yes, and you're so pretty!" Ninyani was gazing at her with wide eyes.

"Well, thank you very much," she replied with an elegant smile. "Now, what would you like to eat?"

Dotty Marbles stepped up and said, "Four large should do it for all of us," and she wiggled the corresponding amount of fingers.

"Right you are, Dot," Zular replied.

"Come on, kids, let's go grab a table," Auntie Peg said.

A few minutes later, four large identical plates of food were brought to them.

"Zular makes small or large platters; those are the only two options," Auntie Peg informed the children.

Each plate held two very large fried oysters, two fried shrimp, and a pile of fried clam strips on a bed of sweet potato fries. Wedged in on the plates among the crispy food were little steaming dishes with buttery baked whitefish.

Auntie Peg jumped up, grabbed two extra plates, and the queens began distributing the food.

After lunch, it was time for...

"Six iced mistcreams, if you please!" Dotty Marbles said to a girl behind the counter inside the little parlor called Frozone the Frozen Zone. The queens and four children were shivering.

The storefront was set up in an Oselian cooler that was perpetually kept below freezing, and the space had remained so for over two centuries. No one in Teshon City knew how the Oselians managed to chill the space, nor why it remained cold for so long after they were gone, but Frozone the Frozen Zone utilized the low temperatures.

The employees were each bundled up in winter clothing meant to protect against the most brutal cold, and the girl's voice was muffled behind a scarf as she asked, "Sparkles or infusions for any of them?"

"I'll take mine with phong petal drops," Auntie Peg requested.

"And please, top mine with a little fizzing dust," Dotty Marbles added. "Make the other four regular."

The queens were given a tray holding the six chilled treats, and the group quickly headed back out into the sun.

"What is *that?*" Jzuna asked in wonder. Her huge eye was focused on the iced mistcreams.

"You're gonna love it!" Ninyani declared.

"To the pool!" Auntie Peg said with a laugh.

Condensation from the interior of Frozone the Frozen Zone was collected and funneled out through a series of tubes that dripped their chilly waters into a shallow pool. Quite a few people were already enjoying the water, which only came up to their ankles.

The queens kicked off their heels, and Ninyani and Fennah removed their shoes. They all stepped into the water, and Thech joined them beside Dotty Marbles.

Auntie Peg pointed at the boy's feet. "Dot, what are we looking at?"

Although Thech was standing up to his ankles, the liquid seemed to not want to touch him. It was as if the water was Thech-*phobic*, or like some sort of thin invisible shield was blocking his slime from the water.

Dotty Marbles shrugged at her beloved with a smile. She scooped a bit of the iced mistcream and said to Thech, "It's cold," as she fed it to him.

He began to chomp, but he paused and let out a little steaming breath of surprise.

Jzuna's giggles suddenly filled the air all around them. "He loves it! *He loves it!*"

Auntie Peg laughed. "We thought you might."

"Don't eat it too fast," Fennah warned, "or it'll make your head cold on the inside!"

"But don't eat it too slow," Ninyani countered, "because it's already starting to melt."

A few hours later, the group had visited a flower garden, a teahouse, and a petting zoo with a few goats and a pigmy pig, then the six of them ate a lovely dinner of breakfast foods. It was already early night when the group arrived back at the queens' house, and faster than either of the ladies expected, the four children were asleep.

Dotty Marbles poured two glasses of wine, smiled at Auntie Peg, and said, "This *is* going to work, isn't it?"

"Yes, Dot, I think it is."✪

Chapter 17 – Unadi & Olona, Part Two

After Ilya flew off with Lahari's unconscious body, Olona began testing Unadi's photonova gland to see if it was indeed no longer active. The two of them were still close to the edge of his lifeless grey realm, with the living forest surrounding it.

Olona was not feeling ill at all.

When Unadi and Lahari collapsed to the earth, Unadi had gotten right back up again, but Lahari was unresponsive to anything Olona or Ilya tried to do to help her recover.

"I'm so sorry about your friend," Unadi said to Olona. He had said it many times in the few minutes since Ilya flew off with Lahari.

Olona did not reply. She was shocked at the effect her devices had on Lahari, but she was keeping her emotions hidden. "I don't feel any symptoms from your power," she told Unadi in as strong a voice as her emotions would allow. "I think it worked; I think you're not a Shift anymore. I'm not getting any readings at all." She was looking down at a device connected to the cable from the organic machine inside her forearm.

Unadi was hopeful. "You really don't feel anything?"

Olona took a deep breath of fresh air and said, "I feel completely fine." A lump threatened to rise in her throat at the thought of Lahari's condition. She forced a cough and continued. "But what do *you* feel? You told me you could feel the life forces you absorb; can you feel yourself absorbing anything now? The trees or plants," she asked, waving toward the living part of the forest outside of his ring of death, "or any animals, or even me?"

Unadi hesitated. "No, I can't. I can't feel anything at all." A wide smile spread across his face that made his eyes squint almost completely shut. "I'm not a curse anymore!" he declared, and he began to cry with joy. "Thank you, thank you! I have no way to repay you for this incredible gift you've given me!" He took one of Olona's hands and repeated himself through his sobs. "Thank you! I'm so overwhelmed right now that I've completely forgotten your name, but thank you a thousand times!"

Olona laughed. "It's Olona," she reminded him. "And I'm so happy it worked. I'm sure Lahari is going to be okay. Her father is a healer and will know what to do." She gave him a smile that she hoped did not look halfhearted. "Since it'll be a long time before Ilya returns, why don't we head back to your place so we can get to know each other a bit?" Olona picked up the tent in its carrying case and the sack of remaining food.

"I would love that! Follow me," Unadi replied, and he started to lead.

Olona lit a joint as they walked, and after a short time, they arrived at his shack. Olona returned his books to their shelves, and she sat on a floor cushion positioned at a low table.

Unadi sat across from her.

"How old were you when you left Bahlim Town?" Olona asked. She added, "I found the old photograph and the article about the so-called ghost sickness in one of your books."

Unadi nodded. "Yeah, that's what the villagers called what was happening to people before they realized it was coming from my mother, while she was pregnant with me."

"I was so surprised to read how your mantis gland activated before you were born," Olona continued. "I've never heard of something like that happening."

"Yes, as a child, none of my tutors or nurses had ever heard of someone with my condition. None of my history books have accounts of a single Shift's mantis gland activating before puberty." He waved over at the shelves lined with old volumes. "The Oselians knew so much, but I guess they never came across anyone like me."

"You're an anomaly," Olona agreed. "You mentioned tutors and nurses; do you mind telling me what your childhood was like?"

"I haven't thought about those days in a long time," Unadi replied. "My earliest memories are a blur of people who cycled through my youth. Since no one could remain in my presence for any extended period of time, there was a constant flow of adults coming and going. As I got older, teachers eventually replaced most of my nurses, and I got *some* education until I was 15 when I left, but I never spent any time with anyone my own age."

"No one?" Olona asked.

"My powers are worst for Shifts, but children and the elderly also experience the sickness intensely, so the only people who came up the mountain were healthy adults who could deal with my powers for a little while before returning to the valley below. Eventually I left Bahlim and ventured into this wilderness. I've been here for over two decades."

Olona was taken aback. "You've been out here for 20 years?!"

Unadi sighed and shrugged. "Yeah, I'm used to being alone."

Olona shook her head and continued. "You just said that your powers *are* worst for Shifts, but I think you meant *were* worst," she corrected with a kind smile. "The ghost sickness is gone."

Unadi's hands came to his face as another sob of joy threatened to bring him to tears, and he whispered, "Yes, it's gone."

Olona took one of his hands and gave it a squeeze. "You're not going to make anyone sick anymore." She looked around. "Unadi, why don't you show me how you normally spend your days?" Olona stood. "Where do you make food?"

There was a fireplace but no stove, no pots or pans, no kitchen at all. There was no lavatory or privy chamber. The little house did not even have a bedroom. Olona had not noticed these peculiar facts when she was there before and Unadi's powers had been beginning to affect her. Now the shack seemed odd; it was little more than an oversized shed.

"Oh," Unadi replied, recognizing her confusion, "I don't need to eat. My powers absorb life energy and make it so I don't need food."

Olona furrowed her brow. "Well, now that you don't have your power anymore, you're probably going to need to eat."

Unadi scrunched up his nose. "Really? You think so?"

"I guess if your stomach starts grumbling in a few hours, we'll know you're hungry. So," Olona pivoted, "can you run through what your typical days have been like out here in the forest?"

Unadi pointed at a small desk in one corner. "Mostly I write poetry, but I always burn them up."

"What?" Olona responded. "What do you mean?"

He looked at his books. "I've read them all," he stated, "but the ones you took while you waited for Ilya to return are the ones I find least interesting. I have several books of poetry and short story collections, and I love to read them."

"Then you write your own, and you burn them?"

"Yes," Unadi confirmed, "I burn them. I was certain no one would ever read them. Also, any time I go back and reread my own writing, it never seemed as good as the writing in my books." He looked over at them again. "I could never write like them."

"Do you have any poems that you didn't burn? I'd love to read one." She did not know why she said it; Olona did not like poetry.

"No, I've burned it all."

"Well, I hope you'll write something someday that you'll share," Olona replied with a smile. "Listen, I don't think we should expect Ilya back tonight, and I'm getting tired. Incidentally, where do you sleep?" She yawned and looked around the small hut.

"Oh, *sleep*," Unadi replied, as if being reminded of some long-forgotten memory, "I don't sleep. My powers make it so I don't need to."

Olona was concerned. "What other human requirements have been negated by your power? I suspect going forward you'll need both food and sleep." She paused and thought for a moment. "Since you're not used to sleep, but *I* certainly need some, why don't I set this up?" and she patted the tent Ilya left behind. "I can sleep and you can stay awake if you want to."

She took out another joint, lit it, and she set about assembling the tent with Unadi watching her.

"Can you tell me about where you're from?" he asked.

"Do you mean where I was born down in Xin, or where I live now in Teshon City?"

"The city, yes, where you three live."

"Ilya and Lahari are both from that region," Olona answered, "but I moved there two years ago. No, a little less than that," she corrected.

Olona told him about the Teshon City neighborhoods and inhabitants. She informed him of the attack on the underground and the Battle of Gate Town the following year. Olona explained how *many* of the worst people in the city had been killed or driven away, and that there was a new brightness to the place. She made Teshon City sound very enticing to Unadi.

Not long after Olona started assembling the tent, her sturdy little fabric structure was standing.

"You sure you don't want some food?" she offered.

Unadi furrowed his brow. "I'm not ready for that yet. It all seems so weird."

"Okay, well, I'm gonna eat a little something and get some sleep, but I'm looking forward to bringing you to Teshon City with us tomorrow." Olona smiled at him again and closed the flap of the tent.

A few hours later in the middle of the night, Olona was awakened, and she was surprised to hear the sounds of talking. She sat up in the darkness and listened. Unadi's voice was speaking, but Olona could not make out the words. It sounded like he was in the middle of a conversation, and she peeked out the flap of the tent.

Ilya was back! She was inside Unadi's house.

Olona entered the shack and interrupted their quiet discussion. "What are you doing back here so soon?"

"Oh no, I'm sorry," Ilya replied. "Did we wake you? We were trying to keep it down."

"It's okay," Olona said. "Why didn't you stay the night in Teshon?"

"I left Lahari with her father, but I was so worried because of how badly everything went here, that I figured I should come straight back and check on you both, but Unadi says it worked."

Olona felt very worried about Lahari, but she wanted to sound upbeat and opted for, "We're fine, aren't we, Unadi? I still don't feel anything, and Ilya, you seem fine, too. Unadi, can you feel yourself absorbing any lifeforce?"

"No, nothing," he replied. "Ilya and I were just discussing where I should go."

"Go?" Olona asked. "What do you mean?"

He smiled. "When you invited me to Teshon City last night, it got me thinking. Ever since Ilya first found me here in the forest, I've been planning to go back to Bahlim. But *should* I return to my village?" Unadi looked at each of the young women. "I'd love to see Bahlim again, but what you've both told me about the city, it just sounds so good."

Olona flashed him a smile. "Well, what are your thoughts? Do you want to come to the big city, or go back home again?" she asked.

"That's just it," Unadi replied, "I don't think I want to return to Bahlim Town."★

Chapter 18 – Lonklam & the Other

Lonklam left the mutilated corpse of the Shift boy in the forest at the edge of Hazel Cove, and Ronging followed him into the wilderness. With Lonklam's craving satiated and Ronging's not to rise again for some time, the two began to follow their secondary urge, the draw to be with others of their kind. The pull had always coaxed them back to Gunge, but it now made them travel north.

They remained in the forested tracts of land and avoided the few other human habitations that lay between Hazel Cove and Teshon City. Lonklam and Ronging could feel another monster, but it was not hiding in the populated areas, and at the dilapidated sight of the old ruins that the locals called Ilin, Lonklam and Ronging's senses told them they were near one of their own kind. For a brief moment, there was no sign of the other to whom they were drawn, but then the two were attacked.

A hideous mutant that had once been a woman flailed out with her many limbs. She crashed into Lonklam and Ronging and sent them sprawling across the terrace of the old ruins. She sprang onto them and was stronger than both, and she managed to hold them down.

"*What are you!?*" she raged, focusing her weird eyes on Lonklam.

"We are others like you," he replied.

"No one... is like me," she retorted. She scrutinized him and added, "No one is... like *you*." She climbed off them.

Lonklam looked from her to Ronging, who rose and stood but paid no attention to the other two.

"Indeed," Lonklam replied to the female monster, "I am Lonklam."

"Riam... is my... name. Riam," she repeated. Every word out of her bizarre mouth seemed like a struggle, but somehow, Riam had managed to keep more of her humanity than any other monster besides Lonklam.

"How have you not become like the others?" Lonklam asked, glancing back at Ronging. He picked at the metal crown that was embedded in the flesh of his head. "An organic mechanic built this for me," he explained. "It has helped my mind deteriorate more slowly than the others, but how have you maintained yourself despite your many changes?" His eyes moved over her.

The thing that used to be a woman was made up of more body parts than Lonklam had ever seen on one of his fellow monsters. Somewhere underneath it all was the original human form that Riam was born with, but she was far more mutated than any of the creatures of Gunge.

Her right shoulder supported not one, but four separate arms, and beneath them, an entire leg protruded out from her ribs and hung heavy. The multiple limbs forced Riam to stand with a pronounced lean. Another leg had grown from the back of her neck, and it hung down along her spine. Still a third unnatural leg stuck out of the left side of her stomach, and two full arms extended from her right hip.

Riam's left shoulder was even more bizarre than her right one. A partial face had grown into it, complete with a fully-formed mouth and half of a nose. The single nostril sniffed at the air and the mouth snapped, clacking its teeth together with a constant unnerving sound from her shoulder.

Three extra fingers poked out from the wrist of her left hand, and another thumb had grown beside Riam's pinky, mirroring her natural thumb. Another cluster of six fingers wiggled at the air together from the side of her neck, and one of her original thighs was covered in a small collection of toes in various sizes. The leg was also graced by a row of teeth. They protruded from her skin in a straight line and ran from her inner knee up to her crotch. Several undersized and malformed limbs protruded from her torso as bizarre chunks of undeveloped flesh.

Riam had also grown multiple extra breasts during her transformations, one right on top of her normal left breast, and another very large one that bulged from the right side of her stomach opposite the stomach-leg. There were still two other breasts that had grown on her back, one up by her shoulder blade and the other at the center of her low back with the foot of her neck-leg always resting on the breast. Beneath her left buttock was a final additional weird lumpy breast that had four separate nipples.

Despite all of her bodily mutations, Riam's face was worst of all. One of her eyes bulged with an extra eyeball within the orbital socket. Her secondary eye was fused to the eye she was born with, and her side by side irises created the shape of an infinity symbol. Nothing about the bones of her skull had changed, and her weird double-eye did not fit in her head; she could not fully close her eyelid and constantly dripped tears. A separate trio of glassy eyes blinked in her neck near the finger cluster, but the three were cloudy and could not focus. There was still another eye that peered out from a bald patch of hair on her scalp.

Not only did Riam have an entire extra mouth on one shoulder, but there was another half-formed mouth that grew from her second natural eye. The lower eyelid was a partial lip, and several teeth pressed against the orb of her eyeball, squeezing it into a strange shape. The half-mouth extended to her temple where a tongue remained perpetually lolled out, dangling by her ear, which had grown thick black whiskery hairs. Her opposite ear hung floppy like a dog's.

From the tip of Riam's nose extended a single finger that sometimes pointed straight forward at Lonklam, and it sometimes curled up toward her forehead. Another finger grew along her jaw, but it was partially fused with the side of her face, and it barely moved; only its fingertip could wiggle by her chin.

Riam's normal mouth had at some point developed multiple rows of teeth on both the top and bottom, like the layered teeth of a shark, and she could no longer close her mouth completely. The teeth stuck out at strange angles and made it very difficult for her to speak.

"I was a… Demifae before I… became a Messiah," she explained.

"And at some point you ate another mantis gland," Lonklam finished for her, thinking he understood how Riam became the way she was.

"*17*," she corrected in a hissing voice.

Lonklam was taken aback. The child he slaughtered in Hazel Cove for its photonova gland was only his sixth victim, and none of the monsters of Gunge had even reached as many as 10 before they were all slaughtered.

"I need…" Riam declared to Lonklam, and she hesitated before she added, "more… and always."✪

Chapter 19 – Dotty Marbles, Auntie Peg, & Heavyfeather

Theolan and the mystic were preparing a treatment for Lahari when they heard a quiet knock at their front door.

"I'll get it, honey," Theolan said to his husband, trying to make his voice sound less hollow.

He opened it and was greeted by Dotty Marbles and Auntie Peg with the three children. Thech, Jzuna, and Fennah had been with the queens and Ninyani since the evening two days prior.

"Hello, lovely people," Theolan said to them, "Lahari is still... resting."

"I'm sorry," Dotty Marbles replied. "Peggy and I have an appointment, and we've kept these three wonderful individuals for as long as we could." She looked down at them. "Thech, Jzuna, and Fennah, Peggy and I loved having you spend the last couple of days with us, and we'd love to have you over again tomorrow. We just need to run right now, but we'll be back in the morning."

"It's no problem at all," the mystic said, walking up to the little group. "Welcome back, kids. Are any of you hungry? We can make a snack if you'd like."

Just as Auntie Peg and Dotty Marbles were heading back out the mystic's front door, Sumi and Harakin came up the path toward the house. Sumi was holding a beaten and bloody child. The two young women warned the queens that the child's skin was burning hot to the touch, and that they suspected the child was a Shift. Auntie Peg escorted them inside, then she and Dotty Marbles left the group again and headed back out into the Shifton streets.

"I feel bad making Theolan and the mystic take care of all those kids," Dotty Marbles said.

"They can handle it. *I* feel bad making people wait. I hope Heavyfeather hasn't been at the space for too long."

Dotty Marbles let out a laugh. "It'll be just fine if she gets there before us. What we're doing is very important. I'm sure she won't mind waiting."

"I know it's important," Auntie Peg agreed. "That's why I want everything to be perfect."

"Peggy, it will be; it will be!"

A few minutes later, the two queens turned down a narrow alley and opened a door partway along it. They stepped into a dark hallway with a faint light at the end and headed in its direction. The two turned the corner, and the glow of several torches illuminated an immense woman.

Auntie Peg and Dotty Marbles stepped into the torchlight and looked up. Both of them were smiling.

"Hello, Heavyfeather," Auntie Peg said up to the giantess.

"Sorry we're late," Dotty Marbles added.

"You ladies aren't late for anything," Heavyfeather replied in her booming voice. "I haven't been waiting here even five minutes."

Auntie Peg, Dotty Marbles, and Heavyfeather were standing together in a room that could accommodate the giantess. She was easily three times the height of the queens.

"Glad to hear you weren't here long," Auntie Peg said, giving Dotty Marbles a look, which she ignored.

"I think this space is going to be absolutely magnificent!" Dotty Marbles declared. "The back entrance where we came in is very convenient, and the big wooden main doors open onto Lesser Teshon Way; I couldn't be happier. What do you suppose the Oselians used this place for?"

"Haven't got a clue," Heavyfeather rumbled. "This room must have been some sort of auditorium."

The ceiling was very high and there was a large stage set into one of the walls, but there were no chairs or seating of any kind in the room.

"I used to explore this building," the giantess said, and she added with a reverberating chuckle, "back when I was little. I don't know why the second floor has all those matching empty rooms. The construction seemed odd to me as a child. They aren't barracks; those are on the other side of Teshon City."

"I can't wait to see the rooms," Auntie Peg replied. "When you told me about the upstairs of this building, it just sounded perfect! Do you mind waiting here, Heavyfeather, while Dot and I head up and check them out?"

A different booming voice interrupted the three women.

"Hello?"

Auntie Peg, Dotty Marbles, and Heavyfeather turned to the set of large glass doors that led out onto a wide enclosed pavilion beside the building.

A giant man was kneeling in the open space. He was looking in at the trio with a very surprised expression.

"Who are you?" he asked in a curious rumble.

The queens looked back at Heavyfeather.

"Another giant?" Dotty Marbles whispered.

"I'm sorry," the huge man said. "I didn't mean to interrupt you ladies, but may I please speak with you?" He was staring at Heavyfeather.

She turned to Auntie Peg and Dotty Marbles. "Check on the upstairs and I'll go out there with him."

The glass doors to the pavilion were much taller than the wooden doors at the front of the building, and they had been Heavyfeather's entrance. She ducked and exited through them, and the two giants stood facing each other. The walls that surrounded the space barely came up to either of their waists.

Heavyfeather asked the giant man, "Who are you?"

"I've never met anyone like you," he stated. "My name's Ogomo."

"I'm Heavyfeather," she replied. "How is it we've never crossed paths?"

"I was born in Teshon City, but my sister and I left when I was 12 and I began to grow. I haven't been back since."

"Why didn't you move into the underground?" Heavyfeather asked. "There were huge chambers below that could accommodate even me. Why did you leave the city?"

Ogomo looked confused. "What underground?"

His response surprised Heavyfeather. "You didn't know about the underground? It's where all the Bio-Shifts of Teshon City lived. I think the community was established over a century ago." She then added in a growl, "A lot of our kind have been murdered over the years. I'm glad you escaped and were able to survive." She smiled. "And I guess I should say, welcome back to Teshon City!"

Inside the old Oselian building, Auntie Peg and Dotty Marbles climbed a wide set of concrete stairs that led to the rooms on the second floor.

"Another giant?" Dotty Marbles whispered again.

"*I know!*" Auntie Peg replied dramatically.

"Could there be romance in the air?"

Auntie Peg paused and held up a hand. "Honey, Heavyfeather is a lesbian."

"Oh?" Dotty Marbles replied, then realization came. "*Oh!*"

"Yeah," Auntie Peg said.

"She and..."

Auntie Peg let out an amused laugh. "Yes!"

"They're a couple?! They're a couple! You're totally right, Peggy," and Dotty Marbles snickered at herself. "I think *I'm* just so into men, I never realized that she wasn't! Heavyfeather is with Pinga, who knew? Well, I guess you did." She chuckled again. "Sometimes I'm so oblivious."

Auntie Peg laughed at her beloved, as the two poked their heads into the first room.

There was not much to it.

"It's just an empty square with a window."

Dotty Marbles looked into the next room and Auntie Peg checked the one across the hall.

"This one's the same. It's all so bland and grey."

"Maybe we should paint it."

Auntie Peg and Dotty Marbles stepped up to one of the windows that looked out over the city, and they embraced.

"It's going to be perfect, isn't it?"

"I think it is."★

Chapter 20 – Sumi & Harakin

It was night.

The former child-soldiers Sumi and Harakin were making their way through the streets of Gate Town. They headed along the quiet narrow alleys that led away from Red Raven's and toward a little eatery overlooking the water.

"Sumi, why didn't you just open one of your doorways and teleport us to Mermaid's Pleasure?" Harakin asked. "I'm hungry."

"It's nice out; I felt like walking." Sumi chuckled. "You're always hungry."

Harakin replied, "The baked winkies they make at Mermaid's Pleasure have been calling to me!"

"Really? I thought we were headed there for the tolgofish. That's what I'm getting."

"Oh, yeah, you're right; that's also good," Harakin agreed, "but no one makes winkies like they do at Mermaid's Pleasure."

"I actually prefer the ones from the street vendor with the little cart a few blocks from the mystic's house," Sumi said.

Harakin looked surprised. "But the vinegar flavor is too strong in theirs."

"That's what I like about..."

A brief scream issued from a side alleyway. Sumi and Harakin paused, and they peered into the shadows as a bruised and bloody child came clambering into view.

Three men and a woman carrying blades were in hot pursuit.

The panic-stricken child stumbled and fell to the pavement, as one of the men raged, "No child of ours will be one of those *freaks!*" He looked at the woman and she pounced.

Sumi and Harakin both reacted instantly.

Harakin caused a shell of physical light to manifest over the child, and as the woman's blade connected, it was deflected. The child's mother futilely stabbed at the protective shielding, and she screamed in fury, but then Sumi's whole body blinked and the raging screams of the four attackers were silenced. Sumi teleported them *inside* the concrete wall of one of the old military structures. Pieces of the four people stuck out like weird art; one whole arm, part of three different legs, the back of one man's head, an elbow...

"Good, they can't hurt anyone again," Harakin said. She caused her shell of light to vanish and asked, "Are you okay?" but the child collapsed.

"I'll get her," Sumi said, and she reached down.

"Isn't that a boy?" Harakin asked.

Sumi cried out in pain as soon as her fingertips came into contact with the child, and she winced back. "She burned me! Her skin is hot. She must be a Shift."

Harakin carefully extended an arm and let her hand hover over the child's forehead. "Oh, you're right. I can feel the heat coming off... her? Are you sure it's a girl?"

"My fingers, there are blisters forming. Maybe I'm wrong. Is he a boy?"

"What do we do with him?"

Sumi's fingertips were screaming in pain, but she tried to ignore them. "We should probably take him to the mystic. The only other healer we know is Olona, but since the mystic has lots of experience with Shifts, I think he's our best bet." She slid her leather jacket off and placed it over the child. "Give me yours, too," Sumi said. "These will at least give me a little protection from his heat."

"Be careful picking him up," Harakin said. She also laid her jacket over the child.

"Muunith," the child whispered.

"What?" Sumi replied quietly.

"My name is Muunith."

"Be careful picking him up," Harakin warned.

"I'm not a boy," Muunith murmured.

"Oh, I'm so sorry," Sumi replied, tucking the jackets around Muunith.

"Mind her skin," Harakin said.

Muunith added in a hoarse whisper, "I'm not a girl," and the child lapsed back into unconsciousness.

Sumi and Harakin looked at each other.

"Okay," Sumi replied. She carefully scooped up the abused child with skin like fire, and she opened one of her doorways and teleported them right to the mystic's house.

Dotty Marbles and Auntie Peg were coming out the door.

"Hey there, gals!" Dotty Marbles said, then she saw the condition of the child in Sumi's arms. "Oh, no, what happened to the little one?" She reached for Muunith.

"Be careful!" Harakin blurted out. "Don't touch him! Erm... I mean *them*."

"This is Muunith," Sumi added. "I think she's a Shift. Oh, right, I think *they* are a Shift."

Harakin added, "Muunith's skin is really hot. There were these people after him." She growled at herself. "Sorry, *them*."

Sumi asked Dotty Marbles and Auntie Peg, "Is the mystic home? Muunith is not in great shape."

The queens looked at each other.

"He is, but he's already got his hands full, and Lahari is still in a coma."

"But what should we do with Muunith?" Sumi asked urgently. "The mystic knows how to handle Shifts, so he seems like the best option."

Auntie Peg nodded, knocked on the front door, and she reentered. "Sorry!" she called in, "but we've got more to add," and she stepped aside.

"This is Muunith," Sumi said to the mystic as she entered, "but don't touch them. Their skin is really hot."

"Some men were attacking them," Harakin added.

"Sorry," Dotty Marbles interrupted, "we really need to run, so we're going to get out of your *wigs*." She and Auntie Peg left again.

Theolan, the mystic, and Bivon were in the house with Thech, Jzuna, and Fennah.

Harakin informed the group, "Muunith's parents did this. We heard two of the grownups say Muunith was their child."

"And there's four fewer cruel people in the world," Sumi added.

Bivon furrowed his brow. "What does that mean?"

"There were two other people with Muunith's parents," Harakin explained, "and the four of them are now inside a wall."

No one spoke for a moment.

Bivon repeated himself hesitantly. "What... does *that* mean?"

Sumi replied, "I put them into the concrete."

"Oh, okay, well, right," Bivon said.

"What should I do with Muunith?" Sumi asked.

Theolan stepped up and recommended, "Maybe we should lay the child onto the tiles in the privy chamber."

Sumi entered the room, lowered Muunith to the floor, and she looked at her hands. "Do you have a burn treatment?" she asked the mystic.

He was staring at the unconscious form of the beaten child, but he turned from Muunith and gently took Sumi's wrists to examine her hands. He looked over at his husband. "Theolan, will you please open a packet of silver mustard for Sumi's burns?" He added to her, "It'll hurt, but it'll make the healing much faster."

"Thech, Jzuna, Fennah," Bivon said to them, "why don't we head into the kitchen?"

Theolan led Sumi into the sitting room, and he began to prepare the burn treatments.

The mystic knelt beside Muunith, and Harakin stepped up behind him.

"Careful, they're really hot," she said.

Muunith's eyes fluttered open.

"Hello, little one," the mystic said in a quiet voice. "I'm a healer. May I look over your body and check how bad your injuries are?"

Muunith nodded and whispered, "Be careful. Don't get burned."

"Okay," the mystic replied, "I'll be careful." He lifted the two jackets off the child and handed them to Harakin.

"Oh, honey," the mystic said to Muunith, looking over the many wounds, "I'm so sorry this happened to you."

In the room's bright light, it was evident Muunith had suffered. Injuries covered much of their little body, and Harakin was brought to tears at the sight of them.

"May I please apply wound patches and bruise relief ointment to some of the places where you're hurt?" the mystic asked, and the child nodded again. "My goodness, I can feel your heat," the mystic said as he brought his hands close to Muunith's skin. "I wonder how the salve will work." He used a little wooden paddle to dab a tiny bit on one of the many bruises and it sizzled. "Muunith, did that hurt?"

They shook their head that it did not.

"It's already burned up," the mystic commented, looking down at his little jar of ointment and then at the bruise. "I don't know if this will help at all, but let me apply some more." The salve continued to evaporate as he treated the wounds.

A few minutes later, the mystic rose and returned the jars to his medicine cabinet. Muunith had drifted back into unconsciousness again on the cool tile floor, and Harakin and the mystic left the child to rest.

Theolan was just finishing the burn treatments on Sumi's hands, and tears were running down her cheeks. "This'll help?" she asked in a voice quavering with pain, looking over at the mystic.

"It will, and I'm sorry the silver mustard is painful to apply, but it will speed your healing. In a moment, it should diminish the pain almost entirely." He stepped up to examine his husband's treatment of her wounds.

"Sumi, Harakin, would you two like to join the kids and us for a little dinner?" Theolan offered. He nodded toward his husband and Bivon, as he applied the final bandage. "We've had a massive pot of oxtail curry simmering for hours."

"Oh, yes, please join us!" Fennah called out, peeking around the corner from the kitchen and hoping to get a glimpse of what was happening.

"There's plenty of food," the mystic urged, "and I'd love the company." He looked up toward the ceiling; Lahari was unconscious in her room upstairs.

Sumi and Harakin accepted the invitation, and they crowded around the kitchen table with the three children.

"Bivon, do you mind ladling everyone's food?" the mystic requested.

"Not at all," he replied with a smile.

"Harakin, there's a little bottle of hot sauce in the cabinet behind you," Theolan added. "Could you please grab it for us?"

"These are for Jzuna and Fennah," Bivon said, handing two bowls to the mystic, who placed them in front of the girls. "This one's for Thech," Bivon continued. He scooped a larger bowlful next and added, "This one can be for Sumi or Harakin."

A moment later, steaming dishes of curry were in front of everyone.

Jzuna floated beside her brother's chair. She was still using one of her tentacles to cradle the stump of her limb that had been chopped off, but she reached out with several of her other arms to take hold of Thech's bowl.

Everyone else could not help but watch her.

She poured some of the rich broth into Thech's mouth, a little at a time, until it was gone and the bowl only held two fatty chunks of oxtail.

"It's very sweet how you help your brother, Jzuna," the mystic said to her with a smile. "You are both very compassionate little..."

-Kgrunkch!-

Thech had managed to grab one of the pieces of oxtail, and he shoved it into his mouth, bone and all. He was chomping it up with a horrible crunching noise. The others expected him to make a mess, but the unusual boy was not sloppy at all, and a moment later he swallowed and reached out for the second oxtail.

"Wow! You ate the bone!" Fennah declared.

The mystic chuckled in disbelief, and he watched Jzuna focus on her own food. Without touching it, her bowl of curry drained down to the pieces of oxtail, and they dematerialized.

"Aren't you two just so unique? I'm so glad you're both enjoying your..."

-Kgrunkch!-

Thech ate his second piece of oxtail with the same brutal noise.

"Thank you," Jzuna's voice said all around them, "this is really yummy."

Harakin suddenly gasped and made a hissing noise. Everyone looked at her. "*Sorry*," she wheezed, "too much hot sauce!" She grabbed her mug of water.

A weak voice called out from the other room, "Hello?"

"Lahari?!" the mystic cried, jumping up from the table, but Theolan shook his head.

"It's the child." He looked at Sumi and Harakin. "I'm sorry, please remind me their name."

"Muunith."

"I'll check on them," the mystic said, heading toward the privy chamber. He peeked in and was surprised by the radiant heat that filled the room.

Muunith was sitting up.

"Hi, there," the mystic said gently. His eyes moved over the child's many injuries. "How are you feeling?"

Muunith groaned. "My body hurts."

"Would you like a little more medicine? Or are you hungry? We're all eating dinner right now." The mystic gestured toward the table and Bivon waved at Muunith.

Theolan stepped up behind his husband. "So many orphans," he whispered.

"It's heartbreaking," the mystic replied✪

Chapter 21 – Let's Have a Kiki

It was night. Sumi had teleported herself and Harakin home, and the others at the mystic's house were getting settled for bed.

Inspired by the queens' creativity with Thech and Jzuna's sleeping arrangement at their house, Theolan made the same recommendation to Muunith. "Honey, would you like to sleep in our nice cool bathtub?"

Muunith liked the idea very much.

Thech and Jzuna curled up together in their basin, and Fennah headed into the room she shared with Tchama, even though Tchama rarely stayed at the house at that time.

The following morning, Bivon came out of the mystic and Theolan's bedroom.

"I think we should move Lahari down to our room, honey," the mystic said to his husband as he began to make coffee.

"I'll prep the space and we can move her," Theolan replied.

There was a knock at the front door.

"I'll get it!" Fennah called out from her room.

Bivon chuckled at her enthusiasm, and the mystic said, "I didn't realize she was already awake." They watched the little girl skip out into the hall and were both surprised when Jzuna floated out behind her. Quite a lot of Jzuna's tentacles had ribbons tied on them, and Bivon brought a hand to his heart, as a little sob of joy mixed with relief threatened to bring him to tears.

Auntie Peg and Dotty Marbles were on the other side of the front door.

"Hello, princess," Dotty Marbles said to Fennah, who giggled as she let the two queens into the house.

"Morning!" Auntie Peg called out in a bright voice. "Jzuna, don't you look lovely? Your bows are so pretty. Did Fennah tie them for you?" She looked down at the girl.

"I did!"

"Yeah, except for around my hurt arm," Jzuna added, extending it toward the queens.

"Welcome," the mystic replied, "thanks for coming back so early."

"It's our pleasure. Thech and Jzuna and Fennah are just delightful!"

Theolan stepped out of the bedroom and said to his husband, "It's ready for Lahari. Hello, Peggy and Dot."

Bivon asked the mystic, "Would you like me to carry Lahari down?" He was by far the strongest of the group.

A few minutes later, Lahari's unconscious body was in her father's room.

"This'll be easier," he said. "One of us can stay up there, and I don't mind sleeping in her room."

"Neither do I, honey," agreed Theolan. "Can I pour anyone a cup of coffee?"

"Oh, no, thank you," Dotty Marbles said emphatically. "This one's already got me all jittery from *her* potent brew." She wiggled her fingers at Auntie Peg, who struck an elegant pose and smiled.

"I wish I could just give Lahari some of your strong coffee and that it would wake her up," the mystic said.

Auntie Peg stepped up and wrapped the man in a tight hug. "I know, honey."

"*Gurls!*" Dotty Marbles gasped to Theolan, the mystic, and Bivon in a dramatic whisper, indicating she had a secret. "Let's kiki!" The three men and Auntie Peg turned toward Dotty Marbles and she said, "There was another giant!"

"What?!" Theolan squawked. "You mean, besides Heavyfeather?"

"Exactly!" Dotty Marbles replied. "This enormous man just turned up while we were with her. I thought there might be something there, you know, relationship-*wise?*"

"Heavyfeather's with Pinga," the mystic stated.

Dotty Marbles gawked at him. "Did *everyone* know except me?! They're together," she said to herself, "but they're so different."

"That's one of the things," Auntie Peg replied to her beloved, "that makes their relationship so beautiful. Pinga and Heavyfeather make it work."

"Wait," Dotty Marbles interjected, "they've lived together since..."

"Yes, Dot," Auntie Peg said with a pandering face, indicating the obviousness. "They've *been* together since they started living together."

"But that's got to have been a year ago! Am I an idiot?"

Auntie Peg cackled, and Theolan and the mystic laughed.

Dotty Marbles pulled a silly face at the children, and Fennah and Jzuna giggled. Thech huffed and walked right up and stood next to her. Dotty Marbles reached down and took his slimy hand in hers. "Anywhizzle," she said merrily, "kids, how would you like to come with us again today? Peggy and I have something we'd like you to see."

"Ninyani is going to meet us over there," Auntie Peg added.

Several minutes later, the queens were leading the three children through the Shifton Streets.

"Where are we going?" Fennah squeaked.

"Someplace special," Dotty Marbles replied.

"Dot's right," Auntie Peg added. "It is special, although it may not look special when you first see it. You'll have to use your imaginations."

"Thech has a really strong imagination!" Jzuna declared.

"Oh, good!" Dotty Marbles replied. She was still holding his hand, and she gave his fingers a little squeeze. "Maybe you can help us all to see its potential, Thech. And what do you kids think we should have for breakfast?"

"I want iced mistcream!" Fennah declared.

"It's probably a little early for that," Auntie Peg replied.

"What about mistcream lattes?" Jzuna chimed in from the air all around them.

Thech let out a single grunt.

Dotty Marbles looked down at the unusual boy. "You think so?" she asked. She then looked at the two girls. "Thech says mistcream lattes are a marvelous idea!"

Jzuna's single eye grew wider. "*Thech can talk to you, too?*"

"Oh, no, honey," Dotty Marbles replied with a chuckle. "Sorry, he can't, I just inferred his meaning; I understood him. He's an expressive little guy, got a lot of emotions."

"Yes, he does!" Jzuna replied in a bright voice.

Auntie Peg added, "I also think mistcream lattes sound like a wonderful way to start the day, but we are right around the corner from what Dot and I want to show you. Do you mind if we pop over there first?" She pointed down a wide side street just as Ninyani came walking up from the opposite direction, and he greeted them.

"Good morning, Fennah. Good morning, Jzuna and Thech."

"Good morning!" Jzuna and Fennah said almost in unison.

All of them giggled.

Auntie Peg leaned down and planted a kiss on Ninyani's forehead.

"Thech, stay right here," Dotty Marbles said, releasing his hand and stepping up to a gray building. It had large wooden doors and a row of small windows set high in the wall. "*Ta-da!*"

"What is it?" Ninyani asked. He sounded unimpressed.

"Yeah," Fennah added, repeating Ninyani, "what is it?"

"This is *it*; this is where *it* will be," Auntie Peg replied.

"But what is *it?*" Fennah squeaked.

"This building hasn't gotten any love in a long *long* time," Dotty Marbles said, not answering their questions. "Do you kids think you can help us give it a little love?"

"Are we going inside?" Ninyani asked.

"Later," Auntie Peg answered, "we'll get breakfast and mistcream lattes first." The children began to protest, but the queen repeated herself with a silly smirk, "*Later!*"

"And we've got a few supplies to pick up," Dotty Marbles added. "We also have several more folks who can help us, then we'll all head inside and check it out."

Auntie Peg wrapped an arm around Ninyani's shoulders. "It's a great location and will be exactly what we need."

He pursed his lips and replied, "It's very plain."

"That's the spirit!" Dotty Marbles declared. "You can see it, can't you? It'll be marvelous! Now, let's head to breakfast. Who's hungry?"

"But what is it?!" Ninyani and Fennah squawked.

Thech let out a little huff.

"*See?*" Auntie Peg jeered playfully. "Thech thinks it's going to be just fabulous!"

Jzuna giggled. "That's not what he said! What's this place gonna be?"

Dotty Marbles and Auntie Peg smiled at the four children. "I guess you'll just have to wait and see."★

Chapter 22 – Dozi

It was just after 8am, and Dozi had already done quite a lot of business at her mushroom table, when she noticed Ilya and Olona heading through the crowd toward her stall. She had not seen either of them in several days, and she did not know much of what had transpired. Dozi smiled and waved at them, but she noticed that a man seemed to be walking over with the pair. He looked a bit older, and Dozi guessed he was about Theolan's age.

"Hey, Dozi," Ilya said in a voice Dozi could tell was forced. "This is Unadi."

"Hi," Dozi said dismissively, focusing on Ilya. She could tell something was bothering her. "Ilya, what's wrong?"

"It's Lahari!" she cried out. "Something happened, I don't know, but she's in a coma."

Dozi was shocked. "What?!" she barked.

"It worked," Olona interjected. "The process worked and Lahari was able to turn off Unadi's mantis gland, but she passed out and we weren't able to wake her."

"I brought Lahari back to her fathers," Ilya informed Dozi. "Hopefully the mystic can do something."

Dozi furrowed her brow and looked from Ilya to Olona to Unadi and then back to Ilya. "Okay, why don't I pack up my mushrooms, and we can all go grab a bite to eat so we can talk some more."

It took her only a moment to close her vendor table, and the four of them headed through the streets of Gate Town.

"This is Shifton," Ilya said to Unadi as the quartet passed a little sign indicating the border to the neighborhood. "We're almost to Red Raven's."

A few minutes later, they entered the pub and seated themselves around a table.

Olona asked, "Unadi, what would you like to try and eat?"

He scrunched up his face. "The whole idea of it is so unappealing."

Dozi asked, "Food?"

Unadi explained, "My curse always made eating unnecessary."

Dozi pressed him further. "You don't eat?"

"Never. Even when I was an infant, I apparently couldn't keep anything down. The midwives eventually stopped *trying* to feed me, but I was fine. That's what they told me. I've never eaten anything."

Dozi again looked at Ilya and Olona and then at Unadi.

"You're probably going to need to eat soon," Olona said, "since your mantis gland is no longer consuming the energy of other living things."

One of the regular barkeeps stepped up to their table. "Hello, you three," he said to Ilya, Dozi, and Olona, and he added, "I see you've brought a fella with you today. What can I get for you all?"

"Why don't you bring us four fizzyreds to get started?" Dozi requested.

"Be right out with them!"

"What's that?" Unadi asked.

Olona lit a joint, took a puff, and explained, "Fizzyred is a fermented fruit beverage with only a little kick of alcohol."

"It's good," Dozi added. She eyed Unadi uncertainly. She had been trying to be more trusting of new people, but she still thought to herself, *I don't fucking trust this guy, and he better not have hurt Lahari.*

Tchama appeared at the door to the tavern, and she saw Dozi, Ilya, and Olona. She was wearing a black and white striped scarf draped over the healed remains of her shoulder. "What are you three doing here so early?" she asked as she approached their table. It took her an extra second to register that a strange man was with them. She focused on him. "Oh, hello."

"Tchama, this is Unadi," Ilya said.

"Oi, Tchama!" called a jolly woman from behind the bar, and she waved.

"Nice to meet you, Unadi," Tchama said quickly. "Be right back!" She skipped over to the woman.

"What's... wrong... with her?" Unadi asked in a quavering voice.

The three women with him did not know how to answer.

"Do you mean," Olona ventured, "*what happened to her arm?* Because there's nothing wrong with Tchama."

"She lost it during a battle, less than six months ago," Dozi added.

"There's something evil about her," Unadi stated.

Dozi scoffed.

"No, there isn't," Ilya countered. "Tchama's just missing an arm. What are you talking about, Unadi?"

"She's…" he started, but he did not finish his thought, as Tchama returned to the table with a bowl of walnuts.

"Oooh," Dozi cooed, "crack a few of those for me, will you?"

"My pleasure," Tchama replied, and she grabbed one, crushing it in her bare hand. "Here you go."

Unadi picked up one of the nuts and pinched it between his thumb and first finger. His fingertips squeezed the stony exterior of the shell, but it was unbreakable.

"I'll do it!" Tchama said. She snatched it from his hand and crushed it for him.

To the surprise of the four women, Unadi stood up from the table with a start and backed away from Tchama.

"What's your problem?!" Dozi asked in a tone that was a little harsher than she meant. She was trying to be more understanding of people, but she already did not like Unadi.

"How did you… how is that possible?" Unadi stammered. "How are you so strong?"

"Unadi, you're a Shift," Olona replied. "Why is it strange to meet someone who is stronger than you? You're fully aware of the world we live in, which is *full* of powerful people. You used to be one of them."

Tchama eyed Unadi curiously as she popped a shelled walnut into her mouth and crushed another.

Unadi whispered, "Vile demon."

"Whoa, whoa, *whoa!*" Dozi snapped. "What the fuck are you talking about?"

"She's some sort of monster," Unadi said under his breath.

Tchama let out a laugh, did not say a word, and she walked away from the table. Seconds later, she was at the bar again, chatting and joking with the barmaid who had called her over a moment earlier. Unadi's words seemed not to have bothered her one bit.

"*Why would you say that?*" Ilya hissed at him.

"There's something wrong with her," Unadi declared.

Olona was trying to make sense of the situation. "Okay, Unadi, tell us what's wrong with her."

He looked across the pub towards Tchama. "No, no, no," he began repeating quietly. "No, no…"

"Hey!" Dozi barked, snapping her fingers at him, and he turned back to them.

"Unadi, are you okay?" Ilya asked, but he left the three seated at the table and stormed over toward Tchama.

"Now what?!" Dozi asked the universe at large.

Unadi stepped right up to Tchama, stood with his face a little too close to her face, and he yelled at the top of his lungs, *"You should be dead!"*

The tavern grew quiet and all eyes turned to Unadi.

Ilya rushed over to him, grabbed his arm, and said through her teeth, "What's your problem?! Tchama's our friend!" and she urged him out of the tavern and into the street.

The room full of startled breakfasters got back to their morning meals.

During the commotion, Dozi and Olona did not realize a teenage boy had stepped up and was standing at their table. "Excuse me," he said.

The two of them turned to him.

He was gawking at Olona✪

Chapter 23 – Red Raven's

"Almost there, boys," Z'Matri said over his shoulder to Kosephaji and Relliduna as he led them through the Shifton streets. A moment later, he pulled open a door and waved them into a tavern. "Straight to the back and outside," he directed. He turned and headed up a flight of stairs to the second floor.

Kosephaji and Relliduna walked through the dark interior of the tavern past several tables of people eating their breakfasts. They could see the glow of sunlight ahead, and it guided them to another glass door that opened onto a wide green park.

Ogomo and Nahli were seated in the shade of a massive tree. The tavern was positioned at the border of Teshon City, and the forest that spread across the region grew right up to the edge of the little park.

"Hello again, lads," the giant boomed. "Sorry we couldn't..."

"Is Pelipi with you?" Kosephaji blurted out. "There was a light when you tried to break us out of the prison; was it Pelipi?! Please tell me it was him! Please tell me he's here with you!" Tears began to

well in his eyes as the words flowed from his lips. He had not breathed a single one of these thoughts to Relliduna.

"I'm sorry, boys," Ogomo said in a sympathetic rumble.

Nahli rose from where she was seated beside her huge brother, and she stepped up to Kosephaji and Relliduna. "We had a torch," she explained. "When we came up to the cell wall, Ogomo was holding it, and he handed it to me to use his hammer. I gave it back to him as we headed down to the water, and we doused it before climbing in our submersible." She added quietly, "I'm sorry we got your hopes up about him."

"Z'Matri already told us about Pelipi," Relliduna whispered to Kosephaji. "He's gone."

Kosephaji began to sob. "No! Don't say that, Duna!"

Relliduna wrapped his arms around Kosephaji.

"I'm so sorry," Ogomo repeated.

Kosephaji cried against Relliduna's shoulder, and he could not stop his own tears. The two embraced for several minutes, and they poured out their sorrow.

When they calmed down again, Ogomo recommended, "Lads, head inside and order yourselves each a drink called the queen's ecstasy."

"It'll help," Nahli added.

Kosephaji and Relliduna reentered the dark pub and they approached the bar. Behind it, a barmaid was cackling with a young woman who only had one arm. She was wearing a black and white striped sash draped over where her other arm should have been. Relliduna stepped right up beside her, but he noticed that Kosephaji did not follow him to the counter and instead was approaching a table with a few people seated at it.

The barmaid spoke to Relliduna and pulled his attention. "Welcome to Red Raven's, laddie. What can I get for ya?"

He smiled at the woman with one arm and the barmaid. "I was told to order queen's ecstasies for myself and my friend, if you please."

"Be right up!"

Across the dark tavern, Kosephaji stepped up to a seated woman who was smoking a joint. "Excuse me," he said to her in a tone filled with awe. The two people at the table looked up at him.

Kosephaji felt a little nervous and embarrassed, but he pressed on. "May I please see your arm? I've never seen machines like that."

"Oh, well, these are *organic* machines. Some are my own design," she replied with a note of pride in her voice.

"No, sorry," Kosephaji said, "I know what they are; I've just never seen any like *these* before!" He sounded truly amazed.

"You know about organic mechanics?" she asked. "Have you been to my shop? My name's Olona."

"Oh, no, I've never been to your shop," Kosephaji responded. "I'm from Xin, and we just got here." He pointed over at Relliduna, who had joined in the conversation with the barmaid and the one-armed woman.

"I'm also from Xin!" Olona declared in delight. "How did you two get up here to Teshon City?"

"And what's your name?" added a tall muscular woman with an older man beside her. They walked up behind Kosephaji. She gave him a kind smile and rolled her eyes at Olona for not asking his name. "I'm Ilya," she added. "This is Dozi. And this is our new friend Unadi. Sorry, what's your name?"

"Kosephaji," he answered, looking at each of them; however, Unadi was focused on the bar. Kosephaji followed his gaze to Relliduna.

"What a lovely name," Ilya replied. "Kosephaji, Would you like to join us?" She waved to one of the chairs at their table.

Unadi suddenly screamed and rushed at the bar.

"No!" Kosephaji cried. "Duna!"

Unadi snatched up an empty chair and swung it overhead.

Relliduna and the barmaid cringed away from the assault, but Tchama turned right into Unadi's swing. The chair exploded against her and shattered pieces of wood flew around the tavern.

Tchama was unharmed.

Ilya ran over to Unadi and grabbed his arm again, but he howled at her like a beast and ripped himself from her grip. He ran out of the bar and into the city's narrow streets.

"What the fuck is wrong with him?!" Dozi snapped.

Ilya looked confused and upset, and she hurried after Unadi.

Olona sucked air through her teeth. "I'm beginning to think turning off his mantis gland might've had some consequences we didn't anticipate."

"What the fuck?" Dozi repeated. "Sorry about that," she said to Kosephaji. "He is *not* our friend. What's your name again?"

"It's Kosephaji," he repeated.

"You're welcome to join us if you'd like." Dozi looked over at Relliduna, who seemed to be checking on Tchama, and she was smiling at him. "And your friend, too," Dozi added as Relliduna brushed a few wood chips off Tchama's shoulder scarf.

"Thank you," Kosephaji replied to Dozi, "but we've got a couple friends waiting for us outside."

Relliduna stepped up behind Kosephaji. "*That* was exciting, huh? She says she's got some sort of invulnerability." Relliduna indicated Tchama, who was still at the bar. "And Ogomo and Nahli won't mind if we stay inside and make a few new friends and chat for a while." He smiled at the four at the table. "Here's your queen's ecstasy."

Kosephaji took his cocktail.

"Yikes," Dozi commented, "it's a little early for drinks that strong."

"We just lost a friend at sea," Kosephaji said quietly.

"Oh no, I'm so sorry," Tchama replied as she stepped up. "Would you like to tell us about your friend?"

"His name was Pelipi," Relliduna said. "He was a Bio-Shift. The three of us were born down in Xin, and we left together. The ship we were on crashed and sank, and he... was lost."

"That's so hard," Olona said.

"Thank you," Kosephaji replied. "I don't think it has quite hit me yet. We had a rough night."

Kosephaji and Relliduna looked at each other and each took a sip of their drinks.

"Oooh, that's good!" Relliduna said.

Dozi gave them an *I told you so* look. "You won't realize how strong it is until it's too late."

An hour later, Kosephaji and Relliduna were completely drunk. It was barely 9am. They were outside with Ogomo and Nahli.

"Pelipi was my besshht friend," Kosephaji slurred.

"Mine too," Relliduna mumbled in agreement. "He was the best of the three of uzzz."

Kosephaji and Relliduna had sat with Dozi, Tchama, and Olona for part of their first round of queen's ecstasy. However, Ilya had rushed back in after several minutes to say she lost track of Unadi, and the women left with her. The two boys had joined Ogomo and Nahli on their second drink, but they were now halfway through their *fifth* round of queen's ecstasy.

"D'ya think we should've left Pelipi in Xin?" Relliduna asked Kosephaji.

"Where exactly? And with who? Erm... with *whom?* Is it who or whom?"

"I don't know. Maybe we should've never left."

Kosephaji sighed. "We left Xin because Pelipi and I almost lost *you*. How could we have known that we would lose him in the process?"

"Ugh... I think I'm done drinking," Relliduna groaned, and he pushed his remaining half-glass of queen's ecstasy toward the center of the table.

Nahli leaned over to him and Kosephaji. "There's no wrong way for you boys to feel. Pelipi was quite a character, and I'm sorry he's gone."

Kosephaji also decided to abandon the last few sips of his drink. He and Relliduna embraced, and they were both brought to tears again.

When they separated, Kosephaji looked up at Ogomo and said, "We're drunk."

"And it's almost 9:15 in the morning," Ogomo replied with a rumbling chuckle.

"What're we s'pposeta do now that your ship's been smashed?" Relliduna mumbled to him.

Ogomo sighed. "We knew about the underwater barrier, and we have heard about crashes, but after testing my ship in countless challenging conditions, we were confident that it could get through."

"We reinforced the hull and keel," Nahli added, "and it should have been strong enough."

"But it just wasn't," Ogomo concluded. "Our goal was to end up in Teshon City, but not permanently; we were planning on leaving again."

Kosephaji raised his hand.

"We're not in school," Nahli told him with a laugh.

"Oh, right," he mumbled, "so, I guess, well, how come the ship couldn't get through?"

"We observed quite a lot of it from inside our submersible," Nahli said. "The thing goes on for miles, and it looked too precise to be natural. It's some sort of old barricade, we think."

"It was strong enough to resist even *my* ship," Ogomo continued. "The city guard who held you overnight informed the others that there are a number of warning buoys sporadically positioned along the barrier, but because it's so vast, there's no way for them to mark the entire thing."

"So, they dunno what it is either?" Relliduna slurred.

Ogomo shook his massive head. "It's blocked the waters surrounding Teshon Harbor for longer than there's been a Teshon City."

"For now, we're stuck here," Nahli concluded.

"But here is home," Ogomo added, and he smiled.

"Oh, I didn't mean that I don't want to be here," Nahli replied with another laugh. "I meant whenever we decide to leave, we'll need to figure out some other means."

Kosephaji tried to force down the drunken feelings swirling through his body, but he stumbled over his words nonetheless. "D'you wanna stay here? *Tishin Schitty* seems nice." He scrunched up his face at himself and pressed on, "It's nice seeing Shifts and Bio-Shifts out in the open."

"The city went through a pretty brutal conflict that left a lot of people dead," Nahli informed the boys, "but in the end, those who were left, committed to making this place more welcoming."

"And it is," Ogomo boomed with a grin.

"I wish Pelipi was here to see it," Relliduna said.

Kosephaji smacked Relliduna's arm, as tears filled his eyes again. "Duna, stop making me cry!"

"He woulda liked those three who we were drinking with inside," Relliduna added, "the ones with the friend who was *not* their friend, or something; yeah, Pelipi woulda liked them."

"He prob'ly woulda flirted with all three of them," Kosephaji snorted, wiping his eyes hard. "You better not make me cry again, Duna."★

Chapter 24 – Unadi

Unadi ran aimlessly down one narrow street after another. Madness seemed to be his only guide. Ilya had lost track of him shortly after he rushed out of Red Raven's.

He raced under the bright sign at the edge of Gate Town, turned down an alleyway, and at its other end he found himself on an old abandoned airstrip. He kept running. The area was desolate and the pavement was already getting hot, even though the morning sun was still on its climb. Unadi ran straight through the middle, across the vast expanse of concrete, until he reached the coast of Widdershins Bay.

He stopped at the water's edge and looked out at the protruding hulk of the Breakneck Shipwreck. The jagged old metal battleship looked to him like a row of crooked grey teeth, and Unadi's mouth snapped at the air, as if his body was inadvertently attempting the act of chewing for the first time.

A hot wind blew over the flat Oselian runway, and it sounded like faraway voices in his head. They called out, "Hey, are you okay?"

Unadi ignored the voices of the wind.

Another question came from the same direction, and the words of the wind sounded different. "Do you need help?"

As Unadi continued chewing the air, he thought to himself, *The wind is very talkative this particular morning.*

A hand came to his shoulder.

Unadi spun around in shock, but it was just two people.

One of them said, "We saw you run out here," and the other added, "Are you okay?" but Unadi screamed in their faces like a banshee, and he fled.

He ran straight back in the direction from which he came, and he left the two concerned and startled individuals standing on the hot tarmac. He rushed into the tight alleyways again, and soon found himself at the center of Teshon City by the ruins of the Messiah Tower. The rubble blocked his way and forced him east toward the entrance to Gate Town.

Beneath the rainbow sign at the border to the welcoming borough, Unadi came upon a grey-haired peddler who was opening his cart and about to start his day. The old man snapped his fingers, and words appeared in the air that hovered above his head like decorative smoke. They read *NOW OPEN* in pink and silver letters.

Unadi approached the Shift man and attacked✪

Chapter 25 – Dozi, Ilya, & Tchama

"Tchama and I will search the streets while you search from the air," Dozi said to Ilya. "Unadi has to be around here somewhere."

"All of this is my fault," Ilya whispered. She choked down a lump in her throat.

"Don't blame yourself for trying to help someone," Dozi retorted.

"But what I made Olona and Lahari do for Unadi has caused nothing but problems! We shouldn't have messed with his mantis gland."

Tchama extended her single arm toward Ilya with her palm up, and she took her hand. "For a while, half a year in fact, it was just the three of us," Tchama said to them both, and she smiled, "but our family keeps growing. Ilya, I can't even imagine you *not* doing exactly what you did. You had no idea what would happen, but you were trying to make Unadi's life better."

"And we don't really know what's wrong with him," Dozi added. "This may have nothing to do with what you did for him. You told us how messed up his childhood was, coupled with his years of isolation, he's certain to have issues. And he told us that he left his village, but maybe he was kicked out; maybe he did something horrible and they banished or exiled him." Dozi brought her hand to Ilya's arm. "What you did for him was pure compassion. We understand your intentions."

Tears began to run down Ilya's cheeks. "Thank you."

Dozi squeezed her arm. "Now, let's go find him and figure out what's wrong," she encouraged.

Ilya nodded, and without another word, she lifted off the ground and soared into the bright morning sky.

"Come on," Dozi urged, "let's go." She and Tchama headed down one of the main streets of Gate Town. "I can't believe he hit you with a chair."

Tchama shrugged and smiled. "Good thing he couldn't hurt me." She laughed and added, "There's obviously something very wrong with him, like you said, so I didn't take it personal."

Dozi and Tchama talked while they wandered the streets looking for Unadi, a man they barely knew and were not even certain they would recognize. Over an hour later, they found Ilya, and she had found him. She was in a state of shock.

Unadi was unconscious, slumped against a wall, and he was covered in blood★

Chapter 26 – Dozi, Ilya, Tchama, & Unadi

"*What the fuck happened to him?*" Dozi squawked.

Ilya whispered in disbelief, "Unadi killed some old man."

"What?!" Tchama gasped.

"I found him smashing the man's head against the pavement." Ilya looked horrified. "He was already dead by the time I got there, and Unadi was eating chunks…" she swallowed hard and breathed, "of the man's brains."

"What the fuck?" Dozi breathed, staring down at Unadi.

Ilya was looking at the smears of blood on her hands, and she wiped them hard on her trousers. "I knocked him out and dragged him here."

"Where's the body?"

Ilya pointed down an alleyway. "Around those buildings, maybe two blocks. I don't get it," she added, "back in the forest, Olona was asleep in the tent right outside of Unadi's house; if he was some sort of deranged murderer, why didn't he do anything to her?" Another sob had her stuttering, and tears streamed down her cheeks. "Not that… that I would ever… ever want that!" and she wailed, "Why did this happen?!"

Dozi sighed and turned to Ilya and Tchama. "What should we do with him now?"

"I'll carry him," Tchama offered.

"But where should we bring him?"

On the pavement at their feet, Unadi groaned. He pushed himself up to his knees and brought one hand to his head. His other hand was a fist. Without acknowledging the three women, he looked down and slowly uncurled his fingers. Along with a little mucusy grey-pink brain matter, something sparkled in his palm.

"What is that?" Tchama asked.

Dozi and Ilya immediately recognized that what Unadi held was the very same thing they had given Tchama to save her life after the battle of Gate Town.

Unadi was holding a photonova gland. He shoved it into his mouth.

"No!" Ilya yelled, but he swallowed hard, and it was gone.

"Oh, fuck..." Dozi mumbled.

Unadi sucked in a harsh breath, and he screamed, as pain like nothing he had ever felt struck his body. It was like lightning inside of him. He curled up on the pavement, and he groaned, as his limbs seized and his jaw clenched. Unadi's cries of anguish morphed into a gurgling series of grunts, and he took a wheezing breath.

"What the fuck is wrong with him?" Dozi asked again.

"Yeah, why isn't it stopping?" Tchama added.

Ilya spoke under her breath. "It only lasted a moment with you."

Unadi coughed up dark red foam, and he began to claw at his own abdomen. His eyes became cloudy and unfocused, and blood poured from his mouth. The three women stepped back as Unadi rolled onto his back. He pulled up his shirt and began digging his fingers into his skin.

Things were already bad for him, and they were about to get worse.

To the three women's further shock, Unadi's fingers *did* manage to pierce through his flesh, and he began to pull gruesome chunks off his torso.

Tchama let out a noise of alarm.

Ilya screamed.

Dozi vomited.

Unadi's insides were liquefying; his flesh was deteriorating, and he thrust his hands into the mess that used to be his stomach. The blood from his mouth coated much of his face, but his eyes were visible; the three women wished they were not. His eyeballs began to soften like gelatin gummies left out in the sun. As he writhed on the pavement, the gooey orbs of his eyes began to dribble out and run down his face.

Unadi pulled his hands in opposite directions, opening his entire middle and spreading his dissolving body onto the narrow street, but his life was yet to be spent. He continued to dig through his spilled innards, until even the flesh of his fingers had deteriorated away. His bones were becoming soft and spongy, yet he still clawed at his own remains.

The only sounds Unadi could make were bubbly hisses, and his dreadful noises added to the horrible display. Even as his muscles turned to muck, his arms continued to feebly poke at the gloppy tangle of what were once his organs.

"Is he still alive?" Dozi asked.

Pieces kept twitching long after most of Unadi had dissolved to nothing more than a stewy pile.

"What the *fuck!*" Ilya whispered.

Dozi looked at her and agreed, "You said it."

"Now what?" Tchama asked.

"We fucking leave it," Dozi answered.

Ilya looked uncertain. "But that's a person," she said.

"Not anymore," Dozi replied.

"It's still moving and making noise," Tchama added. "Is it… still alive?"

"I'm done with this, and I'm going home," Dozi declared. "Are you two coming?" Without awaiting their reply, she turned and left Unadi's melted remains on the street✪

Chapter 27 – Clean-up Crew

Dotty Marbles and Auntie Peg were with Thech, Jzuna, Fennah, Ninyani, and several adults, whom the pair of queens had rallied, including Bivon. It was late morning. The queens had taken the children to breakfast and ordered mistcream lattes for each of them, and they were now back at the grey building with the large wooden doors. Fennah had asked about it several times before they all returned, but the queens were enjoying keeping their plans secret.

"Okay, boys and girls and everyone," Dotty Marbles said to the group, "let's split up into a few teams to focus on several different projects. We want to deal with this big room," and she waved at the large empty space. "It's very dusty and grimy and the windows are coated in gunk, but it will eventually be our central area." She smiled and looked around.

"Cleaning the entire building is going to be a serious chore," Auntie Peg added, "however, we know exactly what we intend to achieve first. Along with the auditorium, it's important that we get a few of the small rooms upstairs prepped. I know it may all seem overwhelming now, but today we only have to start; we don't have to finish anything. Kids," she said to Thech, Jzuna, Fennah, and Ninyani, "why don't we head upstairs and start cleaning out some of the smaller spaces?"

Fennah eyed Dotty Marbles inquisitively, but Ninyani whispered, "You *know* she's not gonna tell us what we're doing." He rolled his eyes and she giggled.

"Bivon," Dotty Marbles said to the big red-bearded fellow, "will you please help me carry a few of these ladders over and set them up?" She added to the others, "I'd love to deal with the windows first, brighten the place up a little."

Auntie Peg called from the bottom of the stairs, "Dot! I left the glass polish there by the door," and she pointed, before turning back to the kids. "Come on, you four, let's see what's up there." They climbed the stairs and Auntie Peg waved them into the first room. "We'll start in here together? Let me get the window."

The old windowpane may not have been moved in years, and it may have been resistant, but Auntie Peg was still as strong as she had been when she first became a Messiah, and the wood screeched as she forced the window open. Minding her wig, she stuck her head out and looked down at the pavement below.

"Oh, that's perfect. Why don't we start by tossing some of this junk out into the street, so we can collect it later and get rid of it? Here, Fennah and Ninyani, put these on," and Auntie Peg handed the children each a pair of thick leather gloves. "They will probably be a little too big for you, but they will help protect your hands. I have gloves for you two as well," she added, turning to Thech and Jzuna, "but do you need them? Can you even wear them on your tentacles, Jzuna?"

"I don't think so," she replied, "and Thech doesn't need them."

"Let me know if either of you want to try them," Auntie Peg said with a smile. "You can certainly use them if you'd like. Why don't we begin with this?" She took a broom out of a closet in the hallway.

There was some accumulated grit on the floor, and Fennah enthusiastically grabbed the broom handle and began to sweep. "Jzuna and Thech, how old are you?" she asked the unique pair.

"We're 12," Jzuna replied, and Thech huffed in agreement.

Fennah stopped sweeping. "Wow, you two are two years younger than Ninyani, and two *times* older than me! He's 14 and I'm 6!" She then recited, "Twelve plus two is fourteen, and six times two is twelve." Fennah nodded with certainty.

"Those are impressive math skills," Auntie Peg declared. "And you are quite correct, princess!"

Fennah smiled so widely that her eyes squinted shut. "We had to do maths and languages and histories and sciences," she explained, "even me, even though I was the youngest." The little girl asked in an overly casual tone of voice. "So, Peggy, what are these empty rooms gonna be?" Fennah resumed sweeping, glancing at the queen, trying to downplay her curiosity.

Auntie Peg let out a cackle and brought a fingertip to her nose. She winked at Fennah, who repeated Ninyani's eye roll and Auntie Peg only laughed more raucously. Jzuna, Ninyani, and Fennah could not stop themselves from giggling, and Thech hummed. Auntie Peg pinched Fennah's cheek, and the girl stuck her tongue out. "Princess, we'll make a queen of you yet!"

"But not like you and Dot, right, since you're boys underneath?"

"Oh, honey," Auntie Peg replied, "absolutely anyone can be a queen! Now, let's get back to cleaning."

Larger broken chunks of concrete and pieces of debris were strewn about the room, and Jzuna focused on them. The bits levitated, floated out the window, and dropped. A steady flow of refuse made its way out with Jzuna and Thech's powers.

"That is quite astonishing," Auntie Peg said with a chuckle. "Ninyani, why don't you head back down and see if Dot has another broom? Thech and Jzuna have already almost finished clearing this room, and we'll move on to the next in another minute or two. If Dot's got another broom, you can sweep that second room while Fennah finishes this one."

"Okay," Ninyani replied brightly, and he skipped down the stairs.

Fennah continued sweeping, and Jzuna left her brother in the hall and floated into the next room. She used her powers again, and all the little miscellaneous pieces of rubble and twigs and pebbles rose up from the floor. They drifted through the hallway, and they entered the first room, moving through the air past Fennah and Auntie Peg. Jzuna released it, and the rubble fell to the growing pile on the street below.

Auntie Peg began scrubbing the window, and Thech left the hallway and stepped right up to her.

"Would you like to help me, Thech?"

One of his arms shot straight up overhead. He smeared the window with the slime that perpetually covered him.

Auntie Peg replied in a confused voice, "Oh, well, that's something."

Jzuna came to the door of the room and informed Auntie Peg, "Thech used to help our mama clean our home. If you just wipe it off, the glass will be clear."

Auntie Peg looked down at Thech. "Is that right? You used to help your mother clean the windows like this?"

The boy gave her a subtle response, rocking from side to side. He then reached out and slimed the outside of the window as well.

Auntie Peg wiped each side, and sure enough, the boy's slime, along with whatever buildup had accumulated over the 200 years since the fall of Oselia, came right off.

"Wow," Auntie Peg exclaimed, "thank you so much for helping me, Thech. Would you like to clean the windows in the other rooms?" He followed her as Jzuna continued levitating little bits of junk into the first room and out the window.

Auntie Peg looked back in on Fennah. "I'd say you're almost done here, and Jzuna has already picked up what was in the second room. Would you like to move on and sweep in there next?"

Fennah nodded her head, and she concentrated on getting all the remaining grit into a little pile.

"We have a dustpan downstairs that we can use to pick that up later," Auntie Peg informed her. She snapped her fingers. "Should have asked Ninyani to grab it."

"I can get rid of it!" Jzuna called out from the hallway. She entered and focused on the pile Fennah made. The minuscule particles began to lift like a cloud, and Jzuna drifted it out the window.

"Truly wondrous," Auntie Peg said. "And let me open some of the other windows, so you don't need to keep coming back into this room. We just need to make sure there's nothing important and no people below."

Ninyani arrived a few minutes later with another broom, and the four children and the queen cleaned out five of the rooms before lunchtime. They joined everyone downstairs for sandwiches that Theolan and the mystic delivered to them just after noon.

"Say *thank you*," Dotty Marbles said to the four children as they each got their lunch.

"Thank you," Ninyani dutifully repeated.

"Thanks, mystic and Theolan," Fennah squeaked.

"Thech says *thank you* also," Jzuna added.

The afternoon passed in much the same way as the morning, and the group called it a day when the sun began to set.

"I can't begin to tell you how much Peggy and I appreciate all your help today," Dotty Marbles said to everyone. "I'm thrilled with how much we accomplished! If you're up for it, dinner is on us at Red Raven's, and you're all welcome."★

Chapter 28 – Olona, Kosephaji, & Relliduna

It was early in the morning when the knock Olona was expecting came from the front door of her shop, *First Organic Mechanic of Teshon City*. She opened it and said, "Welcome, Relliduna and Kosephaji." She had written down her address on a napkin for them before leaving Red Raven's the day before.

"Thank you for letting us come see you," Kosephaji replied.

"And you can call me *Duna*," Relliduna added.

Olona closed the door behind them. "Come into my workroom." She led them to a space with a couple of tables with quite a lot of equipment on top of them.

"What is all this?" Kosephaji asked. He did not recognize much of what he saw.

"I got kicked out of the organic mechanic apprenticeship for performing those *sacred corruptions* I showed you," Olona said the words thick with sarcasm.

"Can I see again?"

She smiled at Kosephaji, lit a joint, and rolled up her sleeves. Only small portions of her machines were visible, and even though Kosephaji was not permitted by the guild to work as an organic mechanic, he immediately understood the complexity of her devices. She removed the false panel of skin that covered the machine hidden in her forearm.

Kosephaji gasped in awe and gawked at her. "You did all this to yourself? No one helped you?"

Relliduna looked at Kosephaji. "What's so different about what she has done to herself compared to what you did for me?"

Kosephaji looked appalled that his shoddy healing methods were being compared to the avant-garde creativity he was witnessing in Olona's machines.

She smiled, replaced the panel in her forearm, and began looking over Relliduna's healed injuries. "I can see what you were trying to do," she said to Kosephaji in a kind voice. "You kept Duna alive, and I think that's incredible. Don't sell yourself short. There's just more that can be done for each of these various healing modalities you've applied." She turned to Relliduna and said, "The one on your elbow is not even working anymore."

"Once I had recovered a bit and started moving more, it kept popping out," he informed her.

"We'll replace it with a machine that will last longer." She looked over at Kosephaji. "Would you like me to show you how to do it? There are a few additional steps, and they're a little complicated, but you had the basic idea. And hey," she added, "organic mechanic stuff just makes sense to me; I get it." Olona shrugged, and recommended of Relliduna, "Why don't you sit down? None of this should hurt, but some of it might take a while." She waved toward a cushioned chair.

On one of the tables, Olona assembled an exact replica of the machine Kosephaji had made for Relliduna's elbow. It took her less than 90 seconds.

"How did you..." Kosephaji was dumbfounded. "I worked on him for *hours*."

"Please, don't compare yourself to me," Olona said in a tone that was almost apologetic. "I'm the type of person who can sit down for hours and read technical manuals about organowire gauges and external structural components for machines. This stuff all just clicks in my brain." She held up the device. "Now look, these two pieces can't sustain the extended wear and tear of an elbow, so in this replacement machine, why don't you reinforce the smaller part there," and she pointed, "with a little of this organowire, and do the same thing to the other with this thicker gauged wire."

"What if I mess it up?" Kosephaji asked, looking over at Relliduna.

Olona smiled. "You're not going to mess it up. There are just a few extra steps that I'll show you. They will make this replacement more durable and more supportive to Duna's arm."

"Why didn't I know how to do this?" Kosephaji asked.

Olona sighed. "A lot of practices have been restricted by the guild. Take this," she said, handing him a small tool. "Coil the organowire around the first support." She observed his nervous application of the material. "That was good," Olona encouraged. "Now, use this thicker gauged wire for the second. I know that the smaller wire is a little easier to deal with, but you shouldn't have too much trouble." As he completed the task she said, "Good, that looks great."

Kosephaji handed her back the tool and said "But there's a pointy end of the thicker organowire sticking out." He sounded disappointed with himself.

"Let me just remove a tiny piece," Olona replied. He handed the device to her and she folded the wire over on itself, clipping off the excess. "See how it's smooth against the hinge now? That's what you want. You did a great job. Now, let's add a few drops of pringomite to the diziniler."

Kosephaji looked blank. "I don't know what those are."

"Pringomite is a compound the Oselian organic mechanics developed," Olona explained, "but in Tuilii la Ru, the masters of the apprenticeship only ever kept a very small stash of it, and it was always under lock and key. I don't know why they banned and restricted so many of the early OM practices."

Relliduna spoke up. "Maybe the Demifae who run much of Ruburge had something to do with the restrictions. Maybe they viewed organic mechanics as competition, and they've somehow limited what they could do."

Olona raised her eyebrows and considered his idea. "That's not a bad theory."

Kosephaji then asked, "What's the other thing you mentioned?"

"The diziniler?" She pointed at the device. "The energy center in this machine is connected directly to the supports and adjusters. The diziniler is the connection between the two. It needs to be coated in pringomite." She handed him a small container. "Drip a few drops along *this*," and she indicated the connector. "You can use one of these tiny brushes to smooth it out and make sure the whole thing is properly coated."

"Oh, I see," Kosephaji exclaimed as he applied the pringomite. "Does it need to..." He paused.

"Dry?" Olona said with a laugh. "Yeah, as you can see, it dries almost instantly." She stepped up to Relliduna, knelt beside where he was seated, and gently took his arm. "May I?" He nodded to her. "This shouldn't hurt," Olona commented as she began to remove the worn-out device, but Relliduna groaned and tried not to pull away.

"Sorry," Olona and Kosephaji said to him in unison.

A tiny jet of yellow steam hissed as the organic machine detached from Relliduna's elbow. Olona placed it onto one of the tables and stepped back. "Go ahead," she said to Kosephaji.

"Don't you think *you* ought to install the new one?" he replied, extending it toward her.

"No, you do and see how it works," Olona answered with an encouraging nod.

Kosephaji leaned over Relliduna's arm. "Sorry," he mumbled again, but Olona's device perfectly replaced the original.

"Oh!" Relliduna said in surprise.

"I'm sorry!" Kosephaji blurted out.

"No, no, it doesn't hurt," Relliduna explained. "It doesn't hurt at all! Even the dull ache that I'd kind of gotten used to is gone!"

Olona smiled at the two young men.

Kosephaji looked like he was about to cry.

For the rest of the morning, he helped Olona repair or replace each of Relliduna's organic machines that needed upgrading, and noon was approaching when they finished their final adjustment. At that point, Olona recommended the three of them head out and grab some lunch from one of the countless street food vendors.

Relliduna still walked with the phallic fish cane, but he strode with more vigor than since the attack. His vast improvement overjoyed Kosephaji.

The trio stopped at a pod of food carts. "Can I buy your lunches?" Olona offered.

"What? Certainly not!" Relliduna replied. "After everything you did for me, we need to get your lunch for you!"

"I don't mind, and the shop is doing really well," Olona explained. "It'd be my pleasure." She handed them each a few coins. "Get whatever you want," and she waved at the row of food carts. "I'm having a noodle bowl!" She lit a joint and stepped up to the vendor.

Kosephaji and Relliduna left Olona to place her order, and they wandered by quite a few carts. Relliduna stopped at one to order kabobs, and Kosephaji walked two booths farther and ordered dumplings stuffed with roast wild boar.

The three of them reconvened at an empty table and dug into their meals, but almost immediately, Tisa came rushing up to them. "Olona!"

"What's wrong?" Olona asked out of the corner of her mouth, trying not to dribble.

"There was an attack!"

Olona furrowed her brow. "Does someone need healing?"

"No, you don't understand! Some*thing* ate a Shift's mantis gland."

"Gunge?" Olona said, pausing between bites.

"Yes," Tisa responded, "I think so. There are two separate accounts. One is from a few days ago down in Hazel Cove. There was a witness who claims there were two monsters." She paused. "The other happened at Ilin."

Olona furrowed her brow. "Those ruins to the north of the city?"

"Yes, a mangled and headless body was found on the path leading up to them. Some travelers were talking about seeing several human-like monsters."

"Headless?" Kosephaji asked with his mouth full.

"Monsters?" Relliduna added.

Tisa and Olona looked at them.

"Let me explain," Olona said. "I know that the people where we're from down in Xin don't talk about Shifts, but whether by Demifae or Messiahs or monsters, Shifts are often murdered for their mantis glands."

Kosephaji and Relliduna made eye contact, and Kosephaji asked, "Do you think that's why you were attacked in Ruburge, for your mantis gland?"

Relliduna did not reply.

Olona continued. "Most people in Xin have at least heard of Gunge and the monsters, but Tisa here was from Kestapoli, the monster's nearest hunting grounds. She had a few run-ins with them while living there, but we've never heard of them coming up here." She turned to Tisa. "How reliable is this information?"

"Like I said, in Hazel Cove, someone actually *saw* two monsters. At Ilin, the accounts were more vague, but the descriptions were reminiscent of what we know about the inhabitants of Gunge."

Olona finished her lunch, and she set her spoon and pair of chopsticks onto the table beside her empty bowl. "Why would they come up here? The monsters have never hunted in Teshon City before."

"We changed their status quo," Tisa said matter of factly. "Who knows what they'll do now?"

"And we obviously didn't get them all," Olona added.

Kosephaji and Relliduna also finished eating, and Olona collected their dirty dishes to deposit them in one of several bins filled with soapy water. After an excessive show of appreciation from Kosephaji and Relliduna for everything Olona had done, the boys headed back to where they were staying with the giant and his crew, and Tisa and Olona made their way home✪

Chapter 29 – Riam, Part One

Lonklam and Ronging struggled to keep pace with Riam. Despite her severely twisted body, she was much stronger and faster than either of them. The three were headed down the Pinewood Path away from the ruins of Ilin, but Riam was far ahead of Lonklam and

Ronging. They moved as quickly as their strange bodies allowed, and yet Riam continued to pull away from them.

She reached Bloodwater Crossing, and in an instant, she had forded the Lonely River. The pull toward her prey was all-consuming. Riam sensed the many photonova glands in Gate Town, and as she approached a tiny shack at the very edge of the city, she honed in on two Shifts who were inside. Without stopping, Riam smashed into and through the wall of the little building. She collided with and incapacitated the individuals; her strength was terrible.

The two Shifts were slammed against the ground, and the fingertips of Riam's multiple hands dug into and penetrated the meat of their necks, rupturing their flesh. Blood sprayed over the mutated woman. It took her almost no effort to rip both of their heads from their bodies, and she discarded the convulsing corpses without another thought.

Riam screamed with vicious ecstasy, and she peeled one of the skulls like a hideous fruit. She ripped the face and scalp from the bone, and two of her other hands came slamming together with the skull between them, popping the head like a pomegranate. Brains, blood, and bone shards sprayed through the air in a gruesome arc. Riam ripped her hands apart with the same force, and she snatched at the mess with yet another set of unnatural fingers. She found the photonova gland, shoved it into her mouth, and swallowed hard.

With the other severed head tucked under one of her many arms, Riam felt herself beginning to change. She made her way back toward the forests that surrounded Teshon City, as a new arm thrust out from her right collarbone. An oversized eye with no lashes formed on the back of one of her many hands. The weird extra mouth on her temple developed a second tongue, both of which perpetually hung toward her whiskered ear. Yet another breast grew from the side of her torso, and it had three nipples. On the back of her head, a large patch of hair dropped out, and from her scalp sprouted a new pair of thumbs.

"I see you've got a snack for later," Lonklam said as he and Ronging finally caught up with Riam in the forest outside of town.

"I will need... again... soon," she struggled to say.

"How soon?" Lonklam pointed with one of his hands at the severed head. "Will that allow you to travel?" He looked at Ronging, then back at Riam, and a bizarre smile stretched across his double mouth. "I think we should bring you to Xin."★

Chapter 30 – The Kids & the Queens, Part Two

Thech, Jzuna, and Fennah stayed the night with Ninyani, Auntie Peg, and Dotty Marbles again, after spending the day with them cleaning out the old Oselian building. The following morning, the group was back at the site, and they continued where they had left off the day before. That second day was much like the first, and it ended again with a meal at Red Raven's. On the third morning, the group started to paint.

"This may seem boring to begin with," Auntie Peg said to the children, "but this is just the base coat. The fun colors will go on later."

"Are you two gonna tell us what this place is gonna be, or what?" Fennah squeaked up at the queens, but they both just grinned.

"It's gonna be great!" Dotty Marbles proclaimed. "Grab a brush or a roller, and let's get to it."

Quite a few additional friends were there to help, and Auntie Peg directed them into the auditorium, as Dotty Marbles led the children upstairs.

Several large cans of basic primer were stacked in each of the cleaned rooms. She popped the top off of one and poured a little of the bland paint into several trays. Dotty Marbles dipped the tip of one finger into it, and to the children's surprise, the queen swiped pale grey stripes under each of her eyes, right on top of her gorgeous makeup!

Ninyani, Fennah, and Jzuna all burst out with giggles and Thech lumbered up to Dotty Marbles. She reached out and poked Fennah in the nose, dabbing her with a little grey spot. She also dotted Ninyani's forehead.

Thech leaned toward Dotty Marbles, and his sister's voice squealed from the air all around them, "Thech wants you to get him too!"

"Oh, does he, now?" She asked with a silly smirk, and she stuck her painty fingertip into the slime on his chest. "*Ding!*" she said, and she drew back her finger. A tiny bit of the pale paint remained, and it slowly began to slide down the slime on his torso.

Thech moaned a happy noise and Jzuna let out a peal of laughter. "That's so funny!" she declared.

Dotty Marbles laughed and said, "Alrighty, kids, let's get started." She tousled Fennah's hair. "We need to begin by painting the wall with the window, and we'll make our way toward the door a little at a time until we get there."

They did just that. The five of them painted the first room, and they were well into the second when lunch was called. After eating, Auntie Peg joined them upstairs for the rest of the day. When the group stopped for the evening, four of the empty upper rooms were painted, and the adults in the auditorium had painted almost a third of it.

The next three days were filled with a lot more painting, and each ended back at Red Raven's for food and fun.

On the fourth morning, Auntie Peg declared, "This is our last day of grey. It's almost time for the exciting colors! In a few days, we are going to invite some people to come see all the work you've done, but Dot and I would just love for each of you to put your own personal touches on the building. However, the two of us need to take care of a few things first."

That night, the queens brought Thech, Jzuna, and Fennah back to stay with the mystic and Theolan for a couple of days. They also dropped Ninyani off with Zular.

"Thank you for agreeing to keep Ninyani for a while," Auntie Peg said to Zular.

"I'm so excited to get to know him," she replied, giving the boy a dainty hug. "Especially now that I know Ninyani is a fan of my performances!" Zular framed her face with her hands and blew him a kiss. The queens and Ninyani laughed.

Two days later, to Auntie Peg and Dotty Marbles' delight, everything that they hoped to accomplish was completed. Before they headed to the pub that evening with their helpers, Dotty Marbles ushered the group into the auditorium. She stepped up onto the stage that was set into the wall. However, as she tried to speak, a sob of joy choked her, and she brought her hands to her mouth. Auntie Peg jumped up beside her beloved.

"I'm okay," Dotty Marbles whispered. She then spoke aloud. "I'm just so overwhelmed by everything we've accomplished. This space is going to be so special. Thank you, all, very much!"

"We would love to take everyone to Red Raven's once again in celebration," Auntie Peg added.

After a lovely meal and plenty of sassy banter, the queens headed home for the night. The next morning, Auntie Peg and Dotty Marbles made their way to the mystic's house to join Fennah, Jzuna, and Thech for a little breakfast.

"Good morning, you three," said Dotty Marbles.

"And good morning to you, Muunith!" Auntie Peg added.

"Hi," Muunith replied to the two queens.

"Are you feeling a little better?" Auntie Peg asked.

Muunith nodded their head.

"That's wonderful! If you're up for it," she added, "we're having a special event in a few days, and we'd love for you to attend." Auntie Peg smiled at the child.

"Jzuna and Thech, our bathtub has worked perfectly," Dotty Marbles commented to them, "and we haven't needed your tub, but why don't we come back here this evening and take it with us."

"That's a great idea," Auntie Peg added with a knowing nod. "Oh, yeah," she exclaimed, pulling a paper bag from her purse, "we brought goodies; candied fruit!"

The mystic stepped up and helped himself to a few pieces.

Bivon turned to Dotty Marbles. "You know, Dot, I've been wondering, how *do* you get your hair so high?"

She let out a shocked gasp and replied playfully, "It's so rude of you to ask a dame to divulge her secrets!" and she laughed again. "I joke! Ha!" Dotty Marbles turned her head from side to side. "It's just an illusion. There's a thin cage framework hidden under the hair. Could you imagine how cumbersome this ridiculous thing would be if it was solid? No, thank you!" She scoffed and the children giggled.

Bivon looked surprised by her answer. "That's not solid?" He reached up toward her hair.

"Ah, ah, *ah*," Auntie Peg interjected, "thou shalt never lay a finger 'pon a queen's wig."

Bivon pulled his hands back in a placating gesture. "My mistake, *my mistake*," he replied with a chuckle.

There was a knock at their front door.

"I've got it," Theolan said.

The others started to nibble on the sweet treats the queens had brought.

Olona was on the other side of the door.

"Hey," she said sheepishly, "I hope it's okay that I'm here. I just wanted to check in on Lahari. Has there been any change in her condition?"

"No, honey," Theolan replied. "Please, join us."

"Come *in?* You're not... mad at me?" she asked quietly, looking at both of Lahari's fathers.

"Oh, Olona, of course not," the mystic replied. He scurried over and wrapped her in a warm embrace. She burst into tears and he held her close. "I know you were helping someone else," the mystic said in a kind voice. "I don't blame you," and Olona sobbed for several minutes. "And to answer your question," the mystic eventually added, "Lahari still hasn't woken up."

Jzuna's voice issued from the corner where she and Thech quietly waited by their basin. "Can I try to wake her up?"

Everyone looked over at the two unique children, and Olona rubbed the tears from her eyes with the sleeve of her shirt.

"Jzuna, honey, Lahari is more than just asleep," Theolan explained gently.

"But I think I might be able to wake her." Jzuna's one huge eye turned toward the mystic. "Would it be okay if I talked to her?"

He gave her a kind and pandering smile, and he shrugged at his husband. "Yes, Jzuna," he conceded, "go ahead."

Thech stayed in the corner as Jzuna drifted into the bedroom and over to Lahari's unconscious form.

The mystic and Theolan watched from the doorframe with Fennah and Olona. Bivon, Auntie Peg, and Dotty Marbles stepped up behind them.

Jzuna floated above Lahari. She turned in the air so she was looking down with her tendrils reaching up toward the ceiling, and her mysterious disembodied voice began, "Lahari, wake..." but she stopped and rotated in the air to look back at the mystic. "Lahari's not there," she said in a definitive tone.

"We know," he replied in a low voice full of sadness. "She's in a coma."

"No, she's not," Jzuna stated. "That's just her body, but the thing that makes her Lahari is not with it. The *Lahari* of Lahari is gone."

The mystic entered the room, stepped up to Jzuna, and he reached out and took one of her slimy tentacles. "Can you please tell me what that means?" he asked her.

"She's in the..." Jzuna paused. She floated higher until she was almost to the ceiling, and she looked past everyone in the doorway, right at her brother. The mystic was reaching up to her and still holding one of her tentacles.

There was a silent moment.

Everyone followed Jzuna's gaze over to Thech.

Nothing happened.

"Honey?" the mystic said to Jzuna.

There was only silence.

Then Jzuna's enormous eye blinked, and she lowered again. She focused back on the little round man. "Lahari is in the imagination place."

"What is the imagination place?"

"It's where Thech and me can talk."

They all looked back over at the motionless boy in the corner with his weird gaping mouth and his blank eyes.

"Thech can talk to you in the imagination place?" Theolan asked.

"Yes, we don't go there often, but sometimes we need to talk."

Olona spoke up. "Is it an alternate dimension?"

Jzuna looked at the young woman. "I don't know what that means."

Olona bit her lip in concentration and took a thoughtful breath. "When you go there to talk with your brother, is it a place *not* in this world?"

"Yes," Jzuna replied.

Olona turned to the others and said, "Maybe it's something like Sumi's teleportation doorways into her congruent reality. Jzuna, can you tell us *where* the imagination place is located?"

Jzuna rose toward the ceiling again to look at Thech.

There was another silence and Olona whispered to the others, "I think Jzuna is talking to her brother in the imagination place."

Then Jzuna lowered and answered. "Thech thinks it might be inside our heads. We just think it, and we go there."

"Alright, so if Lahari is in the imagination place, too," Olona continued, "can you think yourself to *her?* Can you find her?"

"Not like that," Jzuna replied. Without another word, she drifted toward the bedroom door, and everyone stepped back so she could float out of the room and over to the corner with her brother.

"Okay," Olona said to the mystic, "if Lahari's consciousness is in an alternate dimension or some other plane of existence, we may need to find a Shift with mental abilities, maybe someone like Tisa's companion from her days living in the forest." Olona snapped her fingers. "What was the name of the Bio-Shift woman who those villagers called a witch?" She looked at the ceiling, as if the answer would reveal itself. "Huh..." She shook her head in frustration. "Or maybe someone like Tilby. Tisa doesn't know whatever happened to him, but he... oh, Liovia! That was her name! Anyway, both she and Tilby had some sort of psychic..."

A shocking light came suddenly from the two unusual children in the corner. Jzuna was attached to Thech's chest with her many arms securing her to him. Their three eyes were glowing, but Jzuna closed her single huge eye, and the light from Thech's intensified until it was so bright that the others had to shield their eyes and look away✪

Chapter 31 – The Little Girl & the Little Girl

In a grey world of nothing, a little girl was all alone. She was squatted down, hugging her knees, and she was whimpering.

"Hi," said a voice.

The girl looked up and cuffed the tears from her eyes.

There was nothing.

All around her, the ground stretched out flat until it faded to grey in the impossible distance.

"Hi," the voice said again, this time, from over the girl's shoulder.

She stood and turned around. The girl was young, no more than 12. Her hair was red and curly and her cheeks were freckled. She was dressed in a plain shirt and trousers, and her feet were bare.

Walking up to her was another little girl; the girls were identical.

"Hi!" the new girl said brightly.

"Why do you look like me?"

"Why do *you* look like *me?*" the other girl repeated with a giggle.

"Where'd you come from?"

"Where'd *you* come from?"

The girl was immediately irritated with the annoying game, and she declared, "I don't like this place, and I don't like you messing with me."

The second girl's expression fell. "I'm sorry. I was just trying to play so we could be friends. I'm a Bio-Shift, like you, and I just want to help."

The little redhead's curiosity piqued. "A Bio-Shift…"

"I don't like this place the way it is either," the other redhead added.

"What do you mean? Is it sometimes not like this?" The girl looked around at the blurry grey horizon. "It makes me feel unhappy."

"Yeah, sometimes it's… I don't know, different than how it is now. This isn't how it should be. Do you wanna leave?"

"Can we do that?" the first girl asked.

"Not exactly," the other girl answered, "there's no way to just leave this place. We're gonna have to make this place not exist, so we won't be here anymore."

The girl did not like the sound of that. "I don't want to not exist," she replied.

"But this *place* shouldn't exist, and together we can make it go away so it never bothers you or anybody again."

"How do we do that?" the redhead asked hesitantly.

"By letting it go," the other redhead answered.

The girl paused and said, "That sounds scary."

The second girl sighed. "It is, a little," she admitted. "I don't want to be here anymore, and I think you should go, too." She reached out her hand.

"I don't wanna just *go*."

"It's gonna be scary, but then it's gonna be better."

For a moment, there was no sound.

The first little girl gazed at the vast emptiness, and she tentatively reached out to take the identical hand of the other girl. Their fingers connected, and the blurry grey horizon slowly began to close in on them from all directions.

The girl looked around in panic. "I changed my mind! I don't like this at all!"

The faded distance drew closer and closer.

"Don't let it get me! Stop this!" she pleaded with the other girl, who remained silent.

The grey was almost upon them.

"Please, don't! I just want to stay! I can stay here! *No!*" the girl screamed, as the grey enveloped them both, and they were no more★

Chapter 32 – Lahari, Part Three

The intense radiance from Thech's eyes faded, and everyone turned to look back at the two unique children in the corner. Jzuna opened her one huge eye, released the grip of her tentacles on her brother, and the two of them separated.

"Ada?" Lahari's weak voice said from behind the mystic and his husband.

"*My little moth?*" He spun around and rushed into his bedroom.

Lahari's yellow eyes were fluttering open.

The mystic knelt beside his daughter. "Are you okay? How do you feel?" he asked gently.

Lahari whispered the name she used for her father again, "Ada," as her eyes closed, but she shifted her blue scaly hand across the bed and interlaced her fingers with his. Tears streamed down her father's cheeks, and he kissed her knuckles over and over again. Theolan stepped up and placed his hands on his husband's shuddering shoulders.

Everyone else was staring at Thech and Jzuna. Dotty Marbles stepped up and placed her hand on the boy's slimy shoulder. "How did you two do that?" she asked.

"Thech and me had to go into a *weird* imagination place," Jzuna replied. "It was not the happy place we were used to, but that's where we found Lahari."

"Your powers are astounding," Dotty Marbles declared in awe. "Thank you for helping her."

Auntie Peg quietly said to the children, "Kids, let's head into the kitchen and give them a little space."

"Peggy, let's make some tea," Dotty Marbles recommended.

"I think that's a lovely idea. Would you four each like a cup as well?"

Fennah and Muunith both nodded and Jzuna said, "Yes, please."

Bivon stepped into the doorframe of the bedroom and quietly said, "Welcome back, Lahari." He smiled and added, "I'll leave you three alone and be outside by my cart."

Olona joined the queens and the kids a moment later and said, "Lahari is talking. She's weak but she seems okay." Olona was suddenly overcome with emotion, and she began to sob again.

"Oh, honey," Dotty Marbles exclaimed, wrapping her in a tight embrace. Olona cried into the queen's cardigan, as relief washed over her.

"I never meant for Lahari to get hurt," Olona managed between her ragged breaths.

"We know," Auntie Peg replied. She stepped up and gently rubbed Olona's back. Dotty Marbles added, "Every one of us understands that what happened *happened* while you were helping someone."

Auntie Peg kissed the top of the young woman's head and said, "No one blames you, and Olona, you certainly shouldn't blame yourself."

The queens' compassion only made Olona cry harder, and Dotty Marbles led her into the sitting room to sob in her arms.

Auntie Peg stayed with the children in the kitchen. "Hey kids, what do you know? We've got four lovely options for tea, and there are four of you! First up, would you like peppermint? Smell this," she offered, holding the first tin so they could all put their little noses close for a sniff.

"That's a strong one," Auntie Peg added. "It's one of my favorites."

"Mine too," Muunith added.

Auntie Peg winked. "We've also got a citrus ginger tea. *Mmmm*," she hummed, breathing in the aroma. She put down the peppermint tin and let the kids smell the citrus ginger tea.

"I like that!" Jzuna's voice declared. "It smells yummy!"

Auntie Peg chuckled at her enthusiasm. "Up next, we've got a vanilla tea, and finally a cocoa tea. You can all smell them both."

"Thech likes the smell of the cocoa," Jzuna informed Auntie Peg.

"And may I please have vanilla?" Fennah asked.

Auntie Peg smiled at them. "You can all have exactly what you'd like! One cup of each type of tea, coming right up!"

Theolan came out of the bedroom with a beaming smile, just as Olona and Dotty Marbles returned from the lounge.

"Lahari is sitting up," Theolan informed them. "She drank some water and I think she's going to try and eat a little food. Jzuna and Thech, I don't know how you two kids woke her up," he said, looking over at the two Biological Shift children, "but thank you for whatever you did!"

"I'm sorry," Olona whispered, trying not to burst into tears again.

"Enough of that," Theolan said, wrapping her in his own tight hug. "No more *I'm sorrys*." He held her as she again broke down and sobbed. After another moment, Olona calmed down, and Theolan offered, "Would you like to go see Lahari?"

"Can I?" she asked nervously.

"Of course!" Theolan replied with a kind smile.

Olona entered the bedroom and slowly approached Lahari.

"Thanks for letting me nap on my flight back," Lahari mumbled.

Olona did not understand.

Lahari let out a hoarse chuckle. Her voice was weak, but she continued. "Ilya may not have told you, but I did *not* like flying with her at all. I made her fly really low." She paused and smirked at

Olona. "I got to sleep the whole way back and missed it entirely, so... thanks."

"Jokes?!" Olona blurted out as a fresh sob wracked her body, this time, a sob of joy. "You've been in a coma, and you're making jokes?" Tears streamed from her eyes.

"It wasn't much of a joke," Lahari admitted with a little laugh that turned into a wheezy cough. "I'm feeling pretty out of it."

Olona pounced onto the bed and wrapped her arms around Lahari. "I'm sorry, I'm sorry, I'm sorry!" she repeated over and over. She kissed Lahari's spiny cheeks and forehead and temples.

Lahari let out another laugh, and she was also brought to tears.

In the kitchen, Dotty Marbles stepped up to Auntie Peg and recommended, "Why don't we take the kids and head out after they drink their tea?"

"*No!*" Lahari called from the other room with a little more energy. She added to Olona, "Please, tell Peggy and Dot to stay. I don't want them to go yet."

Lahari ate a little food, then her father and Theolan helped her into the sitting room. Her fathers sat on either side of her, sandwiching her between them, and she liked the comfort.

The queens and kids joined them in the lounge, and Lahari focused on Thech and Jzuna. She looked over at Olona and said, "I don't remember anything after being in the forest with you and Ilya," and she turned back to her fellow Biological Shifts, "but you're the ones, aren't you? You two brought me back. Somehow, I know it was you, wasn't it?"

Jzuna replied with a shy, "Yes," and Lahari was amazed at hearing her speak for the first time. Her disembodied voice added, "We didn't want you to be stuck in the imagination place anymore."

Lahari furrowed her brow. "Stuck?"

Olona spoke up. "It sounds like your consciousness was trapped in an alternate plane of reality, one that Thech and Jzuna can access."

"Lahari, are you up for all this information?" Theolan asked.

She smiled, gave him a peck on the cheek, and looked back at the children. "Please, tell me your names; they sounded so lovely when Olona just said them."

"I'm Jzuna, and this is my brother Thech." She wiggled her tentacles at the strange-looking boy.

"It's very nice to meet you both," Lahari said. "And thank you for what you did."

The mystic ran his fingers over the black quills that extended from Lahari's cheek. "I'm so glad you're okay," he whispered to her.

She wrapped her arms around him and squeezed him tight.

Fennah stepped up to Lahari, placed her little hand on Lahari's scaly blue knee, and she squeaked, "Good morning!"

"Hello, bunny rabbit." Lahari reached down and pulled Fennah into her lap.

Auntie Peg took Dotty Marbles' hand. They looked at each other and she nodded.

"I think now is a good time for all of us to head out," Dotty Marbles said to the group.

"No, please stay a while longer," Lahari implored.

"Sorry, honey, but we need to pick up Ninyani and take care of a few things." The queen turned to Thech and Jzuna. "Hey, kids, we've got a surprise for you, and you too, Fennah. Muunith, if you're up for it, we'd love for you to join us also."

"I don't really feel good," the child replied.

"Don't you worry at all, honey," the mystic said, "you are more than welcome to stay here with us."

Fennah gave Lahari another squeeze and hopped down from her lap, then the queens and the three children said their goodbyes, and they headed out into the city under the rising sun✪

Chapter 33 – Paint

The kids and queens stopped right outside the mystic's house where Bivon's cart was still parked, and he knelt down in front of the girly phenomenon and her bizarre brother. "Jzuna, Thech, thank you both for what you did in there for Lahari."

"We just wanted to help her," Jzuna replied.

"What you can do is stunning!" he declared to them both. The charred and blackened corpse they left in Brokenpointe flashed into his mind, and he tried not to picture it.

"Bivon, you aren't leaving town, are you?" Dotty Marbles asked him. "Our event is only a couple of days away, and we're about to take these three on an adventure. We gals and Thech would love for you to join us."

"*Yeah!*" Fennah shrieked. "Please, come with us, Bivon!"

The big red-bearded man laughed, and he replied to Auntie Peg, "No, I'm not leaving yet, just wanted to give Lahari and her dads their space. It was quite a long journey from Hazel Cove, so Tophilogin and Theolan invited me to stay for a while."

"Every time you say the mystic's name," Dotty Marbles replied, "it's like my brain hiccups, and it takes me a second to register who you're talking about." She pulled a silly face and laughed at herself.

Bivon chuckled and turned to little Fennah. "And I'd be delighted to join the five of you for an *adventure*."

"First, we need to pick up Ninyani," Auntie Peg stated. "He's been staying with a friend of ours. She doesn't live far, just across the neighborhood."

Soon they arrived, and Ninyani scurried out of the house when he saw the queens and the children coming up the path. He ran over and said, "Zular is so glam!"

Auntie Peg snickered. "Did *she* teach you that word?"

"You know I did!" Zular declared, stepping out into the sun behind the boy. "I'm glamtastic and fabulicious!"

"Mmm, mmm, *mmm*," Auntie Peg hummed at Zular, "you are indeed!"

Dotty Marbles pouted dramatically at the four children and asked in a whiny voice, "We might not be as exciting as Zular, but you kids like spending time with us, don't you?"

"Oh, yes!" Fennah cried in delight.

Jzuna added, "Thech and I like you both so much!"

Ninyani dutifully repeated something Auntie Peg had said to him when they first met. "Well done, you must always give a compliment to someone who goes fishing for one."

The queens and Zular burst into cackling laughter that made the four children giggle, and Bivon could not help but chuckle along as well.

"Righty-oh, off we go, little ones!" Auntie Peg said, and the group of seven headed out in the morning sunshine.

"Bye, Zular!" Ninyani called back to her, and she blew him a kiss.

After just a short walk, the group arrived at the supply depot in Shifton where the queens had gotten most of what they used to clean and prep the large empty building over the past several days. Auntie Peg led them to the paint section.

"Kids, this is where artists come to get everything they use to create the lovely murals that are all over Gate Town. Dot and I are happy to announce that we are done with grey paint, and we would like each of you to pick out two colors. They can be any colors you'd like." She stepped back and let the three children see the rainbow of options.

"What's this about?" Bivon whispered to her, and Fennah eyed the queen in case she was about to divulge the details she had kept from them all, but Dotty Marbles replied to Bivon in a singsong voice.

"*Can't tell!* It's a secret!"

Fennah rolled her eyes, and Auntie Peg laughed as she positioned a flatbed cart by the shelves of paint. "Once you select the colors you each want, we can put them in this to wheel over to the space," Auntie Peg informed them.

"Thech would like green and green," Jzuna stated.

"Perfect," Auntie Peg said, "I suspect he wants two different shades of green." She pointed at the lightest yellow-green. "You'll let me know when I get to the colors you like, won't you Thech? This one?"

He did not reply.

She moved her finger to the next slightly darker shade, but he did not move. However, as she shifted between *chartreuse* and *emerald*, Thech began to quiver.

"Let's doublecheck," Auntie Peg told him. She pointed at *chartreuse* and he fell still, but sliding her fingertip back to *emerald* caused him to sway. "You've got it! And what's next?"

"He likes the really dark green," Jzuna said.

"Dark green," Auntie Peg repeated, and she pointed at the paint can at the opposite end of the hue's spectrum. It was labeled *deep aquamarine.*

Thech did not react.

She moved on to the next. "How about this one?" she asked, but again, Thech did not give her any sign. Then her finger landed on a rich earthy color called *chocolate mint,* and Thech hummed. "We've got our second green! Are you happy with these two?" she asked, holding up the cans of different greens.

Thech responded by lumbering over to stand beside Dotty Marbles, who replied for him. "I think he is indeed! Peggy, do you want to take the cart once these three have chosen as well, or should I?"

"Why don't I take it, and I can meet all of you after at Edgecity Park?"

"We're going to a park?" Fennah asked in delight.

"We most certainly are," Dotty Marbles replied.

Jzuna's voice stated, "I'd like yellow."

"Righty-oh," Auntie Peg said to her, "which shade brings you joy?"

The can of *golden sunshine* lifted off the shelf, hovered, and it floated down onto the wagon.

"Wondrous," Dotty Marbles marveled.

"Ummm..." Jzuna's voice hummed as she considered her options.

"I want this one!" Fennah stated, grabbing the handle of a can labeled *lightning lavender*. It was very heavy and almost slipped from her little fingers, but she managed to get it onto the flatbed beside the other cans of paint.

Ninyani followed Fennah and picked up the color right beside the one she had chosen. It was labeled *soft pink*. He placed it with the others, and in the section of blues he found the color's match, *soft blue*.

"I think I'd like this one," Jzuna said, levitating a can of *midnight purple* off the shelf.

"Can I pick black?" Fennah asked.

"Honey," Dotty Marbles answered with a grin, "you can pick any color you'd like, but don't you want something bright and more, I don't know, fun?"

Fennah's exuberant expression fell ever so slightly. "But I like black."

"Oh, I'm sorry," Dotty Marbles said, "don't listen to silly old me. If you want black, you take black!"

With the colors of paint selected, Auntie Peg headed off in one direction with the cart rolling behind her, and Dotty Marbles led Bivon and the children another way.

"Dot, where's the park?" Fennah asked.

"It's not far. We'll be there shortly, but first, let's get coffee and surprise Peggy with a cup."

"You know where I'd love to go," Bivon commented, "the Shifton Drinkery."

"Delightful," Dotty Marbles replied, "why don't we head there?"

"What are we doing with the paint?" Ninyani asked.

"*Yeah*, what are we doing with the paint?" Fennah repeated.

Dotty Marbles answered with a smirk. "That's a surprise for everyone!"★

Chapter 34 – Ilya, Part Two

"You don't have to do this!" Dozi implored.

"Yes, I do," Ilya replied. She took hold of Dozi's hands.

"But why?" Tchama asked with tears welling in her eyes.

"I just need..." Ilya paused, took a deep breath, and she sighed. "Everything was my fault."

Dozi furrowed her brow. "Lahari is conscious again."

"I know," Ilya said. "I visited her and her dads before coming here. I told them my plans."

"And they didn't try to convince you to stay?!" Dozi squawked.

"Of course they did," Ilya replied gently.

"But *why* do you have to do this?" Tchama pleaded.

Ilya answered in a hollow voice. "Two people are dead because of me."

"That wasn't your fault," Tchama retorted. She was starting to sob.

"It was," Ilya replied. "I should never have interfered with Unadi; I should have just left him alone in his isolation. He's dead, and he killed someone, and who knows who *that* was. I need to leave."

"What does that mean?" Tchama managed to ask between her shuddering breaths. She reached out and brought her one hand to Ilya and Dozi's hands. "You're just going to fly off around the world someplace?"

Ilya did not answer.

"Where are you planning on going?"

"Telling you won't make any difference," Ilya replied. "There's no way for anyone to follow me. I just wanted to let you both know that I won't be back for a while."

Dozi and Tchama did not know what to say.

"You can't blame yourself," Tchama pleaded.

"I do," Ilya replied. "It's my fault that things went so badly. I'm just... leaving."

"So we don't get to know where you're going or when you're coming back?" Dozi asked.

Ilya looked at the concrete pavement. "I'm sorry," she said quietly. She released their hands, stepped back, and lifted into the air. Ilya hovered above their heads for a moment and said, "I love you, Dozi, and I love you, Tchama," and before they could reply, she commanded her powers to launch her into the cloudy skies and out of sight.

Tears streamed down Ilya's cheeks as she flew. She did not fly north, south, east, or west; she flew straight up. In a matter of moments, Ilya was beyond the layer of clouds, and the bright moon shone above her. Like on the night she first came across Unadi and his dead spot in the forest, the night everything started going wrong, Ilya now climbed in the dark sky until she reached the very edge of space.

She paused her flight, testing that she was indeed protected by the powers from deep within her. Ilya did not know what was out there, but she pushed herself beyond the borders of the earth's atmosphere, and she soared into space.

The vacuum of the void, the cosmic radiation all around her, the solitude, none of it seemed to have any effect on Ilya. She altered her angle in order to head toward the only other possible destination in the immediate vicinity. The moon looked only slightly larger than it normally did, even though she was so far above the earth's surface, but as she flew, the moon did not seem to be getting much bigger.

Ilya reached into her powers and accessed depths in them that she had never experienced. She flew far faster than she could have imagined, racing through the emptiness at astonishing speeds and closing the gap with the moon growing larger and larger in front of her. There was no way for her to know how fast she was traveling, but less than an hour after breaking through the edge of the earth's atmosphere, Ilya slowed her flight and came to a hover above the surface of the moon.

Her feet touched down, and she looked up at the enormous round of the earth. It filled the sky above her, and she sighed without a sound. Ilya realized she was not breathing air, and yet, she could feel the same movement in her lungs as when she was on the earth. She had decided not to bring any food with her, and she suspected that she would need to return in a few hours when she became hungry again.

Ilya took a seat on a large smooth boulder. She brought her head to her hands, and she was overwhelmed by her sorrow. Ilya mourned the death of Unadi, whom she had been trying to help. She felt guilty and responsible for the death of the unknown person Unadi had murdered. Ilya was relieved that Lahari had recovered, and yet she was ashamed of her decisions and all the misery they caused. Long moments she sat, and a single tear appeared on her cheek. It froze and fell to the moon's surface as shards of ice.

After Ilya's emotions were released, she again took a deep breath of nothing and let out another silent sigh. She did not understand her powers, did not know why they granted her resistance to the brutality of space, but she was grateful that they gave her a means to be so far away, and so alone.

Ilya rose from the rock, and she began to walk in a straight line with no destination in mind; she simply walked for the sake of walking. The gray wastes of the moon passed beneath her feet, one step after another, and her thoughts became a void. She thought of nothing.

Day and night on the moon are not like they are on the earth, and Ilya walked for hours and hours in the moon's daylight. She could have flown the distance, and walking on the moon was strange with the low gravity, but her abilities were a defiance of that particular universal force. Hunger never *did* rear its ugly head, despite the fact that she spent 37 hours walking, without a single break.

Maybe I'm like Unadi in some way, she thought. *On earth I needed to eat and sleep, but up here, I haven't felt hungry or tired at all.*

Eventually she reached the edge of the perpetual light, and Ilya came upon the dark side of the moon. It was as if her body, her very heart had *wanted* her to spend time with her feet on solid ground, because of what she was going to do next.

Ilya looked up at the earth again, but then she turned her gaze to the glowing orb of burning cosmic gas behind it, and Ilya activated her powers. She finally lifted off the moon's surface, and she felt filled with new vibrant energies. Ilya began to fly through the vast expanse of the solar system toward the blazing inferno at its heart.

Again she told her powers to fly her faster, *much* faster, and she moved through the void of space at speeds that defied the laws of physics. Three hours later, she reached the vicinity of the sun. It no longer appeared the size of a small coin on the inky blackness of space. It had grown in size to a gargantuan raging brilliance of fusion before her; it filled her view. The radiance from the sun at that distance should have blinded Ilya, its cosmic energies should have eviscerated her, but she hovered in space near to the burning giant. The powers of the sun did not affect her, as if the sun were nothing more than an illusion to Ilya. It neither powered her nor damaged her.

Ilya sighed to herself again, turned her back on the sun, and she flew. She flew for the *life* that filled her as she used her powers, the joy and the freedom. She pushed them further, and they took her farther than she could have ever imagined.

With the sun shrinking behind her and only the cosmic emptiness ahead, Ilya flew✪

Chapter 35 – Riam, Part Two

In the distance, Riam could hear muffled chanting through the trees. It was not what drew her to this location, but it now led her to what she sought. Within a small hut at the edge of an isolated community, she could sense a photonova gland. Several people were outside of the little building, but they were young, not adults yet, and none of them possessed what could satisfy her wicked craving.

Slow repetitive thumping noises came from the little shack, and those inside repeated in unison, "Consume! Consume!"

Riam did not hold herself back, and she rushed the youths, slamming into them and sending them hurtling around the clearing. Two of them were soft, and their bodies were ripped and twisted by her devastating assault, but the others were hardened. As Riam impacted with them, her massive strength managed to launch them away from the small structure, but they were unharmed.

The wooden walls were nothing to the monster, and she smashed her way into the building. The chanting died.

Riam's entire being honed in on the thing she needed, currently being swallowed by a blood-soaked boy, barely on the cusp of adulthood. He was on his knees, and he was surrounded by a large group of very surprised-looking adults. Every one of them appeared completely normal, in fact, they all looked similar.

"*What is that?!*" one of them squawked.

The photonova gland that was intended to turn the boy into a Messiah was traveling down his gullet, and Riam attacked him. In a matter of seconds, the boy would have become nigh invincible, just like the elders of the Lovegood cult. He would have been unharmed by the assault, and strong enough to fight back, but he was too late. He had hesitated too long after watching one of his little cousins slaughtered right before his eyes.

Riam grabbed the boy by his wrists with two of her many arms, and two others grabbed him by the torso. He let out the briefest scream, but his cry and his life were instantly extinguished, as Riam pulled the boy apart. She roared and ripped him in half, and his body exploded from collarbones to hips. The boy's head dangled attached to one of the gruesome sides, and his organs poured out and splashed into an enormous pool of blood at Riam's feet.

She dug through the boy's meat, but then she was attacked.

Messiahs are strong and nearly invincible, but Riam was a Messiah before she became a monster, and her power was greater.

A sword collided with her and was deflected without leaving a mark on her skin. A club was swung down upon her head, but it shattered. Hands gripped her and fingers tried to dig into her skin, and she brushed them off as she hunted for the little stone that the boy had partially swallowed. She located the gem within the ruined flesh of the meaty esophagus, and even as the other cultists tried to pull Riam from the corpse, she thrust the photonova gland into her mouth.

Riam laughed at the measly human Messiahs, laughed at the glorious pain that radiated through her with the consumption of the tiny gemstone, and she laughed at her superiority. Riam was a monstrous goddess of death.

Lonklam and Ronging lumbered up to the edge of the isolated community as Riam stepped out of the ruined hut. Messiahs were viciously attacking her, but their brutal assaults were futile. She swatted, and several of them were knocked away from her; she ignored the rest.

"There are… more," Riam managed to say.

"More what?" Lonklam asked.

She sniffed the air with her natural nose and also the bizarre single nostril that grew from her shoulder. "Can't… you smell the sweet glands?" she asked, and she turned. "They're keeping Shifts… right in there." Riam roared again, and she charged another building.

A large man in red robes and with blood up to his elbows cried, "*Not our temple of sleep!*"

Riam smashed through the wall, instantly grabbed three unconscious bodies that were within, and she rushed out into the woods.

"*No!*" the Lovegood priest wailed. "Our corrupt children! Our coma children! Nooo!"

Riam was gone. She left the community and her fellow monsters behind, and she raced into the trackless wilderness. Many cultists pursued her, but she proved far too fast for them, and she escaped.

Deep in the high mountain forest, Riam slaughtered the three unconscious Shifts. They may have been little more than youths, but Riam knew what she needed. She smashed their heads open on jagged rocks, and the three did not even experience any pain as they were massacred. She collected their photonova glands from within the mess of their ruined skulls, and one of her many hands formed an impenetrable fist with the trio of gems at its center. There they would remain until she needed one again, and she would need one again soon.

In the forest, she waited. She knew Lonklam and Ronging would eventually find her, and with three extra photonova glands in her possession, she considered that she might indeed be able to follow them on their journey to Xin. Three might be enough to get her through the extended time without access to more Shifts.

The new flesh that had grown after eating the photonova gland that was meant for the cultist boy, added two new arms and two new legs to Riam. The thick black whiskers that grew from one of her ears spread down onto the side of her neck near the cluster of fingers and trio of glassy eyes. She was a mess of weird flesh, and she liked the way she was. She looked forward to someday eating Xinitian Shifts. Riam was ready to travel south★

Chapter 36 – Shifton Youth Outreach Center

"Welcome, everyone," Dotty Marbles called out to the gathered crowd. "Thank you all for joining us this morning for the ribbon-cutting ceremony of the Shifton Youth Outreach Center!"

The small group of onlookers replied with boisterous applause. Several of the queens' *queeniest* friends were there, and they were exuberant. Among them were Miss Cleopatra, Mrs. Venus, Madame Petunia, and Dame Angelica. Zular was also there and Ninyani was beside her.

"Dot and I," Auntie Peg attempted, but the cheering would not diminish. "*Gurls, please!*" she said with a playful scowl, then she flashed her beaming smile at everyone and continued. "We are so pleased to be able to provide a home for the city's abandoned. The two of us are the house mothers, and some of our favorite young people are the first residents!"

The mystic and Theolan were standing with the group of children. Dotty Marbles reached out toward the little ones and said, "Fennah, Thech, Jzuna, Ninyani, and Muunith, would you five like to join us?"

They sheepishly approached.

"Sumi and Harakin," Auntie Peg added, "have also decided to become permanent residents here at the Outreach Center."

Dozi grabbed Harakin and Sumi's hands. "What's this?" she whispered. "You don't want to live with me anymore?"

"Actually, Dozi," Auntie Peg interjected with a smile, "Dot and I haven't had the opportunity to talk to you yet, but since we'll be living here now with the children, we'd like to offer *our* home to you and Tchama and Ilya. We know you're very fond of your basement, but we thought we'd give you the option of moving into Shifton."

Dozi was stunned. She did not know what to say, and she did not mention that Ilya was gone.

"*Really?*" Tchama exclaimed.

"And Dozi," Dotty Marbles added, "you don't have to make any major decisions right this moment."

"Why don't we all head inside so the kids can show you what they've done to the place?" Auntie Peg recommended, and she opened the large wooden doors that led into the building.

The foyer was bright, and the room was welcoming.

Dotty Marbles indicated several different spaces the guests could see. "This will be our greeting area, and over here is a lounge with a few games and things for the kids. Those stairs lead to the dorms, but let's go into the auditorium before heading up."

"This way!" Auntie Peg called, and she entered the grand room.

Dotty Marbles continued explaining things to the group. "The auditorium will be our primary space. We'll serve meals in here. We'll host events and parties; this is the heart of the Shifton Youth Outreach Center." A little sob threatened to bring her to tears, and she tapped her cheeks with her fingertips. "Hold it together," she whispered to herself very loud and dramatically. "This old bitch promised herself she wouldn't cry!"

The other queens cackled.

Auntie Peg took Dotty Marbles' hand and said, "Many of us have spent time living on the Teshon City streets. Some of you grew up on them. This place is here to help relieve even just a tiny fraction of that burden. The lost and abandoned children who live in the gutters deserve a better life, a safe place, and we want to offer that here." Auntie Peg turned to the two unique Biological Shift children and said, "Thech, Jzuna, will you please join us?"

Thech shuffled over and stood next to Dotty Marbles, and she put her hand on his slimy shoulder. Jzuna floated beside Auntie Peg.

"Thech and Jzuna have told us a lot about their mother, who very recently died, and it sounds like she was a rare and compassionate woman. She loved them for exactly who they are, and they want to provide for others those same feelings of acceptance."

Jzuna's voice came from all around the auditorium. "Our mama took good care of us, even though we're different, and we want to help all the kids who are different like us and don't have a mommy who takes care of them." She repeated a little quieter, "Our mama took good care of us."

"Yes, she did," Bivon confirmed with an emotional smile. He was standing with the mystic and Theolan. Lahari was also with them, and Dozi and Tchama were beside her.

The sunlight was shining into the auditorium from the large glass doors that led out onto the patio.

"There are others like you," Auntie Peg said to Thech and Jzuna, "and also like you, Fennah and Ninyani. Those other kids who don't have a mommy or daddy to take care of them anymore; those little ones will find a home here."

Theolan let out a little chuckle of disbelief. "Wow, you two ladies are pretty fabulous."

Both queens smiled and curtsied.

"Kids, why don't you lead the way upstairs," Dotty Marbles suggested, "and show everyone what you've got to show them."

Fennah made a squeaky noise of delight and scampered to the bottom of the stairs. Jzuna floated behind her and Thech followed.

"Off you go," Auntie Peg said to Ninyani and Muunith, and they joined the other children.

At the top of the stairs, the mystic commented to Auntie Peg, "This place is more incredible than I could have imagined."

"Here's my room!" Fennah declared with a toothy smile as she stepped through the first doorway. The interior was painted in light purple with accents of black.

"It's just lovely," Theolan said to her.

"Peggy," the mystic continued, "what about the clinic?"

Auntie Peg smiled at him. "I've run it for almost eight years, and several on my team have come a long way. They've been interested in taking over for a while. And Dot has had the idea for this center since before we were together. We've been looking for a building a little more seriously since we moved into Shifton with Ninyani a few months ago, but we've been keeping the details under wraps."

"Peggy has eased enough people through their passing from the blood corruption," Dotty Marbles added, "and I think its time for her to have something a little brighter in her life, feeding her soul." She gave her beloved a peck on the cheek.

Auntie Peg let out a contented sigh. "I *am* ready for a change."

"Excuse me, mystic?" Jzuna's voice said from behind him and the queens, and he turned to face her.

"Yes, my dear?"

"Thech and I have never had our own rooms before, but Peggy and Dot said we could have side by side rooms that are our very own!"

"That is a tremendous idea," the mystic replied, stepping into the doorframe.

"And I love your color selection," Lahari added.

"Yes, indeed," her father agreed, "the yellow and royal purple are so vibrant!"

Jzuna's one enormous eye squinted a little, and if the girl possessed a mouth, the mystic thought Jzuna would be smiling. "Let's go see Thech's pretty colors."

The mystic laughed. "Sounds fabulous, Jzuna, lead the way!"

She floated to the next doorway and waved her tentacles in the direction of her brother, but the mystic paused.

"Oh my goodness, Jzuna, it's been a few days since I've seen you and I meant to ask, how is your hurt arm doing?"

Jzuna extended her damaged limb and said, "It's getting much better, thank you. It's not perfect yet, and I don't think it'll ever grow back, but it doesn't hurt so much now."

Bivon stepped up behind the mystic and said, "That is so good to hear, honey."

Jzuna led them into her brother's room. Thech was standing in the middle of it, facing them, and he was not moving. His walls were painted with green on green swirls that snaked all the way around and even stretched up across the ceiling.

"I love these designs, Thech," Bivon declared. "The monochromatic vibe is very classy."

Thech let out a single hum and Jzuna giggled.

"Do you want to see my room?" Ninyani asked quietly.

"Yes, please, show us!" Theolan replied.

Ninyani's walls were decorated with three wide bands of color. The top third was pale pink; the bottom third was pale blue, and in between, the off-white tone of the primer was allowed to show through.

"Oh, I just love it!" Zular cried out, stepping through the doorframe and wrapping the boy in a tight embrace.

"Thanks again for letting Ninyani stay with you," Dotty Marbles whispered to Zular, "while we've been putting the finishing touches on this place."

Zular made a dramatic face like she was surprised to even be thanked. "I adore this little duckling!" she cooed, and she squeezed Ninyani, pressing her cheek against his and making him laugh.

"Zular, I've loved getting to know you for the past couple days!" he squeaked.

Fennah was bouncing around everyone, and she declared in her bright voice, "We're all going to live here now!" She was very excited.

Each of the rooms was furnished with a bed and a little desk positioned under the window, and even the empty rooms that did not yet have lost children living in them already held the same two pieces of furniture. In Jzuna's room, a brand new net hung above where the bed would have been, and she and her brother's tub was in Thech's green-patterned room. There were 18 rooms in all, ready to house the abandoned youth of Teshon City.

"These others are finished," Fennah said to whoever would listen to her, "and someday there will be kids who will come and stay in them with us here, and they can pick out colors to paint their rooms also!"

Harakin laughed. "Yes, that's all true. The other lost children out there will be welcome in here."

Fennah scurried to the next doorway. "But this room will be Muunith's!"

Muunith smiled.

"We like them a lot!" Fennah added.

Muunith was still in rough shape from being attacked a few days earlier, and they were still staying with the mystic and Theolan.

"You're a special little one, Muunith," Sumi said, "and you fit in perfectly here with us."

"We can all help you paint your room later this week when you're feeling better," Fennah added.

In the hallway, Auntie Peg and Dotty Marbles stepped up side by side and each wrapped an arm around the other.

"This place is just wonderful," Theolan said to them, "and you are both wonderful!"

"Well, as you know," Auntie Peg replied with a smirk, "we do all of this for the praise!"

Dotty Marbles laughed at her beloved, and the mystic and his husband joined their frivolity.

The booming voice of a woman came from outside. "Hello, everyone."

Fennah scampered over to the room's open window, and her entire view was filled with an enormous face. "You must be Heavyfeather!" The little girl was almost nose to nose with the giantess. "Peggy and Dot have told us all about you!"

Heavyfeather let out a booming laugh that knocked Fennah to her backside, and the girl shrieked with glee. "You are correct, *very* little one," she said in her booming voice. "I am Heavyfeather, and it's lovely to meet you. I'm so happy for you to have this new home with the queens."

"So am I!" Fennah jumped up and screamed in joy.

Heavyfeather laughed again. "What's your name, little one?"

"I'm Fennah!"

Heavyfeather smiled, looked past her, and said, "Peggy, Dot, this place is remarkably different from how it was when the three of us met here. I'm astonished at all you've accomplished!"

"Thank you, Heavyfeather," Auntie Peg replied. "This building really is perfect. Oh, and we haven't told you; we figured out what it used to be! Ninyani found some records in an old filing cabinet tucked away in one of the closets."

Dotty Marbles smiled warmly and said, "This building used to be a school."

"Oh, that makes sense," Heavyfeather replied with a rumbling chuckle, "of course it was a school, and it has again become a place for children!"

"*Everyone*," Auntie Peg called out, "why don't we head down to the back pavilion area outside where we've got some drinks and treats. Our other friends have arrived, and they're excited to join in the celebration with us! Fennah, would you like to lead the way back downstairs?"

"Follow me!" The beaming child skipped off through the adults and led the way. Once in the auditorium again, Fennah turned toward the large glass doors that opened out onto the patio, and she skipped through them, waving at Heavyfeather. To the child's surprise, there was a *second* giant with the gargantuan woman, as well as quite a few normal-sized people.

Auntie Peg and Dotty Marbles followed the other children out onto the patio, and the rest of the adults were behind them.

"Fennah, it's such a pleasure to make your acquaintance," Heavyfeather boomed. "And this is Pinga," the giantess added, indicating the woman beside her.

Fennah repeated Heavyfeather's words with unbridled glee. "*Pinga, it's such a pleasure to make your acquaintance!*"

Pinga chuckled. "Hey there, kiddo!" She had a shaved head and a piercing in each nostril.

Lahari let out a little laugh at Fennah's joy, and Auntie Peg strode past her, whispering, "What a firecracker, huh?" She stepped up and gave Pinga a peck on the cheek. "Hey, gals!" she said, looking up at Heavyfeather. Auntie Peg then stepped off to one side with Dotty Marbles.

"Fennah, please allow me to introduce you to some other folks," Heavyfeather continued with a wide smile, "including a few new friends I've made. This is Ogomo."

"Hello, Ogomo!" Fennah called up to him, jumping as high as she could.

"My, aren't you an energetic little sprite?" Ogomo replied. "This is my big sister Nahli and my first mate Z'Matri."

"Hello! Hello!" Fennah said with excessive waving.

Ogomo let out a loud chuckle and Fennah giggled with him. "There are a couple of boys over by the food, of course," the giant said with a grin. "You should introduce yourself to them, Kosephaji and Duna. They're a little older than you kids, but they're good lads."

"Do they need a place to stay?" Fennah squeaked. "Maybe they should move in here with us!"

Dotty Marbles squeezed Auntie Peg's hand and whispered to her beloved, "She's just the sweetest pumpkin!"

"That's very thoughtful of you," Ogomo replied to Fennah, "but right now they've got a place with me and my crew." He nodded his gigantic head toward his sister.

"Yeah," Nahli added, "all of us are set with lodging. But go say *hello*. They're right there," and she pointed.

Kosephaji and Relliduna were talking to Olona. She was smoking a joint.

Jzuna floated beside Thech, and they made their way over to the table with the snacks.

Fennah trotted up and said, "Thech and Jzuna, this is Kosephaji and Duna."

The two 17 year olds looked down at the little girl, who they did not know. "That's correct," Relliduna replied with a confused smile. "I'm Relliduna, but my friends all call me *Duna*. This is Kosephaji, and this is Olona. Do you three already know Olona?"

"Of course, silly!" Fennah replied with a chirping laugh.

"You two are Bio-Shifts, right?" Kosephaji asked Thech and Jzuna.

"Yes," Jzuna replied.

"Our friend was one, too."

"He was very unique," Relliduna added, "just like you both."

"Where is he?" Fennah asked.

Relliduna and Kosephaji's faces fell.

"He's gone."

"Our ship crashed," Relliduna explained. "A few people were lost at sea, and he was among them."

"Did you look for him?" Fennah asked.

"One of Ogomo's crew is a Shift, Z'Matri," and he pointed over toward the man beside the giant. "He can sense other Shifts," Relliduna continued. "He can feel Shifts on the other side of the world, but he can't feel our friend anymore."

Thech had remained motionless and silent, but he let out a single low grunt, and his sister turned in the air and faced him. For a moment, the two did not move or make a sound.

"Jzuna, Thech, are you okay?" Fennah asked.

Nothing happened.

Kosephaji and Relliduna looked at each other, but then Jzuna's eye blinked and she turned to them.

"Thech says he isn't strong enough."

"What is Thech not strong enough to do?" Olona asked.

Jzuna's eye looked like it was frowning. "No, not Thech," she said, "*Z'Matri*."

Kosephaji and Relliduna looked at each other again.

"Z'Matri isn't strong enough?" Kosephaji asked.

"Yes," Jzuna confirmed.

"But we just told you, he can sense Shifts all around the world."

"Thech says he's not strong enough to feel your friend."

Kosephaji, Relliduna, and Olona all turned to look at the man beside the giant.

Suddenly, a radiant luminescence shined throughout the courtyard, and all conversations ceased, as everyone's eyes turned to the unique pair of Biological Shift children.

Jzuna was attached to her brother's chest. She closed her huge eye, and Thech's eyes again brightened to a point that had everyone else averting or shielding their eyes.

Across the courtyard, Z'Matri's limbs seized, and he became rigid where he stood. A gentle light surrounded him like the glow of the moon, and his feet lifted off the ground, so that he hovered in a standing position.

Z'Matri spoke into the silent courtyard, and his voice was a strange forced monotone. "Pelipi is alive."

His feet lowered, the illumination disappeared, and his body released its grip. He staggered but managed to keep his footing. "*What just happened to me?*" he snapped. Then he added in a surprised tone, "I can feel Pelipi!"✪

Chapter 37 – Pelipi

The radiance from Thech faded as Jzuna opened her huge eye. The children separated and Jzuna hovered beside her brother.

Z'Matri looked shocked, and his voice sounded startled. "What did you two just do to me?"

Jzuna looked around the silent courtyard; everyone was staring at her and Thech. Her voice sounded nervous as she answered. "We reached into you and told your power to find their friend." She rotated in the air to look at Kosephaji and Relliduna.

Olona stepped up and asked Jzuna, "What exactly is your power?"

The hovering tentacled eyeball turned and faced her brother.

The two of them stared at each other for a moment.

Everyone else continued to watch them.

Then Jzuna blinked and turned back to Olona. "We tell things to do stuff."

Olona furrowed her brow. "What stuff?"

"We can tell fire and water and air and the ground all to do stuff," Jzuna explained. "We can hear the things everyone says to themselves, but they don't say out loud. We can move things and touch things without touching them for real. We can see what people see." Jzuna stopped talking.

"You can control natural elements and manipulate objects without physically touching them? That makes you like some sort of, I don't know, *omni*-kinetic," Olona mused.

"What does that mean?" Dotty Marbles replied.

"How did you tap into my powers?" Z'Matri asked Jzuna.

"Thech could see what you see, and he could tell that you couldn't see strong enough, so we made you see stronger."

"You two must also be ultra psychic," Olona commented, pondering aloud all the information Jzuna shared.

Z'Matri turned to Ogomo, bewildered. "Cap'n, the lad is underwater at the bottom of a cove. The tide must've washed his body to the coast. I don't understand how he's still alive, or why I couldn't see him," and Z'Matri looked at Kosephaji and Relliduna, "but Pelipi is alive!"

The two boys were dumbfounded.

"How do we find him?!" Kosephaji squawked.

"I can still see him," Z'Matri said. "I know exactly where he is, but I don't know how we're going to get to him. The submersible could take us down to where he is, but it has no way to bring him up."

"Mystic!" Dozi suddenly cried out. "You're the one! You're the one who needs to get Pelipi!"

"Me, honey? What on earth do you mean? Oh!" he said, as realization came to him.

"Yes!" Olona declared. "Jzuna, Thech, you can control water, correct? Do you think you could make the water take the mystic straight to Pelipi, and can you make it so the water doesn't hurt him? The pressure of the water above the mystic will be dangerous, but that's a lot to handle."

"It's okay," Jzuna replied. "Water listens to us."

"I've got a pair of old Oselian diving goggles hung on my wall," Dozi added. "I found them a while ago with a bunch of underwater stuff, including a thermometer."

"The one in our tub?" Tchama asked, and Dozi nodded at her.

"Mystic, it's going to be dark as you get deeper," Harakin commented, "so I can make you a light to bring."

The mystic took Dozi's hand. "You're so clever, aren't you? This is why I have the silly ridiculous power to hold my breath for a long period of time. This is why I became a Demifae all those years ago. This is it." He turned and looked at Kosephaji and Relliduna. "Let's go find your friend. Please, tell us his name again."

"Pelipi," Relliduna answered.

"*Pelipi*," the mystic repeated. "Let's go find Pelipi!"

Ogomo looked down at Z'Matri and asked, "Where are we headed?"

"The boy is in a cove a little way past the Grey Shallows almost to Brokenpointe. It'll take a while to get there."

"Let's think about who needs to be involved in the search party," Olona recommended. "Thech and Jzuna need to be there to control the water for the mystic. Harakin needs to be there for her light. Z'Matri will guide us, in case Pelipi's body drifts from where he is right now. We'll likely need to resuscitate him, so mystic, we'll probably need some of your treatments, and I'll bring my gear, as well," Olona added.

"I'm coming too," Bivon stated. "Jzuna and Thech, you can ride there in the back of my cart."

"I'll stay with Lahari," Theolan said to his husband.

After several hours of walking along the Great Southtrack, Z'Matri told the group that it was time to leave the path and head toward the water. He led Kosephaji, Relliduna, the mystic, Olona,

Harakin, and Bivon with Thech and Jzuna in his cart onto the rough and uneven coastal lands that stretched to the water's edge.

They reached a rocky outcrop and Z'Matri pointed out to the water. "Pelipi is down there."

Kosephaji brought his hands to his mouth and smothered a sob of joy and relief that wracked his body. "Pelipi," he whispered.

Relliduna wrapped his arms around Kosephaji.

Jzuna floated over to Z'Matri. "We're sorry," she said sheepishly. "Before we left the city, Peggy told Thech and me it was wrong to use our powers on you without asking. We just knew we could help, but we didn't mean to force you."

Z'Matri stared at the enormous hovering eyeball with tentacles, and he looked at the bizarre little boy behind her. The two slimy children were so strange and so unique, and they were powerful. "She's right," Z'Matri managed to say. "You should always get permission if you ever intend to use your powers on another person like that again someday." He added in a tone of admiration, "You two are very strong, and I know you did it for the right reasons."

"Here, mystic," Harakin said as she formed a wand made of light, "this will let you see in the darkness." She extended it to him.

"What an astonishing power you have," he said as he marveled at the solidified light beam in his hand. He turned to Thech and Jzuna. "All of you Shifts are so incredible. Okay, kids, I'll get in the water, and you take me to Pelipi."

The mystic took off his shoes, socks, shirt, and trousers. Wearing only his undergarments and a little pouch on a belt around his waist that held a few tools and items, he stepped into the water. "Chilly," he commented. He waded out until the water was up to his chest, took a deep breath, and he submerged. The mystic had been swimming many times in his life, but the sensation he experienced was nothing like any of those times.

As if a whirlpool appeared in front of him, he was suddenly drawn forward and down, deep into the dark water. His ears did not pop, nor did the weight of water put any pressure on his chest as he sank. The two children did not create a tunnel of air for the mystic, but it felt as if he were merely underwater in the shallows, and not being drawn deeper and deeper into the crushing depths.

The mystic's goggled eyes were attracted to something beyond the glowing wand, and he was certain that he could see another light ahead of him, down on the ocean floor. All was darkness in every direction around him except for the light in his hand and the light in front of him, and he was being pulled straight to it.

As the mystic came closer to the bottom, Thech and Jzuna from far above slowed his speed, and they brought him to a hover just above the ocean floor.

There was no body. There was no physical form of any kind, but the mystic focused on the light. Lying on the sand was something he recognized instantly, and even in the darkness of the water he knew what he was seeing. He was looking at a photonova gland. He had never seen one that produced a light of its own, and he tentatively reached a hand out and lifted it from the sand. It did not pulse or flicker; it simply glowed.

Are you Pelipi? the mystic thought to himself.

He took a small glass vial from a pouch at his belt and removed its cork. At that depth, the container, and even the mystic himself should have been crushed to oblivion, but Thech and Jzuna's powers kept him protected. The glass did not shatter, and he sealed the glowing photonova gland within.

The mystic did not know how he was supposed to alert everyone on the surface that he had found what must be Pelipi, but he was suddenly being drawn back up again through the vast column of water, and a moment later he popped out at the surface.

He revealed the little glass vial cradled in his hands.

Kosephaji looked overwhelmed with too many emotions. "Pelipi!" he cried out, and he turned toward Bivon. "Do you have a glass box, or maybe just an empty jar in your cart?"

A moment later, Bivon poured out a container of dried tealeaves and handed it to Kosephaji.

Relliduna took the vial from the mystic, and he removed the cork. He carefully poured the seawater onto his palm and caught the tiny photonova gland. "Pelipi," he whispered, "you're going to be okay."

Kosephaji was holding the jar, and Relliduna carefully let the glowing gemstone fall into it.

To the others' amazement, the crystal did not drop to the bottom of the jar and make the little *clink* sound they all expected. Instead, the light stayed directly in the center of the container and Pelipi's voice blurted out, "Would you just tell Relliduna how you feel, already?!" The illuminating photonova gland blinked in time with the voice. "Wait, where are we?"

"Pelipi!" Kosephaji and Relliduna screamed in unison.

"Weren't we just on the ship?" Pelipi asked.

"You don't know what happened?" Relliduna responded.

"What do you mean? What happened?"

"Oh, Pelipi, it was awful," Kosephaji cried out. "The ship wrecked and your box was lost at sea. You've been on the bottom of the ocean for days! I can't believe you're back; we were sure you were dead!"

"I was underwater?" Pelipi exclaimed. "Wow, liquids really do *not* agree with this bitch, not since I changed." He shined bright.

"Somehow it didn't kill you," Relliduna marveled. "And..."

"Wait," Pelipi interrupted, "if I was on the bottom of the ocean, how did you find me?"

"That's a little confusing and probably will take some explaining," Olona replied.

"We're near Brokenpointe," the mystic said. "Maybe we should head there for dinner and stay the night at one of the inns."

As the group began to make their way the short distance to the seaside fishing village, Relliduna asked, "Pelipi, what did you mean by what you said when we first found you?"

Pelipi let out a laugh and his light blinked bright inside the jar. "I don't remember the shipwreck, but the last thing I do remember is Kosephaji fumbling over his confession of undying love for you."

Kosephaji's voice cracked. "*Pelipi*, what are you talking about?!"

Relliduna pulled Kosephaji to him, and he kissed Kosephaji hard on the lips. When they separated, Relliduna said, "I'm in love with you, too, Kosephaji," and Pelipi laughed in delight★

Epilogue – Months Later

It was quiet at the isolated compound that lay hidden beyond the edge of the Infinite Waste to the west of the Ru River.

Several military men and a few medics were standing over the bodies of three unconscious children strapped to gurneys. One child looked very strange to them.

"I liked that the runaway twins used to call me *the Voice*," the commander said to his officers. "Make these three call me that, too." He turned and left the room.

"Wake up the 13 year old," one of the men ordered the medics. He pointed at a little boy who looked completely normal. "Put him through the initiation ceremony and lock him in one of the black cells."

Less than an hour later, the boy's suffering was ended, but it was ended horribly.

Sobbing in the darkness, after having witnessed the brutal massacre of six bound and gagged prisoners, the little boy was now in a vile battle with countless hoards of insects he could not see. They crawled up his legs and buzzed into his ears, landing on his skin and causing him to scream. He swatted at himself, as their hideous tiny legs scurried all over him.

The boy's punishment was meant to last for hours longer, but a terrible boom startled him momentarily from the onslaught of insects. There was a second louder crash, not like an explosion, but like a building being demolished. Then the wall of the black cell shattered, and concrete shrapnel pummeled the boy, as light suddenly shined into the darkness.

Something that looked like many naked women all squished together into one body came charging through the hole. The monster grabbed the incapacitated child and yanked in several directions with its multiple arms, ripping the boy's body apart. One arm hurtled through the air, back out the hole behind the creature, and one of the child's little legs flew farther into the dark of the cell. The slaughtered boy's head was pulled from his torso, and as soon as the monster had what it needed, it smashed deeper into the building.

Lonklam and Ronging peered through the hole Riam had smashed in the wall, as her wicked senses pulled her toward more of what she craved.

She destroyed another wall and paused. There were two photonova glands beckoning her, but they were in different directions.

A door burst open and a battalion of soldiers rushed Riam. She pounced at them, and the group of warriors collided with her. Their attack was futile. The blades and bludgeons that struck her weird, twisted, and nearly invulnerable body were all bent or shattered. Riam's retaliation against her would-be assailants was terrible.

With a single simultaneous attack of her many limbs, seven people died at once. In an instant, Riam grabbed one man and pulled off both his arms. She also yanked a man's head so far back that the flesh of his throat opened like it had been slit with a jagged blade. Two soldiers were grabbed and slammed together with such force that their torsos burst in a repulsive explosion of guts. One of Riam's legs kicked a man in the side of his hip with such power, his body folded sideways and fell convulsing to the stone floor. Another of her legs stomped, and a fallen soldier's head popped beneath her foot.

In that same moment, with Riam lashing out at six men at once, she also leaned forward, and her vicious mouth, with its rows and rows of teeth, bit the seventh soldier in the face. He tried to scream as she chomped through his flesh and cartilage and bone. Riam spat the mess onto the pile of corpses, and blood sprayed into the air from all of her victims.

The remaining soldiers were stunned at seeing such an incomparable and instantaneous slaughter. A few tried to run, but they were running in the direction that Riam intended to go, there was a photonova gland beyond them.

Several soldiers tried to attack her, but it was like trying to attack a battering ram. Riam rushed forward, trampling two more and shoving another out of her way so hard that his body went through the wall she slammed him into. The fleeing men were overtaken, and she dismissively tossed them aside with such force that wherever they fell, *there* they remained.

Riam spared not a thought for the wake of death behind her as she approached the room that contained a photonova gland she could feel, held inside a Shift's head. She kicked the door open and saw a girl.

The child gasped in horror, but then the little girl was *gone*. Riam felt the child go, long gone before the monster could even react.

A wave of rage exploded in Riam's mind as she suddenly realized the other photonova glands she had felt a moment earlier had escaped and was now also far away. She could feel them getting farther and farther with each instant.

Riam roared. Her wicked toothy mouth let out a rumbling growl, and she smashed the head of the Shift boy she had ripped apart in the black cell still clutched in one of her many hands. Riam found what she needed and shoved the photonova gland past her many teeth. She swallowed hard and pain struck her like lightning. She relished the delicious agony.

Her disgusting body began to change yet again, as she made her way through the corpses and back out of the devastated compound.

Lonklam and Ronging were waiting for her.

"Perhaps this base can be our new Gunge," Lonklam recommended.

"We are... close... to cities," Riam managed to say. "Hunting... grounds are close." Her twisted mouth formed the most violent of smiles, and she reiterated Lonklam's words, "This *is*... New Gunge," and her unearthly laughter sounded like a pack of hyenas, as it rang out across the Infinite Waste✪

Book Five is coming soon!

The Mantis Equilibrium - Book Two

Someone is slaughtering Messiahs, and the Messiahs are investigating. Who will survive this new confrontation and what will be left of them?
Featuring:
GODS, DRAGONS, & DRAG QUEENS!

The Mantis Corruption - Book Three

In the east are MONSTERS. To the north is the WITCH. In the south lies the CAPITAL. To the west is the WASTE. The land is called XIN.
How is this distant land connected to the people and events in Books One & Two? And what will happen with the monsters?

The Mantis Continuum - Book Four

A story of eldritch horror and psychic confrontations. Two weird children go through a significant upheaval in their happy lives. A unique trio of gay 17 year old lads embark on a buccaneer adventure. A man living alone in isolation is found and helped, but with very unexpected consequences.

Coming in 2024 from Danu Books
A sexy new tale begins!

The Starting End - Book One

An epic fantasy adventure in a queer normative universe. The Starting End is a spicy exploration of unique kinks and relationships, and love is experienced in a plethora of beautiful ways. Gender identity and sexuality are celebrated through the diverse cast of characters who come from across the LGBTQIA+ rainbow.

The Hyperspace Enigma - Part 1
Destination Unknown

In a gay reverse-harem in space, a pleasure android has begun developing human emotions, and it causes problems for everyone!

The Hyperspace Enigma - Part 2
Fantastic Voyage

The starship Ulaa-Lah is lost in uncharted Space, but Lyoth and Stawren are sent on a mission to collect rare items from around the universe in order for a group of hyper-advanced scientists to build a deep space scanning computer to look for the lost ship.

www.ingramcontent.com/pod-product-compliance
Ingram Content Group UK Ltd.
Pitfield, Milton Keynes, MK11 3LW, UK
UKHW021909190726
13853UKWH00002B/594

9 798869 388216